
★

"Breathe," Charlie implored Elizabeth, on her knees now, stroking the pale blond hair back from the equally pale face. She wore a black silk nightgown, and Charlie slammed her fist down between the other woman's breasts. "Breathe!" Tom caught her fist when she raised it again.

"She's dead, Charlie."

"Elizabeth?" Charlie spoke softly to the dead girl, the way you whispered to someone who was still asleep. "Why?" She noticed there were other smells in the room. From Elizabeth's parted lips came the smell of wine. But mingled with it, and overpowering it, was the smell of blood. Blood rimmed the white even teeth that showed between the girl's open lips. Blood matted the hair at Elizabeth's temple. When Charlie closed her eyes, all she saw was red, all she smelled was death.

★

BURIED DIAMONDS

APRIL HENRY

WORLDWIDE®

TORONTO • NEW YORK • LONDON
AMSTERDAM • PARIS • SYDNEY • HAMBURG
STOCKHOLM • ATHENS • TOKYO • MILAN
MADRID • WARSAW • BUDAPEST • AUCKLAND

BURIED DIAMONDS

A Worldwide Mystery/June 2005

First published by St. Martin's Press LLC.

ISBN 0-373-26532-8

Printed in U.S.A.

Acknowledgments

My thanks for making this book possible go first to Wendy Schmalz,who can always be counted on to do and say the right thing. My Web mistress Carrie Patten keeps everything organized—my speaking engagements, vanity license plates that readers have shared with me, even my favorite recipes (check out her work at www.AprilHenryMysteries.com). Ruth Cavin has been a wonderful editor—she gets more done than two people half her age. And my work life just isn't the same without Jan Bellis-Squires.

The Southwest Community Connection, the Multnomah Village Post, Ruth Weatherford and Evelyn Knudsen Starr all helped me figure out what Multnomah Village looked like in the early 1950s. For information about strokes, my thanks go to Sharon Wildwind and Carol and Rick Segina. Dr. Louise Mesher, DVM, explained strychnine poisoning to me. At the last minute, Carla Robertson and Kelley Rothenberger volunteered to right the wrongs. As always, any errors are my own.

The past isn't dead. It isn't even past.
—William Faulkner

ONE

THE BLOW CAME OUT of nowhere. The next thing Eddy knew, he was flat on his back. A kid was standing over him, and something green and shiny and slender was heading straight for the side of Eddy's face.

His cheek exploded in pain.

"Go back to where you came from, you wetback!"

Eddy tried to roll away, but the guy ground his foot on Eddy's shoulder and pinned him fast. Two-handed, the guy swung the thing he was holding back over his shoulder, where it caught the light. It was a half-size souvenir bat, made out of metal. Eddy's son had gotten one at PGE Park one time at a baseball game. The bat connected with the bone just above his right eye, and his vision was flooded with blood.

There were three or four of them, he saw with his good eye, standing over him, one of them laughing. And one of them, he realized with dimming horror, held a gun.

Eddy tried to speak, but his throat was filled with hot, salty liquid. *I was born here,* he wanted to say. *I belong here, same as you.* But the thought melted from his mind, as insubstantial as cotton candy. He barely felt the hand tug his wallet from his pocket, didn't hear the rattle and hiss as someone shook and then used a can of spray paint. When light from a passing car washed over them, his three attackers froze and then ran.

He was beyond knowing they were gone. Lying on the wet leaves, he felt his legs dance a little, no longer under his control. And then Eduardo Estrada, second-generation Mexican-American, lost consciousness.

When a jogger found him just before the sun began to rise,

the blood around Eddy's head glowed like a black halo in the sodium shine of the streetlight. Next to him, someone had spray-painted the word "Spic!"

TWO

DETOURING AROUND the flattened carcass of a dead crow, reduced to not much more than feathers, Claire Montrose ran past Portland's Gabriel Park. At every fourth step, she exhaled just as her right heel hit the ground, the rhythm automatic. It was interrupted by a high-pitched squeal that penetrated past the buds of her headphones, startling Claire and temporarily blotting out Tori Amos singing about a man and a gun. Looking over her shoulder, Claire saw a toddler coasting to the bottom of a short orange plastic slide, her chubby arms raised in triumph.

Claire returned her attention to the road, just in time to narrowly miss stepping on the body of a plump squirrel. She leapt over it and then stopped for a moment, jogging in place. The squirrel looked whole and unharmed, if you didn't consider the fact that it wasn't moving and that its black bead eye never blinked. There wasn't any blood that she could see. Overhead, telephone and power lines laced the sky. Poor thing must have lost its footing. Maybe it was only stunned. For a moment Claire imagined the squirrel getting to its feet, shaking itself, and then scampering off.

But when she nudged it with her toe, it skidded a couple of inches, stiff and clearly dead. Another childish squeal made her look up. She couldn't leave the squirrel here, not next to a line of parked cars, each with a car seat in the back. The sight of its lifeless body would surely give some poor kid nightmares for the next few months. A few feet away was a bus shelter with a garbage can. Using only the tips of thumb and forefinger, Claire leaned over and picked up the squirrel's body, splayed and rigid, then quickly dropped it in the garbage can.

If he could see her, Dante would be horrified. Whenever she bought a pretzel from a street vendor on her visits to him in New York, he would shudder elaborately, then inform her that the pretzels had surely been languishing for months in rat-infested warehouses in Jersey. Claire would nod while licking the salt from her fingers. Now she vigorously wiped her hand on the seat of her shorts, then resumed her run. The gesture was probably just as effective as the times she had seen a mother blow on a fallen pacifier before handing it back to her baby.

Past the community center, Claire turned left. The hill rose sharply, and her legs promptly turned to lead. Each breath scoured her lungs. She was pushing forty. The days when she might (with a good tailwind, two cups of coffee, and some fast music to urge her on) possibly run a seven-minute mile were behind her. Well behind her. Finally, Claire was forced to stop and pretend to stretch.

While waiting for her heart rate and breathing to slow, she pressed her palms flat against an old stone wall, stretching her calf. The wall was made up of large gray stones about the size and shape of slightly deflated basketballs. In height, the wall was just a few inches shorter than Claire, who was five-foot-ten. It ran around two sides of a large yard that began well above the street. The yard's edge was lined with arborvitae that formed a second, living wall that began just above the rock wall. Years ago, someone had planted the bushes too close together. Now their stubby branches were interwoven as thick as Velcro. Lengthening her stretch, Claire leaned into the wall, left leg straight behind her, right knee bent, feeling the pull in the Achilles tendon. Stretching, ice, orthotics, special exercises, shoes with so much cushioning they looked like marshmallows—they were all part of Claire's reality now, whether she liked it or not.

As she changed legs, she lifted her head for a moment. This close, the spaces between the trunks of the arborvitae offered her a glimpse of the normally hidden house. The house was two stories, the first made of timber, the second of rough pale stucco diagonally bisected by exposed wood braces. Strips of lead cut the windows into diamond shapes. Claire supposed there was a name for this particular type of architecture, but all she knew was that the house looked English. Shakespearean. At any moment, Juliet could appear on the second-floor balcony. And be surprised to find herself in this neighborhood of sixties ranch-style houses.

Claire reached behind her, grabbed her left foot, and pulled it to her buttock. Right at eye level was an inch-long chink in the wall where a piece of sandy mortar had fallen out. A spider had knit a web across the half-inch-wide opening. Behind it, the hole dipped down, forming a hollow space about the size and shape of a crooked index finger. At that moment, the sun came out from behind a cloud. A ray of light glinted off something inside the chink.

Something silver and round, shining dully.

THREE

SQUINTING, CLAIRE PRESSED her face closer to the wall, then sucked in her breath. She was, she realized, looking at a ring.

First she tried to dig it out with her finger, not even minding the web or that the spider that made it might be nearby. She could just touch the ring's rounded edge, but not hook it. The ground yielded a twig. Farther up the hill, a school bus came to a halt, red lights flashing. Two young girls got off and began to walk toward her, giggling, staggering under the weight of backpacks nearly as big as they were. Claire stopped what she was doing and pretended to stretch again, covering the chink with the flat of her hand until they had passed.

A few minutes later, the ring lay in the palm of her hand. It was heavy, and black with tarnish. She realized it hadn't been a glint from the metal that had caught her eye, but rather a sparkle from one of the three clear faceted stones that were set in the band. The middle one was nearly the size of a dime, the other two as big around as the ends of a pencil eraser. The stones were so big it seemed impossible they were real, yet the ring itself, weighty and substantial, looked like it predated cubic zirconia by at least a hundred years. They must be diamonds. Although the band was wide, it was etched with a delicate filigree. A lady's ring, she thought, not a man's. Without making a conscious decision, Claire tried it on. It slid into place easily on her left ring finger. A lady's diamond ring, a fortune on one woman's finger.

Fingers spread, she held out her hand and turned it this way and that. Claire knew it was her imagination, but the ring made her hand feel so much heavier. Normally, she couldn't stand the feeling of something encircling her finger. There was something about a ring that had always made her feel trapped, like she was wearing a tiny handcuff. Maybe that was why she still wasn't married, even though Dante had made it clear he was ready whenever she was.

Who had owned this ring? Claire had the large hands that went with her height, so whoever it was might have been tall like herself. Or maybe she had been short and stubby, with rings glittering on every finger of her plump hands. But even a woman with a thousand pieces of jewelry would surely have missed a ring like this.

How long had the ring lain there? Claire looked at the house again. It certainly couldn't date back to Shakespeare's time. The oldest houses in this part of Portland had been built about the turn of the last century. The house she shared with her roommate, Charlie, was a few years newer than that. So sometime in the past one hundred years, a woman's ring had somehow become part of this wall. Could she have been helping to build the wall when the ring slid from her finger, its absence unnoticed until it was too late? But would the owner of such a ring have ever gotten her hands dirty, broken her nails, and bruised her knuckles as she lifted the heavy stones into place?

Claire looked at the ring again, turning her hand so that the diamonds caught the light. The ring was so weighty—how could the wearer not have noticed its absence as soon as it was gone? And wouldn't anyone have torn the wall apart, piece by piece, to get such a ring back?

An old woman with a prancing black standard poodle rounded the corner. Claire covered her left hand with her right. Whose ring was it, really? If Claire hadn't seen it, it would have continued to hide in the dark crevice, seen only by the occasional spider. God knows how long it had been there.

There was something about this ring that made her want to keep it, made her want to make a fist and run all the way home, so fast that her hands would be a blur. It wasn't that the ring must be worth thousands of dollars. Her desire couldn't be re-

duced to words. Maybe it was the heaviness of it, the seriousness of it, the thought of the generations of women who must
have worn this ring. Claire's family didn't stretch back generations. She had never even known her father, and no one had
bothered to keep track of her mother's ancestors. The little she
knew of her history began and ended with her grandmother's
generation.

If she kept the ring, no one would be the wiser. And who
would be harmed? She was probably the only living person who
knew of its existence.

Suddenly Claire felt ashamed of herself. This ring looked
like an heirloom. It had a history. Maybe a hundred years ago,
a woman had helped her husband build this wall. By the time
she noticed the ring had fallen from her finger it had been buried somewhere in the line of stones that ran nearly the length
of the block and then turned to angle back toward the hidden
house. Claire imagined how that woman had argued with her
husband that they should simply tear the wall down and find
the ring, the cost be damned. But he had disagreed, and she had
swallowed her anger along with her pride. Or maybe she hadn't
noticed its absence for several hours, didn't know that the minute she had spent helping steady a stone had led to the ring's
loss. Maybe she had thought she had dropped it on the street,
left it by a sink, had it snatched away by some very clever thief.
Maybe that was why they hadn't torn the wall apart until they
found the ring—because she hadn't been absolutely certain
that was where it was. Or maybe they had feared that the ring
had become wedded to the concrete, that no amount of attacking the wall with pickaxes would free it from its tomb.

With her hand still tightly clutched around the ring, Claire
walked around the corner, bordered by more arborvitae, and up
the steep driveway, past a flower garden filled with dozens of different kinds of wildflowers, but none that she could name. There
were no cars parked in the driveway, but the house had a detached
two-car garage, both doors closed. It mimicked the style of the
house, although it was clearly a more recent addition.

She had found the ring on these people's property, and by rights it belonged to them. But what if they had just moved here recently? What if they weren't the descendants of the woman who had once worn this ring? Then they would know nothing about the ring, and it would mean nothing to them. As far as they would know, there was no ring and there had never been a ring. Really, would they have any more right to it than she did? This ring had been hidden all these years, as good as gone. What difference would it make to anyone if Claire held on to it, instead of the wall? Her mind came up with one rationalization after another, but she forced her feet to continue walking to the front door.

In a few seconds, she would show the ring to whoever opened the door. And once she held out her hand, she was sure they would feel the same desire she was still struggling with. There was no bell, just an elaborate knocker that looked like it came straight out of *A Christmas Carol*. Claire picked up the brass ring from the lion's mouth and let it fall, then listened for footsteps.

"Can I help you?" An old man leaned out of the door of the house next door and then walked across the driveway toward her. He was tall and stringy, his posture erect. He gave her a smile and a once-over.

Claire recognized him from previous runs through the neighborhood. He had an old round-edged car, with huge fenders and running boards, that he always seemed to be polishing or tinkering with whenever she ran up the street. Now Claire crossed her arms over the soft fabric of her combination running bra/top, hoping her nipples weren't showing through the flowered fabric. She tucked her left hand in her armpit and out of his sight.

"I'm looking for the people who live here."

He shook his head. "They're not here right now."

"Do you know when they might be back?" Maybe she would come back later this evening. There was no way she was going to entrust someone else with the ring.

"They're in Europe on vacation. They won't be home for a couple of weeks. But I'm looking after their home while they're gone. Can I help you with something?"

Until it bit into her palm, Claire hadn't realized she was tightening her grasp on the ring. "I was just looking at their wall. I wanted to ask them if they knew where the stones came from. They're so…unusual."

He snorted. "Unusual! They're just rocks from the river. Someone just took a truck down to the Willamette and filled up the bed a few times."

"You were here when they built the wall?" Claire asked, curiosity overcoming her annoyance.

"Yup." He extended his hand, and Claire shook it, careful to keep her left hand still tucked out of sight. "I'm Howard Backus. You live around here, don't you? I've seen you out jogging many times."

"I'm Claire Montrose. I live on the other side of Vermont, in Multnomah Village. I've run by this wall a lot, and today I thought I would take a break and ask about it." It sounded lame, but she didn't know what else to tell him. "I thought it was maybe a hundred years old."

He feigned indignation. "What—do I look that old to you?" He paused for a beat, as if expecting a denial, then continued on when none came. "Try about half that, and you'd get it right. They built that wall in the summer of 1951, no, I guess it was 1952, because Allen was just back from Korea and I'd been living here for two years by then. At the beginning of the summer they graded the road down to nothing to make it easier to build some new tract houses and that left the Lisacs' house standing here like an island. Oh, the Lisacs didn't take too kindly to that. They had to put the wall in to stop their yard from sliding away in the next rain. I was lucky that my house was farther up."

The ring must have been the mother's, then, although if she had been old enough to have a son go off to Korea, she must be dead by now.

"So where do the Lisacs live now?"

"What do you mean? They still live here. Allen inherited the house from his folks after they died. The house has been in the family since it was built. His great-great-granddaddy was one of those lumber barons. He built it for his fancy East Coast wife, but they say she only lasted a couple of years before she took sick and died." He waggled his overgrown eyebrows at her. "Of course, some people do say that she just ran off. Whatever, it just left him and his son rattling around in this big house. Things have changed since then. If this house ever came on the market, one of those yuppie people would buy it in a minute. They like all the built-ins and the leaded glass windows. And Allen has made so much money, he makes his great-great-grandfather look like a failure."

Allen Lisac. Claire had heard of him before. He owned a construction company, and signs with his company's logo, an interlocked *L* and *C*, for Lisac Construction, were at half the building sites in Portland. A shiver danced across Claire's damp skin. Now that he had an audience, this Howard guy looked like he could go on talking forever, gossiping about a time long past, when he and the world were both young.

"Well, I certainly appreciate your telling me about the wall. I'd better get started running again before I lose all initiative."

"Feel free to stop by if you think up any more questions."

His expression was wistful, and Claire imagined his day—long stretches of silence broken up talking too long to the grocery store clerk or the guy at the auto parts store. She gave him a little wave with her right hand before turning on her heel and running down the length of the driveway. She was still careful to keep the ring's winking diamonds from betraying that she was taking something that didn't belong to her. Before she could cross the street, she had to wait for a brand-new purple Porsche to pass. The vanity license plate read RUNVS—license-plate-speak for "Are you envious?" Claire, who had once worked as a vanity license plate verifier for the state of Oregon, wondered how long it would be before someone keyed the car in a darkened parking lot. In her opinion, people who used their license plates to brag on themselves—like the Jaguar for which she had once approved plates reading IQ 189—were just asking for it.

On the way home, she had to detour around an unidentifiable dead animal in the gutter that had been rained on, stepped on, and run over so many times the only thing left was a flattened patch of gray fur. Claire thought nothing of it.

FOUR

SKIRTING THE FOOT-WIDE ceramic dog dish emblazoned with the word "Duke" that lay on the front porch, Claire opened the door to the big house she had shared with Charlotte Heidenbruch for more than a half dozen years. Charlie claimed the dog dish was cheaper than a burglar alarm—or a real dog. To add to the verisimilitude, she occasionally even filled it with the cheapest brand of dry dog food. The only drawback was that the stale kibble drew all the neighborhood dogs as well as the occasional raccoon.

Claire found Charlie in the dining room, kneading bread dough on the round wooden table. At four-foot-eleven, Charlie found the kitchen counter impossibly high for the task. The older woman was so full of life that Claire tended to think of her as both taller and younger, certainly not the eighty-one years she really was.

"Look what I found when I was out running today." Claire stretched out her left hand. The ring's diamonds caught the light.

In the ten minutes it had taken her to run home, Claire had had time to picture what Charlie's reaction might be. Surprise, excitement, amazement—all these she had imagined. But not this, not Charlie staggering backward, one floury hand pressed against her chest.

"Where did you get that?" Charlie was regarding the ring the way a gardener might a fallen branch suddenly slithering away with a telltale rattle.

"What's the matter, Charlie?" Claire had never seen her friend look like this before.

"Just tell me where you got this thing." The last words came out *dis ding,* the *th* sound eluding Charlie's tongue as if she were suddenly back in Germany. Her English was nearly flawless. She had immigrated to the United States in 1946 and become a citizen as soon as she could. Whenever anyone asked her what she was, Charlie always answered that she was, of course, an American.

"About ten blocks from here, off Forty-fifth, inside an old rock wall." Claire turned her hand so that the diamonds caught the light. "Why? Have you seen it before?"

"Let me look at it." When Claire put out her hand, Charlie leaned closer, but Claire noticed she was careful not to actually touch the ring. Instead, she scrutinized it for a long time with narrowed eyes, before finally looking up. Claire had expected her expression to be sharp, but instead her friend's eyes were unfocused, her mouth loose and trembling. For once, she looked her age.

"How can this be? Tell me again where you are finding it."

"Why? Do you know what it is?" Claire waited a moment, but when Charlie didn't answer, she continued. "I was on a run when I stopped up the hill from the Southwest Community Center. When I was stretching out I saw something shining inside a chink in this old rock wall where the mortar had fallen out. And it turned out to be this ring. I tried to ask the people who owned the house about it, but the neighbor said they were on vacation. So do you recognize it?"

Charlie was silent for nearly a minute. When she finally spoke, her words were heavy and slow. "It looks so much like the ring that belonged to my friend Elizabeth. Her engagement ring. But the last time I saw it was fifty years ago. When her man came home from Korea, something went wrong between them. She broke off the engagement and gave the ring back to him. And that's the house where he lived." Charlie's faded blue eyes finally focused on Claire's. "So why are you now finding this ring?"

"This Mr. Backus who lived next door, he told me the wall

was made around that time. Maybe she lost the ring somehow while it was being built."

"Backus? Was this Howard Backus?" Pronounced *How-vard*.

"Do you know him?" Claire didn't know why this surprised her. Charlie had lived in this neighborhood since shortly after the war. At the same time, Charlie didn't dwell on the past. The past had stolen her husband and child, and left behind nothing but a green string of numbers tattooed on her forearm. One human being had done that to another, the better to keep track of perishable inventory.

Charlie paid no attention to Claire's question. "Tell me again where this wall was."

"Off Forty-fifth, above the Southwest Community Center. On one of those cross streets that's named after a state."

"And the house, what did it look like?"

"Like one of those English houses, you know, two stories with wooden beams running diagonally through the plaster on the second story."

"That is where my friend lived."

"So do you know where this Elizabeth is now? Can we give her back her ring?" Claire slipped it off and put it on the table, next to the plump dark ball of dough. Now her hand felt light enough to float in midair. "Or maybe it would really belong to the guy she decided not to marry."

"The man she didn't marry still lives in that house. Allen Lisac." Charlie paused. "And for fifty years, Elizabeth has been buried in Finter's Cemetery."

"She's dead? The woman who owned this is dead?" Claire was suddenly glad the ring was no longer on her finger. "What did she die from?"

"She killed herself." Slowly, almost reluctantly, Charlie picked up the ring and weighed it in her hand, her eyes narrowed as if she were appraising it.

A shiver ran through Claire. "Killed herself? What was her name again? And how old was she?"

"Elizabeth Ellsworth. She was only nineteen years old."

"How did she kill herself?" Claire thought of sleeping pills, a quiet slipping into an endless slumber.

"She hung herself." Charlie hesitated, then nearly whispered the next words. "I was the one who found her."

FIVE

1952—"I'VE BROUGHT YOU LUNCH," Charlie said on the day that Elizabeth died and everything changed. She held out the wicker hamper to Tom. Even though it had only taken her a few minutes to walk from her house to the Lisacs' front yard, sweat trickled between her breasts and slipped down the hollow of her spine.

Tom flashed her a smile while carefully setting into place another stone in the wall he had been building for the past six weeks. The stones were only a little larger than a loaf of bread and looked deceptively light. Charlie knew from the time she had tried to lift one that each weighed about twenty kilos, but the only sign they were heavy was the flex of the sinews in Tom's forearms. Rather than putting the stones one right after another in a line, he fitted each into just the right space like a puzzle piece, matching contours so closely that only a little mortar was needed to hold them together.

"Good timing. I was just thinking about how hungry I was." Tom grinned, and the look he gave her, one eyebrow raised, white teeth flashing in his tanned face, made the double meaning clear. They had been lovers since the first day they met, when she had invited him back to her house, talked with him for two hours, fed him, then matter-of-factly invited him upstairs. Now every evening Tom knocked on Charlie's door, dirty and scraped and with a faint gray dusting of cement worked into every pore and crevice. And every evening, Charlie would be waiting for him with a glass of whiskey and a tub filled with tepid water. She knew it would offer cool relief after a day spent laboring under a sky baked such a hard blue it looked like it might crack. Leaning over his powerful back, she would slowly rub the white washcloth along the bunched muscles, then reach around to the strong slabs of his pectorals, then lower, lower, until he finally stood up or pulled her into the tub with him. His hands—strong and callused, the nails bruised and torn—were always gentle when he touched her.

Now he washed those same hands under the outside faucet. No matter how strong their desire for each other, Tom needed this job, and Mr. Lisac frowned on lunch breaks of any duration. There was no question that they would do anything now but eat and talk. In a way, this was Charlie's test, to see how much they had to talk about during the daylight hours, when there was more to say than urgent murmurs on twisted sheets.

They walked a few blocks and then spread their blanket on a grassy strip next to the fenced field of a dairy farm. On the other side of the fence, three brown and white cows watched them without curiosity. Tom and Charlie sat in about the same spot where, fifty years later, the Southwest Community Center's whirlpool would be. But for now there was nothing but a single oak tree, and they sat in its dappled shadow. Charlie had made a picnic for them, with the last of the blueberries and a loaf of her rough bread and some cheese she had recently discovered, real, pale-colored cheese with a strong, sour flavor. She thought she would never get used to America's bland cheeses, dyed unnatural colors as if to camouflage their lack of taste.

The hot air pressed down on them, heavy and still. At the refugee resettlement center, they had told Charlie that it rained a lot in Portland. She had since discovered that Portlanders had a six-week-long secret called Indian summer. Charlie loved the term. It reminded her of her childhood spent reading books set in the American West, featuring noble Indians. It was only recently that she had learned that the man who had written these books had never set foot in America.

"I figure I'll be done with the wall in two weeks. Maybe less." Avoiding her gaze, Tom took a deliberate bite of bread and stared down at the grass as he chewed. His face was expressionless.

A flash of something approaching hatred ran through Charlie. He was as simple as an animal. He ate, drank, slept, and fucked with complete enjoyment, abandoning himself to the moment. She knew what he was trying to say. When the wall was done, Walter Lisac would pay Tom and he would go on his way. He already had a job lined up in Oregon City, forty miles away. As for what would happen to her then, Charlie told herself that Tom was not the first lover she had taken, nor the last.

"Will you miss me?" she said lightly.

"Did I say I was going anyplace?" He looked up at her then, with his golden eyes, and she saw that he was focused only on her answer, watching intently. "Or are you telling me you want me to go?"

Charlie, always so sure of herself, opened her mouth but could not find any words. The words came out anyway, as if someone else were saying them. "No. I do not want you to go." Tears pricked at the back of her eyes. She had never before betrayed Richard with her heart. Seven years after his death, he still came to her in dreams.

Tom covered her hand with his own, his large hand completely enveloping hers, and didn't say any more.

After they finished eating, Charlie couldn't find the flask of iced tea she thought she had packed. She must have left it sitting on her kitchen counter. Her throat was so dry it itched. After she walked Tom back to the Lisacs' house, he set to work immediately, not one for lingering. The city had widened and deepened the street earlier in the year, leaving the Lisacs' house sitting alone on top of an unnaturally sharp-edged hill. Walter was still angry about it. He had to commission the wall to keep his property from washing away when the rains came in November.

Just thinking about rain made Charlie even thirstier. She imagined a cool glass filled with ice water, condensation beading on the surface. Instead of using the heavy brass knocker, she rapped lightly on the door. Somewhere inside, she thought she heard a door close. Someone was at home, then. Probably Elizabeth, who at Allen's parents' urging spent most of her time here rather than her own tumbledown house filled with squabbling children. Or maybe it was Elizabeth's future mother-in-law, Austrid Lisac, who might have been beautiful, with her wide gray eyes, if they hadn't been offset by the thin line of her mouth. She knocked again, then after a minute tried the door and found it unlocked.

"Hello?" Charlie called, then pushed open the door. At first, all she could take in was that something was wrong, out of place. It was more than the chair overturned on the rug, it was the thing that swayed faintly in the draft from the door, something dangling from the huge oak crossbeam.

Then Charlie realized the thing was Elizabeth, her limp form, dressed in a black peignoir, completely lifeless. Her head was bowed, and her pale yellow hair covered her face. Two feet above the ground, her bare feet danced in the air.

Charlie ran forward then, screaming Tom's name as she ran. She grabbed Elizabeth's thighs in a bear hug. They were still warm and wet where the piss had run down them. With all her might, she pushed up. Elizabeth weighed at least twenty kilos more than Charlie, but the strength came to her from somewhere. She wanted Elizabeth to be alive. She willed it.

Tom ran in the still-open door, took one look. Yanking the knife from his belt, he righted the chair even as he stepped on it. With a single slice, he cut the thin white rope that tied Elizabeth to the air.

The full weight of Elizabeth's body shifted and fell onto Charlie. She lost her balance and stumbled sideways, her arms still around Elizabeth's thighs, her face pressed into her soft belly, into the smell of piss and shit. Together, they reeled into the china cabinet. Charlie would forever after remember the sound Elizabeth's head made as it struck one of the etched glass doors, shattering it. A terrible hollow thunk, accompanied by the crack and tinkle of shattered glass. It reminded her of Kristallnacht.

And then they were lying in a tangle of arms and legs, dead woman and live woman. Tom had been through the war. He knew how to act when you must. Without hesitation he clawed his index finger into the narrow white cord that dug into Elizabeth's long neck, slid the flat of the blade under, and then turned it and cut the cord. The edge of the blade nicked her skin, leaving behind a red line two inches long.

"Breathe," Charlie implored Elizabeth, on her knees now, stroking the pale blond hair back from the equally pale face. "Breathe." Elizabeth's eyes were open and dull, the pupils fixed, dwindled down to two dark pinpricks. She wore a black silk nightgown, and Charlie slammed her fist down between the other woman's breasts. "Breathe!" Tom caught her fist when she raised it again.

"She's dead, Charlie." His words were flat, without emotion, and she saw his own pupils had shrunk down so small she couldn't see them anymore, just his golden irises. "You can't help her."

"Elizabeth?" Charlie spoke softly to the dead girl, the way you whispered to someone who was still asleep. "Why?" She noticed there were other smells in the room. From Elizabeth's parted lips came the smell of wine. But mingled with it and overpowering it was the smell of blood. Blood rimmed the white even teeth that showed between the girl's open lips. Blood matted the hair at Elizabeth's temple. When Charlie closed her eyes, all she saw was red, all she smelled was death.

SIX

"HOW DID YOU KNOW HER?" Claire asked softly. Charlie's eyes were closed, but they still moved underneath the pleated lids.

At the sound of Claire's voice, Charlie jumped a little, then opened her eyes. "There was a group of us who were friends, all of us, for one summer. This was in 1952. In September, Elizabeth died, and then everything changed. Wait. I think I still have some photos of us. From the old days." Charlie turned and went upstairs, leaving Claire at the dining room table, staring at the ring, glinting dully next to the smooth brown round of bread dough. After hearing what had happened to its last wearer, she found it no longer drew her.

Overhead, Claire could hear Charlie moving around in the attic. It was another fifteen minutes before Charlie returned with a half-dozen black and white photos beginning to crack with age. She handed one to Claire.

"Here is proof, although I was sure the minute I saw it. What you found is Elizabeth's ring." Her voice was heavy with an emotion Claire couldn't name. Was it loss? The photo showed a young man with his arm around a young woman. Her left hand was extended to the camera, carefully manicured fingers spread to show the ring at best advantage. Claire picked up the ring she had found and held it next to the photo. There could be no doubt. It was the same ring, with the same delicately etched flowers and leaves, with the same three diamonds set directly into the wide band.

Next, Claire looked at the couple's faces. From Claire's perspective, fifty years later, they both looked very young to be getting married. Elizabeth Ellsworth hadn't been traditionally pretty, there were too many angles and planes in her face for that, but she was striking, with high cheekbones and large, light-colored eyes. Her pale hair was pulled back from her face in a ponytail.

Charlie looked at the photo over Claire's shoulder, her face soft with remembering. "Elizabeth was tall, taller even than you. Back in those days, fewer women were tall. I guess we did not have the kind of nutrition girls have nowadays. She told me people used to tease her about it in school, and she did not like all the attention it brought her. She said they called her 'giraffe.' When I first moved here I would see her walking home from school with her shoulders curled over. Then when she started dating Allen she straightened up and you saw that she had a long, white neck. Like a swan's."

With their two heads close together, Allen Lisac made quite a contrast to Elizabeth. He was as dark as Elizabeth had been fair, with jet-black hair cropped close to his head—Claire thought the style might have been called a flattop—and dark eyes. Sunglasses had been pushed to the top of his head.

"We had been talking about the wedding that day. They were to be married in six months. His mother spent her days planning it. It was going to be a real society event."

"If they were talking about getting married, then why do they both look so sad?" Claire asked. "Do you think that even then she was thinking of killing herself?"

"What do you mean?" Charlie looked more closely at the photo.

It was hard for Claire to pinpoint exactly what she saw. The ring dominated the picture and was the only thing truly in focus, leaving Allen and Liz's features slightly blurred, as if to underscore how young they were. While they both wore smiles, they didn't look at each other. Liz's eyes looked at the camera, but there was something about her face that looked frozen, as if at any minute the expression could crack and fall away. Allen's head was turned slightly away from Liz, his gaze fastened on something the camera couldn't see. His smile seemed forced, his lips tightly closed, bracketed by lines too deep for his years.

Slowly, Charlie said, "Of course, the war had changed Allen. He was only in Korea for a few months before he was injured. He nearly lost his leg, and spent more time in a military hospital than he did in Korea. He still walks with a cane. And Elizabeth must have been very unhappy, to do what she did. I do not think she was prepared to deal with how he had changed, both mentally and physically. But she knew that if she did not marry Allen, she would have been ostracized for rejecting a war hero."

Claire realized what had been nagging at her. "Allen Lisac. I've heard that name before," she said slowly. "And not just from those construction site billboards."

Charlie nodded. "Of course you have. He and Mary never had any children, but he is determined to leave behind in this world a legacy. He has his name on that new theater space downtown. He puts up the money for Swingtime, that tennis tournament that benefits children's charities. And he..." she hesitated.

Claire finished the sentence for her. "And he's the one who's promised the Oregon Art Museum a new wing and the Old Masters paintings and drawings to hang on the walls." A new wing that would require a new head curator. The three candidates for the position were Vicki Guinn from the Getty Museum in Los Angeles, Laurel Williams from the Chicago Art Museum, and Dante Bonner, currently with the Metropolitan Museum of Art in New York City. And Claire's long-distance boyfriend.

Claire didn't have much chance to think about what this might mean before Charlie handed her another photo. "This is from the same day. We were all down at the river having a picnic to celebrate Allen's coming home. Ten days later, Elizabeth was dead."

Claire's first impression was of a lot of people, too many crowded into one photograph to make out individuals. She turned and rummaged around in the junk drawer of the dining room's built-in sideboard. Charlie's house, built in 1922, had built-in everything. Charlie had a magnifying glass for when instructions proved too tiny even for her reading glasses. Seven people stood or sat on a blanket spread in the grass. Behind them lay a jumble of large stones and the dark edge of the water. Now raw sewage spilled into the Willamette anytime it rained hard, so you had to be brave, stupid, young, or unable to read English—or all four—to be willing to swim in it. Even the blanket was a reminder of times gone by. It was an Indian-patterned Pendleton, the kind of thing that would fetch hundreds on eBay now, but fifty years ago it had been fine for throwing on the ground and dripping mayonnaise on.

"Is that you, Charlie?" Claire tapped her finger on the couple standing on the left side of the photo. Charlie took the magnifying glass from Claire's hand, then nodded as she looked at where Claire's finger pointed, fifty years in the past. For a woman a few months past eighty-one, Charlie was still a looker, petite and elegant and always put together. But the photo revealed her at her peak, all ripe curves, her black hair framing her face in waves. She wore a form-fitting sleeveless polka-dot shirt topping a gored skirt unbuttoned to show off the matching shorts. The effect was more provocative than Claire had imagined would be seen in the fifties. The man who stood next to her had his arm around Charlie's waist. He was at least a foot taller than she, but since she was so short, that wasn't hard. He wore long pants and a short-sleeve shirt, patterned with palm trees, open to reveal a muscled torso. He had the kind of build that men now spent hours in the gym with a personal trainer in a vain search for, but Claire could tell this guy had come by it honestly. Even in the old black and white photo, his skin looked tanned.

"Who is that you're with?"

"His name was Tom." As she spoke, Charlie turned away to get a red-and-white-checked towel from the linen closet. "He was actually a day laborer whom Allen's father had hired. He was not really part of our little group, but then, for that matter, neither was I. I was thirty-one, quite a bit older than the other girls. They had just been children during the war. Tom was older, too. He had fought in Italy, and liberated one of the camps. We understood each other."

"But you broke up?"

Still not meeting Claire's eyes, Charlie went to the kitchen cupboard. Standing on tiptoe, she took down some shortening. "He wanted to get married." She rubbed the shortening on the inside of a royal blue ceramic bowl, then carried the bowl back into the dining room, plopped the bread dough in, and turned it over. The dough was as round and full of life as a pregnant belly.

Claire had long ago figured out that, for Charlie, there could be no husband to replace the one who had died in a concentration camp, no child to substitute for the son torn from her arms. Charlie had taken many lovers since—and clearly this Tom had been one of them—but Claire guessed that Charlie had not been able to truly start over, to make a new family for herself as if the first one had never existed. Now she covered the ball of dough with the kitchen towel, then tucked it on the bottom shelf of the refrigerator. The secret to Charlie's bread, nutty and sweet, was the three long, slow risings in the fridge.

Claire looked back down at the photo. "I see Elizabeth and Allen, but who are the other people?"

Charlie came to point over Claire's shoulder at the three people who stood next to her old self. "Nova and Elizabeth are with Howard, the one you talked to about the ring. Howard was funny. He had a bitter kind of humor. It could make you laugh if you were in the right mood. Sometimes it was too sharp."

It took a minute for Claire to see the resemblance. Howard was still tall and thin, but fifty years ago he had had all his hair and a fresh, confident look on his face. He stood with his arms hooked around the two women's waists, clowningly pulling them close. They turned toward him, their lips pursed in an exaggerated fashion, mugging for the camera. The one named Nova, another blonde only with shorter hair, had kicked one shapely leg behind her. She wore an off-the-shoulder white peasant blouse over brief shorts, her hair in pin-curled waves. Elizabeth was more modestly dressed in a flowered circle skirt and a sleeveless blouse. Like all the women in the photo, Nova and Elizabeth wore flat, wedge-heeled sandals that wouldn't have been out of place fifty years later.

Charlie smiled down at the photo. "Nova—now, she I liked. She was a bit of a live wire. She had what they called a reputation."

"For what?" Claire asked, intrigued.

"Oh, for things no one would look at twice nowadays. She liked a bit of fun. You know the old sayings. Nova smoked like a chimney and drank like a fish and she went through men like a revolving door."

"Did she ever get married?"

"More than once." Charlie paused to think. "I have been to two weddings for her. Maybe three. Then she had a child, and the girl was retarded. I think that made Nova settle down a little bit. A mongoloid little girl, although now they say Down's syndrome. The girl had heart problems. Nova cosseted that child. The doctor said if it hadn't been for her care, the child would never have lived as long as she did."

"How old was the girl when she died?"

"Eight." Charlie sighed. "Over time, Nova and I have grown apart, but I still get an occasional Christmas card from her."

Claire looked down at the photo again. Allen Lisac sat on the blanket on the far side of the trio, his legs straight out in front of him. Even covered with long pants, one leg was noticeably thinner than the other. His eyes were hidden by dark glasses. Next to his leg was something black and straight, about the size of a short broomstick, ending in a silver cuff. Claire realized it was what she thought of as a "professional crutch" a waist-high metal stick.

Charlie tapped one fingernail, manicured in Petal Pink, on the half-hidden crutch. "That's the reason Allen came home. We heard he had been injured on the battlefield, evacuated to the military hospital. Elizabeth was beside herself. There were skin grafts and surgeries, even after he returned home." Charlie spoke more slowly. "I had known him from the neighborhood before he left. He mowed my lawn the summer before he went to college. Allen was a beautiful young man. He told me he set a state record in high school for running the mile. Then he came back from Korea with that cane. He had to move like an old man, and somehow his spirit was old, too."

In the photo, Allen wore civilian clothing, too formal for a picnic at the river's edge. The long pants presumably hid his crippled leg, but he also wore a dress shirt buttoned up to his neck. To Claire, he was a reminder of another time, when men might spend even their weekends looking as if they were ready to go into the office at any moment. Unsmiling, he looked straight at the camera, ignoring his fiancée clowning with another man, a man who stood easily on well-muscled legs.

There was only one other person in the photo, a horse-faced woman in a full dress who sat next to Allen, her legs curled to one side. Something about her face seemed familiar, but Claire couldn't place what it was.

Charlie pointed at her. "That is Mary. Elizabeth's sister. Two years after Liz died, she married Allen."

Claire was taken aback. "What? Maybe that was the reason Elizabeth broke up with him. Maybe she knew he was fooling around with her sister."

Charlie shook her head. "I do not believe there was anything between them while her sister was alive."

Claire studied the woman named Mary. While the two sisters did look quite a bit alike, it was interesting how the same elements, only altered slightly and arranged a little differently, could add up to so much less. Elizabeth's hair was the palest yellow. Mary's hair was darker, a drab dishwater blond. Elizabeth's face had striking angles and planes. Mary's face was simply bony with a long jaw. Elizabeth's eyes were large, while Mary's were too prominent. Why would Allen have chosen her after having loved her much prettier sister? Had Mary offered the closest approximation of Elizabeth he could find? Or had they been drawn together by their grief? In the photo, Mary seemed to be only miming having fun. Her smile seemed too full to be real, her face turned animatedly toward the others as she watched from the sidelines.

"So how did you know all these people, Charlie?"

"I had known most of them by sight. I had been living here five years by then. We saw each other at John's Market, or the movie theater or the drugstore. And, as I said, Allen had mowed my lawn all one summer. But really, I met them all through Tom."

"Where did you know Tom from?"

Charlie shrugged one shoulder and then looked away. The gesture seemed very European to Claire, revealing and concealing at the same time. "I saw him working on that wall one day when I was out for a walk. He was just beginning to lay the foundation stones. I stopped to talk." Claire could imagine the rest. Charlie had always been drawn to beauty, inanimate or animate. It didn't take much imagination to see Tom, stripped to the waist, tanned, sweat outlining the muscles of his chest and arms and abdomen as he lifted those heavy stones into place one by one. And to imagine Charlie beguiling him with a laugh and the elevation of one perfectly shaped eyebrow.

"It was through Tom that I got to know Elizabeth. Allen's family had invited her to stay with them when he went overseas. Allen's mother, Austrid, said she wanted to plan the wedding, but I think she was really trying to mold Elizabeth into a proper wife for her son. And then, through Elizabeth, I met her circle of friends. There was the Lisacs' neighbor, Howard. Elizabeth's sister, Mary. Elizabeth's best friend, Nova. And Allen when he came back. And he had been home only a short while before Elizabeth killed herself."

There was a long silence, and Claire thought Charlie was saddened, thinking about the death of her young friend. When Charlie spoke again, Claire was startled by her words.

"I went through that goddamn war where people died terribly. I could not stand to think that this beautiful girl had killed herself over what was only a moment's unhappiness. She died with her belly full in a warm house filled with beautiful things. With friends who would have done anything for her. Instead, she went to death and embraced him."

Now Claire identified the emotion that colored her friend's voice. It was anger.

"She was a foolish girl, to take her life over a man, and such a man." Claire wondered if Charlie was thinking of her own man and her little son, gone forever and mourned only in private. "When Allen came back from Korea, he was…damaged. He hardly spoke. It would have killed Elizabeth's spirit to be married to such a one. She would have been like a bird who flies inside a room's open door—and then the door closes, trapping it. It dies beating its wings against the glass. She was right to break off the engagement. But I think she was ashamed, too, ashamed to face her friends and Allen's parents and try to explain why she could not marry him. She chose death because she did not understand that she could have chosen life."

Claire didn't know what to say. Her friend seldom talked about the past, but then again, it wasn't every day that a bit of her past made an unexpected reappearance in her dining room. Instead, Claire picked up another snapshot. The next was much like the first, a group photo of the seven of them, only in this one Howard parodied a he-man pose, standing in profile with his wiry arms and legs bent, muscles flexed in imitation of Charles Atlas.

"That Howard," Charlie said. "He was always joking around. He had a reputation as a playboy, but he never stayed with any one woman for long. One date, two, then he was on to another. After Elizabeth's death, he changed. Well, we all did. But Howard seemed more affected than any of us. Perhaps even Allen. Afterward, I wondered if Howard had secretly been in love with her. He wept so hard at the grave that Tom had to steady him."

"Did you say this was your camera, Charlie?" When the older woman nodded, Claire said, "Then who took these pictures?"

"That is a good question." Charlie looked up, thinking. "I

took most of these, but the photos that show me—I don't know. Wait—it was Frank. Mary and Elizabeth's brother. He was a few years older, but he did not really have many of his own friends. He was always tagging along. Here." She slid over another picture. "Here he is with Nova."

Clad now in a strapless bathing suit, Nova stood with her gleaming lips parted in a smile next to a smoking grill. Her darkly manicured hands rested on her hips, accentuating her hourglass figure. Holding a spatula, a young man stood next to her. Frank's eyes were even with the suit's cone-shaped bra. He was pale and skinny and short, and despite how he was looking at Nova, she smiled at the camera as if it alone existed.

"Frank liked women, but he liked them too much. Do you know what I mean? He did not see you, not as a person, not as an individual. He saw only…woman. That is why I took their picture. I saw the way he was looking at her."

Charlie didn't hand Claire the last photo, so Claire slipped it from her unresisting hand. It showed no people at all, just of a tumble of stones lapped with water, shot close to the water's edge so that the stones loomed above. The photo seemed foreboding, and Claire wondered for a moment what had made Charlie choose such a composition on a sunny outing.

Charlie said, "We all drifted apart after Elizabeth died. When we were together, everything we did reminded us of her. We all questioned ourselves. Was there something we could have said or done that would have stopped her? Even when we tried to talk about other things, we would still end up talking about her and crying. Howard just looked ill all the time. Nova—that was the only time in her life that I knew her not to smile. And I think we all worried that Allen might be tempted to follow Elizabeth. How could any man stand two such terrible blows, one right after another? You asked if there had been anything between him and Mary, but I think it was Elizabeth's death that brought them together. She fussed over him, and he seemed to like it."

Claire picked up the first photo again, the one of Allen and

Elizabeth and the ring, then put it back down on the table.
"Elizabeth killed herself." She was trying to get everything
straight. She picked up the ring, weighing it in her palm, then
closed her fingers over it. "But before she did, she broke off
her engagement with Allen."

"Yes." Charlie nodded, her gaze steady on Claire, as if she
already knew what she would say next.

"But why? Listening to what you say, I can understand her
not wanting to marry Allen. But why did she have to kill herself?"

"It all happened so quickly. She had been nothing but talk,
talk, talk about the wedding the last time I saw her alive. Some
girls focus on the wedding, not on what will happen afterward.
Maybe Elizabeth looked at the future and realized she could not
live with Allen. Not with him being crippled and cold. And then
perhaps she was afraid that everyone would judge her."

Claire opened her fingers, displaying the ring. "Okay. Elizabeth breaks off the wedding. She gives the ring back to Allen.
Then she kills herself. So why did I find it in the wall?"

The ring made a hollow noise when she set it down on the table.

SEVEN

Now and 1952—The last time Charlie saw Elizabeth alive was the Saturday before her death, when the loose group of friends had gone for an impromptu picnic down by the river. The day was warm, eighty degrees by noon, the sky a saturated blue. With Warren Lisac's permission, Tom knocked off at lunchtime. Laughing, the group all piled into Tom's truck. Charlie sat beside him in the cab. Allen's leg prevented him from clambering into the truck bed with the rest. He grunted as he pulled himself onto the bench seat next to Charlie. Elizabeth, Frank, Mary, Howard, and Nova sat in the truck bed. When Tom went around corners, they screamed as if they were on a carnival ride. Tom's hand caressed Charlie's knee every time he changed gears, which he did more than was strictly necessary. Beside Charlie, Allen made a point of looking out the window, away from her bare knees and Tom's big, rough hand, his expression shuttered. He hadn't even been gone a year, but he had left a boy, marching off willingly to defend from Communism a nation he had barely heard of, and came back a quiet man whose every word, expression, and step was now carefully contemplated before it was even begun.

Dozens of people had been drawn to the river—to picnic, to fish, to swim in the water, or at least dangle their toes in it. Austrid had packed them a big wicker picnic basket. Deviled eggs. A Mason jar of home-canned pickles. Ham sandwiches slathered with mustard and wrapped in waxed paper. Charlie wondered a bit at the choice of filling, the way she always wondered when Austrid's eyes lingered on her a little too long, the older woman's face expressionless. A basket of the last of the Selva strawberries, dark red and no bigger than the end of Charlie's thumb, the flavor like a distillation of the entire summer. With his pocketknife, Tom hacked chunks from a heavy watermelon. The men had a contest to see who could spit one of the black seeds the farthest. Everyone laughed when Nova joined in, and then laughed even harder when she won.

Charlie took pictures of them all. Her past was gone, reduced to nothing but memories. Even these she denied herself, for fear that she would drown in them, never surfacing for air. When she had first moved to America she found herself taking pictures of everything. Occasionally of objects, the curve of a hand-carved wooden bowl, two hairpins on the tumbled white sheets of her unmade bed, but more often of people. There was something fundamentally innocent about Americans that drew her. After Elizabeth's death, though, she reached for her camera less and less often.

THERE WAS A BEFORE. And there was an after. And in between there was nothing Charlie could bear to think about. Yet it still haunted her.

Eight thousand miles away, fifty years later, Charlie still found herself studying people's faces, wondering if they would have helped her. The businessman walking briskly past her, who pressed his thin lips together and then looked away. Would he have shared his bread ration with her? The woman with two babies in a double stroller, talking on her cell phone—would she have held Charlie up when she couldn't walk? Generosity came from unexpected places sometimes, she had learned that, but cruelty, too. In the camp, people shriveled or blossomed into something else entirely.

EIGHT

"CLEARLY, WHATEVER HAPPENED," Charlie said as they both regarded the ring, glinting dully on the dining room table, "you must return the ring to Allen Lisac. It belongs to his family."

"That Mr. Backus said the Lisacs wouldn't be back from Europe for a couple of weeks." Claire looked down at the ring, tarnished now not only by time but by her knowledge of its past. "Maybe he won't even want it back. Who would want to wear a ring that belonged to someone who committed suicide?"

"I have read that many suicides come from anger. If she were wanting to hurt Allen, perhaps Elizabeth would have still been wearing this when we found her. But I'm sure there was no ring on her hand when we found her. And I'm sure Allen said she gave it back to him. So why was it in the wall? Everything happened so quickly. One day Elizabeth was chattering away about the wedding, and then a few weeks later she was dead. It made little sense. At the time, I did not ask questions. Perhaps I should have." She straightened up. "Nova and she were as thick as thieves. They shared all their secrets. Not that Elizabeth probably had any to be sharing. I am sure she just listened to Nova's tales of adventure. But if anyone would know why Elizabeth hid the ring instead of giving it back, Nova would."

"Would Nova even still be alive?"

Charlie made a small sound of annoyance. "You seem to forget that I am several years older than she. Besides, I got a Christmas card from her last year."

Claire backpedaled. "You said she smoked and drank, so I..."

Waving her hand in dismissal, Charlie said, "I am only teasing. And Nova is alive, although she is living now in Riverwalk." She grimaced. "I think I would rather be dead than there."

An unknown marketer had sold Charlie's name and address to every company that catered to seniors. Each day's mail brought slick ads for hearing aid centers, coupons for Ensure and Depends, and pleas that Charlie join AARP. One of the most frequent offenders was Riverwalk. It billed itself as "Portland's premiere retirement community!" offering "a new lifestyle for seniors where we supply the adventure, fun and friendship!" Whoever wrote the marketing materials believed fervently in the use of exclamation points.

Claire had looked through one of the brochures once after she ran out of other reading material while eating lunch. As far as she could tell, they roped you in with one of the "Homes on Riverwalk," detached single-story houses with views of the golf course, and discreet ramps leading up to the front porches. Inside were high ceilings, big rooms, and showers with a hidden sit-down option. You didn't have to do any yard work, unless you wanted to tend a plot in the community garden. Each home came with a thirty-meal plan so that you could either "cook in your own kitchen or enjoy dining with your new friends in the Riverwalk dining room."

It wasn't until the brochure's third panel that certain polite phrases began to crop up. "We work with you as your needs increase," or "We offer security for the rest of your life." In other words, Riverwalk was the kind of place where you went to die. Even the home you started out with had emergency call buttons in every room, including one tucked in a corner of the bathroom floor. The guest bedroom with its separate bath could easily be turned into a space for the live-in attendant. And "if your care needs should increase," well, you could move—or be moved—into Riverwalk's separate skilled nursing facility, the secure Alzheimer's ward, or the hospice wing mentioned in small print on the brochure's final panel.

That evening, Charlie unearthed Nova's phone number. When Charlie called, she didn't mention anything about the ring. She simply said she wanted to talk about old times, then mentioned she might bring along a friend. When Charlie hung up, she said, "Nova says it's fine if you come along. She said that Riverwalk is a gated community, and that normally they are very protective about having strangers who aren't"—she hooked her fingers—"'seniors' on 'campus,' but there is to be an open house this weekend."

"What—they all have to be locked up for their own protection? They think that once you're old it's not safe to let you associate with the rest of society?" Claire imagined fast-talking vacuum cleaner door-to-door salesmen lined up three deep.

"Riverwalk is very expensive. Maybe it is not so much to keep them in as to keep the riffraff out."

"How can Nova afford to live there? Did she marry money?"

Charlie grinned. "Divorced money, with the help of a good attorney, which may be even better."

AFTER FINISHING UP at Capitol Hill Elementary, Claire drove to her mom's house. For the past few years, she had been a volunteer with the SMART program—Start Making A Reader Today. For an hour a day, she worked one-on-one with Jason Lutz, a seven-year-old who had attention deficit disorder. Jason came from an impoverished household, both mentally and physically. The books the SMART program gave him were the only ones in Jason's apartment.

People tended to think of southwest Portland residents as having money, but there were pockets of poverty all the same. Just as many people lived among Barbur Boulevard's ragged jumble of cheap restaurants, gas stations, and businesses like Baby Dolls Modeling and Lingerie as had homes in the terraced heights of West Hills. Claire wasn't supposed to get involved in Jason's home life, but driving to her mother's, it was hard for Claire not to fantasize about taking Jason home.

Jason lived with his mechanic dad in one of Barbur's run-down motels. There didn't seem to be a mom, just a seventeen-year-old brother, Matt. From the scraps of information Claire had been able to piece together, Matt probably used, and possibly sold, drugs. Despite the oversized red flannel shirt and dirty jeans that seemed the only clothes Jason had, curiosity and intelligence shone from his face. How long would it be before circumstances snuffed them out?

Despite the sunny day outside—or perhaps because of it— the curtains in Claire's mother's apartment were tightly closed. The only light in the room came from the TV. Although Jean had recently reduced the number of TVs she owned, there was still one in the bedroom, one in the bathroom, one in the kitchen, and one in the living room. On the big screen, a chef was trying to teach a talk show host as well as an actress Claire had never heard of how to make gazpacho. Her mother would never make gazpacho in a million years, but still she kept her eyes on the TV while she talked to Claire.

"Do you want to go garage-saleing with me tomorrow, Claire?"

"Garage-saleing?" Claire could hear the tightness in her own voice. Jean's trucker boyfriend, Zed, had broken up with her two weeks before, leaving Jean for a female pump jockey who had presumably done more than gas up his big rig. Claire knew from painful experience that, left to her own devices, Jean sometimes reverted to bad habits. Her worst vice was shopping. Jean had met Zed in a Shopaholics Anonymous twelve-step program while trying to overcome her addiction to QualProd, a TV shopping network. Her habit had left her with a maxed-out credit card and so many useless knickknacks that she could hold her own garage sale every day for a year and still not run out of stuff.

"Mom, are you sure that's such a good idea? Have you talked to your support group about this?"

"Honey, I only allow myself to bring five dollars in quarters. How much trouble could I get into? Look, it will be fun."

Claire was willing to bet that her mom also brought along her checkbook. If she didn't nip this in the bud, on Saturday, Jean would be hauling home flaking brass-plated headboards, jade-green life-size ceramic jaguars, and paint-by-number numbers done on black velvet.

"I've got a better idea," Claire said quickly. "Charlie and I are going to Riverwalk tomorrow to see an old friend of hers. I've heard you talking before about how nice that place looks. It's an open house—why don't you come with us and see?"

Jean was only sixteen years older than Claire, so she was really too young—as well as far too poor—to be a prime candidate for Riverwalk. At the same time, she had always been fascinated by a place she viewed as a sort of country club, the exclusive privilege of the rich.

Claire could tell Jean was tempted. "Come on," Claire wheedled. "They've got a band, refreshments—and door prizes." She knew this last idea would be the clincher, and it was.

"You're going to have to help me figure out what to wear." Jean finally looked away from the TV and up at Claire. In the half-light, the concealer she had smeared around her deep-set eyes glowed, making Jean resemble some sort of reverse raccoon. "I don't want to look like the local yokel."

NINE

RITCHIE WAS ASLEEP behind the stacks of recycled tires outside the Velvet Wrench when a kick to the gut woke him. Reacting as automatically as a pill bug, he rolled into a ball. But the kicks kept coming, finding all his vulnerable places. When he tried to cover the back of his neck with his right hand, he felt one of his fingers snap. Ignoring the pain of his broken finger, Ritchie rolled to his hands and knees and tried to scuttle behind his shopping cart.

The lights of a passing car picked out something shiny in one of the kids' hands. A gun. Pointed at him. Ritchie froze. He was crouched on his haunches, and now he raised his hands unsteadily beside his head.

The biggest kid swaggered up to him, the gun held confidently in his hand. He stood so close to Ritchie that Ritchie could no longer see the gun. Afraid to move his head, he rolled his eyes, trying to figure out where the gun was. He stilled when he felt its cold kiss on his left temple.

Two more kids stood behind the one with the gun. Young, all three of them, seventeen, eighteen, nineteen tops. In contrast to their buddy with the gun, the other two looked like they might be scared. One had dark stubble across his head and was holding a can of spray paint. The other one, with his blond hair shorn close to his skull, wasn't even looking at Ritchie, but up at the blind white eye of the moon.

"You know what you are, man?" the kid with the gun asked. Tattoos crawled past the ends of his sleeves. Ritchie might have been able to tell him some things—homeless, HIV positive, an alcoholic, finally off the needle, just getting by, old enough to be this kid's father—but the kid didn't wait for an answer. "You're a disgrace to your race! A white man like you shouldn't be begging on the streets."

Ritchie closed his eyes, waiting for the bullet. But what came next was a flurry of kicks, from all sides. He fell over, now as helpless as a beetle on its back. All three of them kicking him, hard kicks, too, none of them holding back. As if their lives depended on kicking him. Right before he lost consciousness, Ritchie saw the look in the eyes of the kid with the gun and thought that maybe their lives did.

TEN

JEAN HAD HAD TO BE dissuaded from buying tennis whites, although Claire could tell from her mother's streaky orange legs as she walked out to the car that she had applied self-tanner the night before with a too-liberal hand. Jean had also managed to come up with a pair of white Keds and footie socks with pink pom-poms. Three "gold" necklaces—mementos from her dalliance with QualProd—nestled on what Jean liked to refer to as her "girls," displayed by the U-shaped neckline on her too-tight short black dress. Jean was the kind of woman who had skinny arms and legs and a squarish middle. Her build was so different from Claire's that it was easy to guess that Claire's father, who had disappeared long before Claire made an appearance, must have been tall, thin, and red-haired.

"This is so exciting!" Jean said, after she had settled down into the Mazda 323's passenger seat. She flipped down the visor, but because Claire's little car had been made as cheaply as possible, it lacked a vanity mirror. (There were also no intermittent wipers, nor a sideview mirror on the passenger's side. A recessed space in the dash was helpfully labeled "quartz," although it was empty of a clock.) Charlie smiled at Jean from the cramped backseat, which was tolerable only for children and really short adults.

Without the reassurance of a mirror, Claire's mother was forced to rely on Claire and Charlie. "Is my lipstick on straight? Do I look okay?"

"You look fine, Mom," Claire said, while Charlie nodded in agreement. In truth, Jean and Tammy Faye Bakker both subscribed to the same makeup philosophy. But according to her own standards, Jean, with her eyelashes mascaraed into five or six clumps, her iridescent shadow glittering, and her lips as shiny as a brand-new cherry-red convertible, did look fine.

After her car had been waved through the gate by a uniformed security guard, Claire discovered that finding a place to park at Riverwalk's open house was like finding a parking space at Washington Square Mall two days before Christmas. As they made ever-widening circles, they passed middle-aged children walking side by side with their elderly parents, or pushing them around the tidy grounds in wheelchairs. For residents, golf carts seemed to be the preferred method of zipping over the concrete paths from one part of the sprawling compound to another.

Jean kept forgetting that she was supposed to be looking for any telltale reverse lights, and instead craned her head to take in all the sights. Contrary to its name, Riverwalk had no river, although it did have a large concrete pond in the courtyard, complete with a couple of ducks. Jean exclaimed over everything they passed—the grounds as carefully manicured as a golf course, the rolling greens that really were a nine-hole golf course, the tennis courts. It all had the slightly fake feeling of a better-quality resort.

After they finally found a place to park, Jean claimed the packet the security guard had given them. Inside were a number of raffle tickets to be dropped off in fishbowls located throughout Riverwalk—at the therapy pool, movie theater, ice cream parlor, air-conditioned pet kennel, and playground for visiting children. The more places you visited, the more chances you had to win prizes. They made plans to meet back at the car in an hour and a half, and Claire and Charlie set off in search of the clubhouse, where they had arranged to meet Nova. In the pocket of her shorts, nestled in a silk drawstring bag, Claire carried the diamond ring. She was conscious of its weight bouncing lightly against her thigh at every step.

"Yoo-hoo! Charlie! Over here! By the pool!" Her hand trailing cigarette smoke, a woman wearing a swim cap festooned with what looked like giant sequins leaned over a white fence to wave vigorously at Charlie and Claire, and then opened the gate to reveal a sparkling blue pool. She wore a purple skirted swimsuit that exposed skinny tanned legs mapped with the blue-green squiggles of varicose veins. The swimsuit jutted forward in the bosom area in a way that was more hypothetical than realistic.

"You look wonderful!" Nova pulled Charlie into a one-armed hug, holding her cigarette out of the way. No air kisses for Nova—she kissed Charlie firmly on both cheeks, then turned to Claire. "And who is this? Charlie, you haven't been hiding something from me, have you? This couldn't be your granddaughter, could it? My, she's tall!"

Claire was surprised to feel herself flushing. While Charlie was easily old enough to be her grandmother, in Claire's secret heart of hearts, she looked upon the older woman as her surrogate mother.

Giving Claire a quick smile as if to take any possible sting out of her words, Charlie said, "Not my granddaughter, I am afraid. I would like you to meet my good friend and housemate, Claire Montrose. Claire, this is Nova—" She stopped and turned to Nova, smiling apologetically. "I am not certain I know your last name any longer."

"Oh, I went and did like all those women libbers used to say. Took my name back. It's Nova Sweeney, just like it used to be when I was a girl. I didn't want to go out of this world with some jerk's last name on my tombstone." With her free hand, Nova pulled off the swim cap, revealing hair a color that Claire was sure the hair dye package had described as platinum. Settling herself onto a white plastic lounge chair, Nova gestured with her cigarette toward the empty chairs on either side.

"So sit down and tell me how your love life is these days, Charlie." Hooking her oversize purple sunglasses, Nova pulled them halfway down her nose. "Because mine stinks." She turned to Claire. "When we were young, this girl could get any guy she wanted. She made me sick. All she had to do was crook her little finger and whoever she wanted would come running with his tongue hanging out."

Charlie looked away, coloring a little. Claire realized she had never seen her friend look embarrassed. "I am not seeing anyone at present." It had been at least two years since Charlie had liked a man well enough to bring him home to meet Claire. The last one had been a retired bank president who had suffered an aneurysm a month after they began dating. Charlie had come home from his funeral dry-eyed, but still moving uncharacteristically slowly.

Nova blew a stream of smoke to one side. "Well, I'm still out there, as they say in the singles world. 'WWF, honest, attractive, happy, healthy, and physically fit, seeks soul mate, fifty-five to seventy. Enjoys dancing, dining, travel. Would like a pleasant man for LTR.' That's my current ad in *Seniors' World*. WWF stands for widowed white female, and LTR is long-term romance, in case you don't understand the whadaucallits."

"Acronyms," Claire supplied.

But Charlie had focused on another part of the ad. "Fifty-five to seventy?" Her expression was mischievous.

Nova shook her finger at her old friend. "Don't you go telling secrets out of school about how old I am, Charlie! I can pass for sixty, and I never let a man see my driver's license. If I owned up to seventy-four, I would be rejected so fast my head would spin. Men have always wanted younger women. Always! Two of my husbands left me for girls young enough to be their daughters! By the time you get to retirement age, all the good men are taken. Or dead. Did you know that that census-thingy shows that when you reach seventy-five, there are four single women for every single man? Four! And don't think they don't know it." She leaned toward Claire as if imparting a secret. "At Charlie's and my age, there are so few men around that we women are willing to accept some short fat guy who's pushing ninety. Why? Because he's a man, damn it! Someone to go out to dinner with, someone to talk to, someone to let you know you're still pretty. Of course, if I had my druthers, I'd want someone younger, too. Not some old man who's only looking for a nurse or a purse."

Claire supposed that the need for companionship, love and maybe even sex never went away. Prior to Dante, Claire's love life had been hit and miss at best. Listening to Nova, she just hoped that she wouldn't be back in the singles game at eighty.

"So, Charlie, are you thinking of moving in here?" Nova lowered her voice to a conspiratorial rasp. "Let me tell you something, you might be better off living in the real world as long as you can. There are no men here. And those that are here have one foot in the grave already. Half of them are wheeling around those oxygen thingamabobs. The other half can't even get out of bed, let alone know what to do with a woman in one. I've decided all those gorgeous men in those pictures in the brochures were models they hired."

"So why are you staying?" Charlie asked.

"I've got to be practical." Nova stubbed out her cigarette and lit a new one as she was talking. "I know what you're thinking—when has Nova ever been practical? But I'm all alone. I've got no one in the world. What's going to happen to me if I get sick, or if I fall and break a hip? It might be two weeks before the mailman gets around to wondering how come my box stays full. But once you sign on for Riverwalk, you realize this is the last stop. If you want to look into the future, you don't even need your glasses to see it. It's as near as these old broads you see doddering around, too out of it to touch up their roots or get out of their house slippers. Even worse are the ones who stare at you from the windows on the second floor of that building over there." She gestured at a structure on the edge of the property. "The ones they never let out. They look so sad." For a moment, Nova looked like she was about to cry herself, but she took a hard drag on her cigarette instead.

Charlie said, "To be honest, I have not been thinking of moving here, Nova. I came because I wanted to ask you about something else."

"What—you stopped by here to talk about old times?"

Charlie lifted one shoulder. "In a manner of speaking. Something has happened that made me want to ask you about Elizabeth. About what happened before she died."

"Elizabeth?" There was a pause. "Do you mean Liz Ellsworth?" Nova offered them a confused smile. "Why, I haven't thought about her in years."

"You were her closest friend."

"That was fifty years ago. Back when we were all young." Nova looked down and slowly let a stream of cigarette smoke out between pursed lips. Her purple lipstick had bled into the little lines around her mouth. "Liz will always be young, won't she? She'll never know what it's like to get washed up and worn out." She looked back up at Charlie. "Why are you thinking about her after all this time?"

Charlie looked over at Claire. "Could you show Nova, please, what you found?" As Claire stood up and took the silk drawstring bag from her pocket, Charlie said to Nova, "Remember the Lisacs' wall, the one Tom was building the summer Elizabeth died?"

"Yes…" Nova let the word trail off. Her expression was hesitant, not as if she didn't remember, but as if she didn't want to go where Charlie was leading her.

"Claire found this where a chunk of mortar had fallen out. All covered in tarnish. I had some photos of Elizabeth, and we compared them. It is the same. I am thinking it has been there since Elizabeth died."

Shaking the ring into her palm, Claire held it out to the two women. She had shined it up with silver polish, and it winked in the sun.

Nova began to shake her head. "It can't be. Liz gave it back." She reached out her hand, then stopped before she touched it and pulled back her fingers, like someone who had gotten too near a hot stove.

Charlie's voice was low and urgent. "Did she tell you she gave it back to Allen? Did Elizabeth tell you that? I do not understand why she would lie."

Nova put her hands over her eyes. "I—I don't remember anymore who told me."

Charlie's voice was low and urgent. "But the ring being in the wall—it does not make sense. The more I think about it, nothing makes sense. Why did Elizabeth break off with Allen, when she had been so eager to marry him? And then why did she kill herself? Claire finding this ring has made me doubt what happened. Austrid looked everyplace for a note, but there wasn't one. Perhaps there was a reason there was no note. Maybe there was something more to her death than we thought."

Nova turned her head to blow out another stream of smoke. "You don't understand, Charlie. There was a reason Liz killed herself. And a reason she'd didn't leave a note. She didn't want everyone knowing her secrets."

"What secret?" Claire asked.

Nova put a new cigarette in her mouth, even though one was still burning in the ashtray. She had to snap her lighter several times before the flame caught. When she exhaled, she turned her face away, but not before Claire saw a tear slide down from behind her sunglasses. Finally Nova sighed and said, "I guess it's been fifty years. Who can it hurt now? Liz was very unhappy and she couldn't see any way out."

"Out of what?" Charlie tipped her head to one side.

Nova puffed furiously on her cigarette before answering. "She was pregnant."

"Pregnant?"

"A week or so before she died, Liz came to me. She told me she was pregnant and that she had to get rid of it. She had tried taking hot baths and hitting herself in the stomach, but of course that kind of thing didn't work. It never does. I told Liz she could go to Mexico, that there were doctors down there who make it as if she had never been pregnant. But it cost five hundred dollars. I'd been there myself once before. I told everyone I was taking a vacation and even came back with a little bit of a tan. If you went to Mexico, then no one back home would even know to gossip. But Liz said she didn't have that kind of money. I would have loaned Liz the money if I'd had it, but I didn't have it." Nova took another drag on her cigarette. Her voice was full of fifty years of remembered pain. "After she died, of course, I started thinking that I could have found a way to get her the money."

"Oh, Nova, so you blamed yourself? But you did not have any idea of what she planned, did you?"

"Of course not. But I should have known that she was desperate. When she came to me, Liz was weeping so hard she could barely breathe. She just kept saying that she had sinned, and that any baby would be a monster. She was out of her head with guilt. I think she barely understood about sex, the poor thing."

"Why didn't they just move up the wedding?" Claire asked.

Nova shook her head. "They had it all planned, a society wedding, everyone would have known why. She couldn't bear that, couldn't bear that people would know. Liz was so ashamed."

Charlie leaned forward. "Then why could not Allen give her the money?"

Nova looked away. "It's complicated. At the time I talked to her, Liz hadn't even told him. She knew he would probably have to borrow it from Warren, and she couldn't stand the thought of that, of other people knowing. And if Warren knew, it meant Austrid would, too. Austrid only tolerated Liz on sufferance. Thought she was low-class just because her family was." She sighed, blowing out a stream of smoke. "Whatever happened between Liz and Allen that night must have put her over the edge. Maybe he couldn't think of a way to get her the money, or maybe he tried to tell her that they could wait, that no one would notice she was ready to pop when she walked down the aisle. Whatever happened, I'm sure she wasn't thinking straight."

Charlie said, "And she had been drinking. Her breath smelled like wine, and on the kitchen counter was an empty bottle."

Claire looked down at the ring. "That still doesn't explain why the engagement ring was in the wall."

Nova shrugged. "Liz was drunk, hysterical. She must have hid it from Allen, knowing how important it was to his family. She must have wanted to punish him." Nova pushed her sunglasses back into place, giving her the look of a purple-eyed bug. Claire decided the older woman looked like a praying mantis with a tan. "Why do you still have it? Why haven't you given it back to Allen?"

"We can't," Claire said. "I tried to talk to him when I found the ring, but the neighbor said he and his wife were in Europe."

"The neighbor was Howard," Charlie interjected. "Howard Backus. Claire didn't tell him about the ring."

"Howard?" Nova put her hand over her mouth. "Oh, I haven't thought about Howard for a long time. We used to have some fun. And even though he was such a flirt, underneath he was a real gentleman. One time he had to take me home from a party because I was absolutely blotto, and he didn't lay a finger on me. Just kissed me on the forehead and left." She leaned forward. "Say, is he still single?"

Charlie rolled her eyes. "I say hello in passing, but I have not exchanged two sentences with the man for years, so I have no idea about his personal life. I am sure you could call him up and ask him yourself. Is there anyone you are still keeping up with from the old days?"

"Not really. Well, I do see Frank here a lot. We say hello, but that's about it."

"Frank? Elizabeth's brother?"

"Our little Frank has come into his own now. He's quite the ballroom dancer—but then again, he doesn't have a lot of competition. Believe it or not, he even has a reputation with the ladies. The management looks the other way when he visits, even though he doesn't live on campus, because the women all like him so. Can you believe it? He got the cold shoulder from girls in high school, but now he's the cock of the walk. Frank can get any woman in this place he wants."

"Is he wealthy?" Claire asked.

Nova shook her head, her lips pursed around a delicious secret. "Frank can drive at night."

ELEVEN

"FRANK CAN DRIVE at night. That's it?" Claire echoed incredulously.

"Honey, at our age, that's a lot," Nora said, lighting a fresh cigarette. "He doesn't realize that this popularity of his will only last until he loses his driver's license—or his health. No one is going to take a bus on a date. And no one is going to sign up with someone who needs to be nursed six months down the road." Nova looked at her watch. "Anyway, if you want to talk to him, you can probably find him at the Top of the World Lounge. I'll take you there—just let me change out of my suit." She picked up her swim cap and pushed open a door marked "Ladies" in the small building next to the pool.

"So, what do you think?" Claire asked Charlie in a low voice.

Charlie shrugged. "She seems sure that Elizabeth killed herself. But I also wonder if perhaps there is something that she is not telling. Nova was always good at keeping secrets. Which probably had something to do with her popularity with married men."

Nova emerged wearing a mauve blouse and purple paisley skirt. Her purple-tipped toes matched her purple high-heeled sandals. She took hungry puffs of a newly lit cigarette, leaving purple stains from her refreshed lipstick. "They don't allow smoking in the lounge anymore. Someday soon they won't even allow smoking in your own private living quarters." Despite the ridiculously high heels, she set off at a fast clip toward the buildings clustered around the artificial lake with its cement banks.

Propped up on an easel in front of the biggest building's double doors was a poster saying, "Appearing Today in the Top of

the World Lounge: Dance to the Music of the Tommy Thoma-
son Trio—Featuring All Your Favorites from the Thirties, For-
ties, and Fifties!" In the accompanying photograph, the trio's
three members wore matching tuxes, desperate smiles, and bad
hairstyles—one comb-over, one bushy perm, and one mullet.

Two smiling women hovered near the entrance. Their gold
blazers and navy skirts made them look like Realtors or stew-
ardesses. They directed people to toss their entry tickets into
the fishbowl for a drawing for the grand prize—a trip for two
on Southwest Airlines anywhere within the contiguous United
States. They had the particular obsequiousness that emanated
from people who would get paid only if you were happy. And
every sentence that wasn't a question sounded like it should end
in an exclamation point.

At the sight of Claire and Charlie, their eyes widened and
their impossibly white smiles glowed even brighter. They tag-
teamed Claire, leaving Nova and Charlie free to go inside.
"How do you and your grandmother like our campus so far?"
the brunette asked.

Before Claire could even begin to explain that Charlie wasn't
her grandmother and also wasn't interested in moving in, the
blonde said, "Did you know that we offer literally hundreds of
activities? All your grandmother would have to do is bring herself!" And, Claire amended silently, her bank account. The fine
print on the brochures said that Riverwalk cost residents up to
twelve thousand dollars a month.

"And we have various service levels and residence options
to match your grandmother's needs and lifestyle, all within
our campus community." The brunette again, talking faster as
if to prevent any pause where Claire might interject a "but."

"And once your grandmother moved in, she would never
need to leave campus," the blonde said. Claire figured the sub-
text here was *no more ferrying Grandma on errands*. "We have
our own barber and beauty shop, gift shop, swimming pool, tennis courts, exercise facility, movie theater, and ballroom.
There's even a convenience store, plus our own grocery shop-

ping service. And of course, we offer twenty-four-hour-a-day nurse coverage."

Claire was finally rescued by the appearance of a middle-aged couple pushing a querulous old lady in a wheelchair who wanted to know why she couldn't have three tickets for the fish-bowl instead of one. With the attention of the two employees diverted, Claire quickly opened the door to the lounge. Inside, a half-dozen couples fox-trotted to the music. They were greatly outnumbered by several dozen women watching them with barely concealed envy. In their flowered skirts, lacy blouses, and pearl earrings, the ladies waited to be asked to dance, but the only men in the place were already on the dance floor. One glance at the room put flesh on Nova's dire statistics about the dearth of older men.

Nova and Charlie waved from a small table in the back. Claire made her way toward them, but Nova continued to wave. Claire realized the older woman was trying to snag the attention of the harried-looking waitress behind her.

"While we wait for Frank to show up, I'm going to order a round of Singapore Slings."

Looking at her watch, Charlie protested, "Nova, it is only eleven-thirty."

"So? The day's not getting any younger, and neither are we. My doctor's always going on about my habits, but I've managed to keep my figure and my teeth, and my eyes are still pretty good—and there's not a lot of people my age who can say that." Nova realized whom she was talking to. "Present company excepted, of course."

A ripple went through the room. The three women turned in time to see a short man enter. He wore a polka-dot bow tie, a crisply pressed short-sleeved white shirt, navy pants, and white leather loafers. All the women straightened up and began to murmur to each other. Several called to him or waved. With an easy confidence, he strolled to the nearest table, his posture ramrod straight, and bowed low before the three ladies who sat around it in wicker chairs. All three smiles widened, until he reached out his hand to the chosen one, leaving the other two behind.

"If you had not guessed, Claire, that is Frank," Charlie said flatly.

Claire tried to match up the seventy-seven-year-old Frank with the one photo she had seen of him at twenty-six. His red hair had faded to pale ginger, and his freckles had blended in with his age spots. He was now dancing as smoothly as any Arthur Murray instructor, with showy steps and little flourishes.

The music ended, and Frank returned his partner to her table, then held out his arms to the next woman at the table. She went into them eagerly. In another four minutes, he repeated the process. As Claire, Charlie, and Nova drank their sweet Singapore Slings, they watched Frank work the room like a bee going from flower to flower. Everywhere he went, women clamored for him, calling out his name, offering to cook him dinner, to play tennis with him, or to take him to the new movie playing that night at the Rec Hall. It wasn't difficult to eavesdrop, since many of the women had the projection of those who were slowly going deaf but resisting hearing aids. Frank responded with nods, pointed index fingers, winks, and half-promises, never letting any one of the women claim him clearly as her own.

Finally, Frank approached their side of the room. He gave Nova a little wave. Claire rated two appreciative blinks, as if he couldn't believe she really existed. But when his gaze came to Charlie, Frank froze for a split second. Then he came over to their table.

"Charlie—is it really you? How long has it been?" He took her right hand, but instead of shaking it he made a show of kissing it.

Charlie snatched her hand back. "A long time."

"Are you still in the old neighborhood?"

"Yes. Still in Multnomah Village. And you?"

"I have a little house near West Portland High. I finally retired when I turned seventy. Insurance adjustor."

"Isn't that near Howard's house?" Nova asked. She leaned forward, her hand rising to her throat. Claire and Charlie exchanged a glance, both thinking that Nova clearly had Howard in her sights.

Frank seemed to wince, and for a moment Claire could imagine him as he must have been fifty years ago, short, frail, and always overlooked. "He lives a few blocks away. We don't really run in the same circles." He turned his attention back to Charlie. "Charlie, you still look wonderful, if I might say so."

"You've become quite the dancer. We were watching you out on the floor."

Claire felt a flash of sympathy at Frank's sudden flush, the pale-skinned redhead's curse. He hid his embarrassment by turning his attention to Claire. "And is this lovely young creature your granddaughter?" He leaned forward and gave her an appreciative smile.

The back of Claire's neck prickled, as if she were being watched. Then she realized that thirty-six pairs of eyes were shooting daggers at her. "I'm a friend of Charlie's."

"Yoo-hoo!" Wearing a wide grin, Jean appeared behind Frank. "I thought I might find you here." Her arms were overflowing with bags, boxes, and brochures, which she let fall into the last empty chair at their table. She had obviously made the best of her time on the Riverwalk campus.

Claire made introductions all around. "This is my mother, Jean. Jean, this is Nova, the woman Charlie came to visit, and Frank, another old friend of theirs."

"Nova, you are so lucky to live here! Look at all the free things I won. I've got the magic touch today!" Jean began to hold up items from the pile on the chair, showing off each one before moving it to the table. Most were emblazoned with the Riverwalk logo, an arch suggesting a bridge over three squiggles that represented the complex's nonexistent river. "I got a pen and pencil set, a gift certificate for a free golf lesson, a six-pack of Ensure in the chocolate flavor, a rubber ball you're supposed to squeeze when you feel stressed out, another coupon for a free bang trim at the beauty salon—did you know they have a beauty salon right here on campus?" Jean rattled on without pausing for an answer. "Another gift certificate for a free meal here when I buy one of equal or greater value, and one of those rubber grippers for opening jars." Jean plopped into the now-empty chair with a sigh, her hands still fondling the things on the table before her.

Frank leaned forward. "If you would be so kind as to excuse me for interrupting, Jean, but might I ask you a question?"

Claire winced to see her mother simper. "Certainly."

"I must have misunderstood Claire. It can't be within the realm of possibility that you would be her mother. You look more like her sister."

With a quick exchange of glances, the other three women at the table commented wordlessly on Frank's too-obvious flattery. Jean, however, was glowing. She dropped her eyes, then looked up at Frank under her lashes—no mean feat, as even sitting, she wasn't much shorter than Frank. She held out her hands toward him, wrists together, miming someone waiting to be handcuffed. "Guilty as charged."

"I can see where her daughter gets her beauty." Frank turned back to Claire and executed a little bow. For a guy who had grown up poor in Portland, Oregon, he seemed to have adopted the manners of some obscure European nobleman. "Would you care to dance, miss?"

"What?" Claire looked around to see if he was talking to Jean, then giggled nervously. Suddenly she was in seventh grade again, where she had endured the humiliation of both towering above all her dance partners and of having feet that were not only size ten, but both left feet. She still remembered the terror on little Billy Reese's face when she caused them both to topple over during an out-of-control polka. "Oh, no. I'm sorry. I can't dance."

"Oh, yes, you can. You've just never had the pleasure of having a good partner." Was Claire imagining it, or was there the faintest hint of a leer in the old man's voice? Not knowing what else to do, Claire stood up. He had to crane his head to look at her. Frank gave her a brisk nod and a smile, then turned and went toward the dance floor. Claire followed, wishing she were anyplace else. Wearing her old Nikes, jeans, and a short-sleeved sweater, she was surrounded by the swish of nylons and full skirts. She felt like a Cinderella who had arrived at the ball without the help of a fairy godmother.

Once on the floor, Frank turned and took her in his arms, his grasp surprisingly firm and sure. She had thought he might hesitate to hold a stranger close—and one nearly forty years younger, at that—but clearly he had no qualms.

At first Claire watched her feet, as well as the other dancers, while also trying to remember whatever bits she hadn't repressed of that seventh-grade PE class. She counted silently, attempting to memorize the patterns and anticipate what she should do next.

Then Frank's whisper reached her from somewhere below her ear. "Stop thinking about where you are going to place your feet. Let my hands tell you what to do." He continued to talk to her, not about how she should move, but instead making observations about the nice weather, recently released movies, and favorite vacation spots. It was the kind of conversation that she could simply mumble an agreement to, or chime in with a brief comment if she felt inspired. Claire stopped watching her feet, stopped thinking about what part she should move next, stopped trying to stay oriented to the rest of the room. She simply concentrated on the top of Frank's head and the low murmur of his words and his hands putting subtle pressure on her back. To her surprise, she found that she was actually moving as smoothly as if she were in a dream or a Ginger Rogers movie.

"So what do you do for a profession?" Frank asked.

"I used to be a custom plate verifier for the state."

He pulled back and looked up into her eyes, "You mean you're the one who approves vanity license plates? Like that one guy who wanted Viagra?"

That plate, requested by a man who had gotten rich from his

Pfizer stock, had ultimately been turned down, a decision covered extensively by the *Oregonian* as well as most of the local radio stations. Claire's old boss had rejected it on the rather dubious grounds that it violated the department's ban on license plates that promoted "controlled substances."

Claire didn't feel comfortable talking about Viagra with a man who might be old enough to need some, so she said, "I liked the clever plates better. The ones you have to spend some time figuring out. Like ML8 ML8 on a white VW Rabbit. Or MTNST on a red sports car." As she spoke, Frank spun her away from him, then reeled her back. Miraculously, Claire didn't miss a step. "You're such a smooth dancer. I guess you were right—it really is all in having a good partner. No wonder the ladies are all vying for your attention."

The music stopped, but Frank made no move to change partners. When a new song began, he again began leading Claire through her paces. Staring down at the top of his right ear, she noticed a streak of what she realized was orange lipstick.

"You know, when I was in high school, no one would date a little runt like me. They were all embarrassed to be seen with me." Frank's voice roughened with emotion. "My social success is a vengeance against everybody." He cleared his throat and then changed the subject. "So is Charlie thinking of moving into Riverwalk?" Frank didn't pause to give Claire time to answer the question. "I don't think I quite caught the connection between you two."

"She's my roommate. And my friend. I understand you knew her a long time ago, when she first came to Portland."

"Did anyone ever really know Charlie? She was always very reserved. It's funny, but in my perception she hasn't changed. She's still the glamorous refugee who moved into the neighborhood and set all the housewives atwitter."

Claire, who had only known Charlie with white hair, was reminded again that Charlie had once been young, younger even than Claire was now. "It sounds like she really stirred things up."

"There weren't many Jews in Portland. Then she comes

here with that kinky hair. No bigger than a child but clearly a woman. And she has that German accent, only she is the good kind of German. Until they met her, I think some people thought Jews had tails and hooves and all the accoutrements. At first she stayed mostly to herself. I myself didn't get to know her well until several years after she moved here. And then later, um"—he paused, and Claire knew he was thinking of his sister's death—"our little group drifted apart. So she and Nova have stayed friends all this time?"

"Nova sends Charlie Christmas cards, but I don't think they've seen each other for years. But something happened recently that Charlie wanted to ask Nova about. Something that reminded her of the past." Claire's words came slower. Elizabeth Ellsworth's death wouldn't be an abstraction to her brother, an interesting conundrum to ponder. Instead, it might well be a wound that had never healed.

"What about the past?"

"Um…" Claire hesitated. Was she imagining it, or did Frank's hands tense against her back as he waited for her answer?

"Was it—was it about my sister?" Frank's step stuttered, and for a moment Claire accidentally pressed her body against his.

They both stepped back an inch or two, and Claire was suddenly conscious of the room again. "I'm afraid so," Claire said.

"Why is Charlie thinking about Liz after all these years?"

Claire pulled back from Frank a little more, enough to look down into his eyes. "Because a few days ago I found your sister's engagement ring."

He missed a step, but quickly recovered. There was a pause before he said, "You mean Allen resold the ring and you saw it in a jewelry store?"

"So your sister gave the ring back to Allen before she killed herself?"

"That's what I heard. And isn't that what you traditionally do when you break off an engagement?"

"Well, the ring's turned up, but not in the way you might think. I was out running and saw something glinting inside an old wall. It might have stayed there forever if the chunk of mortar in front of it hadn't fallen out. Instead, I caught a glimpse of the ring and managed to get it out."

"The ring was in a wall?" He sounded confused.

"The Lisacs' wall."

"What? But that doesn't make any sense." His foot came down squarely on Claire's toe.

"Ow!" Fueled by nervousness, Claire's shriek was louder than she intended. Heads turned.

"A thousand pardons. I'm feeling a little discombobulated. Perhaps I need to take a break."

With his hand under her elbow, Frank steered Claire to the edge of the dance floor. The magic that had allowed her to feel graceful deserted her, and she was again aware of how she towered over him, clomping along in her huge shoes. She felt like a barge being towed by a tugboat.

"I'm sorry I upset you, bringing up your sister unexpectedly like that." Claire noticed beads of sweat at Frank's hairline.

"No, it's not a problem. Liz and I weren't very close. I was five years older. In a big family like ours—there were eleven of us children—five years was a huge gap. We didn't play together when we were kids, and as we grew older, we grew even further apart."

But Claire remembered Charlie saying how Frank had hung around Elizabeth's group of friends for at least that one summer, an integral, if uninvited, part of the group that picnicked and swam and listened to records at the Lisacs' house.

Frank stopped and faced her when they stepped off the dance floor. "I was sure she had given the ring back to Allen. It doesn't make any sense that it was in the wall."

"Nova thought your sister might have put it there because she was angry with Allen." She made no mention of the secret Nova had carried for fifty years, that Elizabeth had been pregnant.

He thought about this. "Perhaps. Isn't suicide supposed to be an act of anger? I think Liz must have been angry with all of them, all of the Lisacs. Or else why did she hang herself in a spot everyone has to pass under? Maybe she found out about him and Mary and didn't want Mary to end up with the ring."

This was an angle Claire hadn't thought about. What if Elizabeth had turned up pregnant just at the time she realized her fiancé was involved with her sister? "So Mary was seeing Allen before Elizabeth died?" Charlie had said no, but it made sense.

Frank dropped his eyes. "Mary always said there wasn't anything between them before. I was never certain." He sighed. "Have you told Allen?"

"He and his wife are out of town and won't be back for another week."

"Where is the ring now?"

Claire watched his eyes widen at her answer. "In my pocket." She pulled out the drawstring bag and took the ring from it.

Frank plucked it from her hand and eyed it closely, or as closely as the soft light of the chandeliers would allow. He was the first person she had shown it to who reacted critically rather than emotionally. "It's a beautiful piece. I wonder, legally, who it belongs to."

"Wouldn't it be Allen Lisac's? After all, Charlie says it has been in his family for generations."

"But he gave it to Liz. Wouldn't it rightfully belong to her heirs?"

If even a few of her ten siblings had reproduced, the slices from the hypothetical pie of the ring would be as thin as slivers. "Sounds like a question for Emily Post," Claire said lightly. She held out her hand, and, after a heartbeat, Frank gave her back the ring. "I'll keep you posted as to what happens."

He took a deep breath, then straightened himself up. "I'm sorry, I shouldn't be monopolizing you." He began to steer Claire back to her table. When they reached it, he gave her a nod and said, "Thank you so much for allowing me the pleasure of escorting you on the dance floor."

"And thank you for being such a good teacher."

Frank bobbed his head in Nova, Charlie, and Jean's direction.

"Ladies." Executing a precise turn on his heel, he was back on the dance floor in a minute, a new and smiling partner in his arms.

"Isn't he the gentleman?" Jean said. Her life had been short on gentlemen. Claire's father had met Jean in a movie line when Jean was just sixteen, and wasted no time in first seducing and then abandoning her. Over the years, Jean had practiced serial monogamy with a sequence of men met in bars. Most of them could be counted on to observe the niceties, like not spitting on the floor, but they didn't approach life with Frank's flourishes and flowery words.

Charlie and Nova both made polite-sounding murmurs, but Claire could tell their opinions of Frank weren't nearly as high as Jean's. Oblivious to their lack of enthusiasm, Jean watched with dreamy eyes as Frank escorted another of the chosen to the dance floor, then excused herself to go to the bathroom.

A part of Claire felt sorry for Frank. It couldn't have been easy growing up short, homely, and red-haired.

"Did you ask Frank about the ring?" Nova leaned forward, her eyes bright. "What did he say?"

"He was surprised. He thought she had given it back to Allen. He seemed mostly concerned about who would own it now."

Nova sat back, shaking her head in exaggerated disbelief. "Don't tell me he thinks it belongs to him."

"He is the oldest living relative of Elizabeth," Charlie reminded her. "It is an interesting question. With those large diamonds, the ring must be very valuable. And its age might make it even more rare."

"But Liz was the one," Nova said, "who broke off the engagement. All the etiquette books say that if you're the one who breaks off the engagement you have to give back the ring. So it belongs to Allen."

"Ah." Charlie sat back in her chair. "But what if she did not really break off with him?"

"But Allen said she did," Nova said. "Why would he lie?"

"I have been thinking. We all know that he came home changed after the war. What if he broke off with her after she told him she was pregnant? That would explain why Elizabeth was so desperate that she hung herself. With no husband, the whole community would whisper about her. And then, after Elizabeth killed herself, Allen felt guilty. Ashamed. So he made up a story so people would not think badly of him for causing her to do what she did. If people had known that he was the one who had broken up with her, that he had been the one who abandoned her after she waited for so long, people might have felt differently. As it was, they were sorry for him. A war hero, and then his fiancée was such a child, she could not deal with a few scars."

"You might be right," Nova said, downing the last of her third Singapore Sling. "Maybe after Liz killed herself, Allen decided to put—what's that word they use?—his own spin on what had happened."

"What do you think, Charlie?" Claire asked. There was a long stretch of silence. "Charlie?"

"Hm?" Charlie said finally.

Claire looked out at the dance floor, following Charlie's gaze. Clasped to her partner's chest, Jean whirled by. Her eyes were closed, her lips were parted, and she looked totally happy. And because her eyes were closed, she couldn't see the three dozen elderly women glaring at her for monopolizing the best dancer in the place—short, solicitous, smooth-stepping Frank Ellsworth.

TWELVE

NOW AND 1944—FOR A long time, it was as if Charlie were frozen like a blade of grass inside a thick coating of ice. Caught immobile, preserved, untouched.

Then, slowly, she let herself melt, and it was the past that was covered in a skin of ice.

There was the self she was now, and the self she had been, and the two were not even related. Sometimes, though, the skin of her new life gave way. And Charlie fell into the past and became Charlotte again.

WOMEN. STANDING IN rows of five, thousands of them. So thin they look like boys. No breasts, no hair. Ribs like hoops, necks nothing but knots and ropes. Frozen to the marrow, filthy, eye sockets filled with black shadows. Numbers tattooed on their arms, to identify them when they are naked and dead.

The night is bright with cold. The moon's blue shadows light up the ice and the dirty snow, here and there spotted with puddles of diarrhea.

They call it the morning roll call, but it really begins at three a.m. and lasts for hours. Every roll call, Charlotte wants to let herself slide into the snow. Into death. Each morning it is the coldest it has ever been. Her bones are made of ice and the wind knifes through them.

It would be so easy to die.

All she has to do is let go of her heart.

THIRTEEN

JEAN WAS QUIET as Claire and Charlie drove her home from Riverwalk. Her arms wrapped tight around all her goodies, she sat smiling to herself in the passenger seat. Claire wished that her mother's smile stemmed from her haul of logo-imprinted gewgaws, but she knew it didn't. Jean had danced with Frank for nearly an hour, finally stopping when the band took a break. Afterward, they had lingered, talking close together at the edge of the dance floor, neither of them seeming to notice that Jean was half a head taller than Frank, and easily fifty pounds heavier. When Frank had finally led Jean back to their table, Jean had surprised everyone but Claire by hugging him good-bye for at least two minutes, pressing him so close that his nose must have been in danger of getting caught in her freckled cleavage.

Claire broke the silence. "I didn't know you knew how to dance like that, Mom." When Jean didn't answer, Claire repeated herself.

"What?" Jean started as if she had dozed off. "Oh, I don't. Not really. Frank is just a marvelous dancer. Didn't you notice how he made you feel when you danced with him? It was like, I don't know, like I was doing something I had always known how to do, only I had forgotten. Except I've never danced like that before." Jean's smile was sleepy, her eyes unfocused.

Claire, who had lived with her mother until she was nearly thirty, had seen that smile far too many times. It usually appeared when Jean was about to be suckered into something that would have been against anyone else's better judgment. Until she had maxed out her credit card, Jean had smiled that same dreamy smile while she watched the QualProd TV shopping network, her hand hovering over the speed-dial button. Each time she got taken by a new scheme, like the times she had decided to make her fortune selling water filters or oxygenated vitamins, Jean had smiled that same slightly dazzled smile as she inwardly counted up all the money she was sure to make. Whenever Jean took up with a new man (at least twenty times, in Claire's experience), the smile had reappeared. Now here she was, grinning like a fifteen-year-old. Except she was really fifty-five. Really, Claire thought, wasn't her mom old enough to know better?

Claire did the math Jean seemed determined to avoid. "He's got to be at least twenty years older than you, Mom." In the backseat, Charlie wisely kept silent.

The smile was replaced by a pout, but at least Jean's eyes were focused again. "Don't get your panties in a twist, young lady. I didn't say I was marrying him. I just liked dancing with him."

Claire didn't point out that Jean had never bothered to marry anyone, including the men who had fathered Claire and her sister Susie. Silence again filled the car, but this time it felt heavy, full of unspoken arguments. When they pulled into the apartment parking lot, Jean muttered good-bye before she flounced away. Charlie took her place in the passenger seat.

As she started the car, Claire said, "I'm sorry. I know that wasn't very diplomatic."

"Your mother is not a child, Claire."

"I didn't say she was a child." Claire shook her head so hard that she felt her hair whip her cheek. "She's more like a permanent teenager. Even when I was little, I had to be the grown-up."

"If I have learned anything in this life, it is that you cannot make anyone do what you think they should."

"You're probably right." Claire thought of her frequent resolve—made and broken on a daily basis—to give up junk food. "I can't even make *me* do what I should." Instead of turning right, which was the way home, Claire turned left, taking the route she had when she had found the ring. She pulled over at the curb, next to the Lisacs' property. The house was barely visible between the tall arborvitae that stood shoulder to shoulder on top of the high wall.

Claire had often walked or driven past this wall without paying any more attention to it than she would a telephone pole or a mailbox. How many thousands of people had done the same thing over the last fifty years?

Claire pointed out the chink in the wall where she had found the ring. It was so small and shadowed, it was a wonder she had seen it at all.

"It was definitely put there around the time of Elizabeth's death," Charlie said. "You can tell how upset Tom was by those last two layers of stones."

Claire saw that what Charlie said was true. The rest of the wall fit as tightly as pieces of a giant jigsaw puzzle, but the top two rows held many more gaps and spaces that had had to be filled in with sandy mortar. It was one of these spaces that had held the ring.

"Since you found that ring," Charlie said, "I keep thinking of Elizabeth. Now I wish I had known what was wrong. I could have helped her."

"I guess I understand why Elizabeth killed herself. But what I still don't understand is why the ring was in the wall. It just doesn't make any sense." Claire paused for a moment, thinking. "So there were—what?—eight of you who were friends when that happened?"

Charlie counted on her fingers. "Yes. If you count Elizabeth. And me."

Claire shifted the car into drive. "And we've talked to Nova and Frank. Mary and Allen are still in Europe. And then there's Howard. What about Tom? The guy who built the wall. Do you ever run into him?"

Charlie busied herself rolling down the window on Claire's old Mazda. "It's been nearly fifty years since I have seen him." She rested her forearm on the doorframe, keeping her head turned away. "We did not stay in touch. I do not know where he lives. I do not even know if he is alive."

Looking at the fragile wings of Charlie's shoulder blades, Claire wondered why Charlie and Tom had broken apart so completely—and whose idea it had been.

"Maybe he knows how the ring ended up where it did. Maybe he even saw who put it there." Claire parked the car, got out, and walked up the steps to their house. Before she reached the door, she was almost bowled over by a big chocolate brown Lab trailing a red leash. It busied itself gobbling up the kibble Charlie had set out that morning.

"Bailey! Come here!" A girl who looked about eleven shouted at the dog from the street, but it paid no attention. She ran up the driveway and grabbed the dog's leash.

"Sorry! I guess Bailey's hungry." The girl's dark brown hair was held back with a shiny scrunchy and there was a spattering of freckles across her nose. "What's your name?" She continued talking without giving them time to answer. "My name's McKenzie Malone. I'm just visiting my aunt and uncle. They live at the end of the block." With her scuffed Nikes braced against the pavement, she began to reel in the dog. "That's weird. My dog's not excited. Usually he would be jumping up and down and barking when he smelled another dog. Do you keep yours inside?"

"We don't keep it anywhere, honey," Claire said. "There is no dog. The dish is more of a deterrent. We figure no burglar is going to want to mess with whatever is big enough to eat out of that dish."

The girl opened her blue-green eyes wider. "You mean it's like a fake? They see the dish and then imagine there's a dog?"

"Yes."

"Cool!" The dog was straining at the leash again, now wanting to go back into the street. "Well, it was nice meeting you!" McKenzie ran down the driveway, half-towed by the dog, her ponytail bouncing behind her. Claire watched her go, wondering if she would ever have children, then turned and went inside. She pulled the white pages from the telephone table's bottom shelf. "What was Tom's last name?"

"Bonfiglio. Thomas Bonfiglio."

"What kind of name is Bonfiglio?"

"It is Italian. The 'bon' is for good, and the 'figlio' I believe has the same root as the English word filial."

"Good child," Claire said. Dante's last name was Bonner. He was Italian-German, and his last name was from the German side, although he looked all Italian. Did "bon" mean "good" in German? Charlie had taught her some German, but Claire didn't think "bon" was one of the words. She flipped open the phone book to the *B*'s.

There it was. Bonfiglio, Thomas. An address in Hillsboro, a Portland suburb thirty minutes to the west. And no woman's name was appended, which made Claire strangely happy. She looked up with a smile. "Why don't you call Tom and see what he remembers?"

Without answering, the older woman took the phone from her. Claire watched Charlie's face as she dialed Tom's number. The last time her friend had called him, the phone had probably been made of Bakelite, black and square and heavy, despite its name. And with a real dial that made a ticking noise when it slid back into place, a sound now as anachronistic as the sound of a typewriter's carriage return. Claire herself, with her fond memories of rotary phones and eight-track tapes, was in danger of being as outdated as someone who lamented the lost sounds of steam engines or Linotype machines.

"May I speak to Tom, please?" Charlie's face had flushed pink, and white tendrils had sprung up around her face, as if the room were suddenly warm. There was a half-smile on her lips.

"Tom, hello, I do not quite know how to put this. This is Charlotte Heidenbruch. Charlie? I do not know if you remember me?"

Whatever Tom answered was enough to make Charlie laugh, the sound surprisingly low and sexy for a petite eighty-one-year-old.

Claire realized it was time for her to leave, and she did so quietly. But judging from the rapt look on her friend's face, she could have had taps on her shoes and bells around her neck and still not have attracted Charlie's attention.

FOURTEEN

"I CAN'T WAIT for next week."

Dante's voice tickled Claire's ear. When had phones gotten so insubstantial that they weighed only a few ounces, not just cell phones but home phones as well? Charlie had recently replaced their ten-year-old portable phone with a new one that weighed two-thirds less and was smaller than a deck of cards. Claire hated it. With nostalgia, she remembered the heavy phone in her grandmother's house. That weighty phone had made any conversation held on it seem important. If she tried to hold this new phone between her shoulder and ear, it slipped away. In a recent issue of the *New York Times* she had read that single-use phones were soon going to be on the market. The article touted them as being cheap, easy to use, and disposable. Was Claire the only one who felt that things were already disposable enough?

"I find myself sitting here and thinking about you and I don't get any work done," Dante continued.

"Are you thinking about me or this curatorship?" Claire reached up to put away a plate, almost losing the phone in the process.

Dante was nothing if not honest. "Both, probably. But mostly you." Dante was one of a team of curators at New York's Metropolitan Museum of Art, all specialists in Old Masters. It seemed like a dream job, and in many ways it was. But if he were named head curator of the planned Old Masters wing for the Oregon Art Museum, he would be able to put his own stamp on things. The position would offer him the chance to design his own exhibits from the ground up. With his many connections in the art world, he could stage shows with famous loaned works that could earn him a national reputation and draw art lovers from all over the country.

"Well, I'm glad to hear that I rank near the top, anyway." Claire bit her lip. She couldn't put off telling him any longer. "Look, something's come up that I need to tell you about."

"What?" Dante's voice was wary. Claire had gotten cold feet about their relationship before, part of a well-honed defense mechanism. As a child, she had learned that it was better to reject than to be rejected.

"The art for the new wing is all being donated by one collector, right?"

"Allen Lisac. I understand he's a big contractor there." He must have read her silence. "Why—do you know him?"

"No. But I need to let you know something that I didn't tell you before." Claire stopped sorting silverware as she tried to find the right way to tell him. "You know that engagement ring I found in the wall? The thing is, see, the man this Elizabeth Ellsworth was engaged to, well…was Allen Lisac."

"What? Why didn't you tell me that before?" There was a pause. "Not that I guess it really makes any difference. It's just a coincidence."

Claire fought the urge to move the phone down closer to her mouth. She still found it hard to believe anyone could hear her. "Anyway, he and his wife are in Europe. Charlie and I are going to return the ring when they come back, which I think is in a couple of weeks."

"Earlier than that," Dante said. "I know for sure they'll be back by a week from Wednesday."

"How do you know that?"

"Because Allen Lisac is one of the people I'll be having an interview with next week."

"Oh." This certainly complicated matters. Courtesy of Dante, Claire had been on the periphery of the art world long enough to know that money drove more decisions than anyone wanted to admit—the same as in the rest of the world. So even though Allen Lisac was not an employee of the Oregon Art Museum, as the donor his word would carry weight.

"So could you wait to return the ring until a decision is made? Technically, he's not the ultimate decision maker—the museum's executive director is—but he could nix any chance I have of getting this. I really want this position, and I'd rather I came at it straight on. Who knows—maybe he would even wonder how you got your hands on the ring in the first place?"

"What?" With her hip, Claire closed the silverware drawer. "Are you saying Allen Lisac would think I would fabricate something just to make contact with him and tell him, *Heh, hire my boyfriend Dante?*"

"No, of course not. It's just that I don't want there to be any confusion. Do you have any idea how rare this kind of chance is? And there will never be another opportunity like this in Portland again."

"I know this is the opportunity of a lifetime. It's just that I keep looking at this ring, trying to figure out why it ended up in the wall." Dante loved a puzzle as much as she did, but he didn't chime in. Claire finally broke the silence. "I'll right, I'll keep out of it. I'll ask Charlie to return it herself and not mention me."

Dante's voice loosened. "I think that would be best all the way around."

FIFTEEN

1944—CHARLOTTE CROUCHES on their tier with the others, the boards used as table, floor, bed.

At night they sleep with no blankets, no pillows, nothing but the cold. Huddled together like animals, taking turns being on the outside.

And talking, always talking. They re-create entire meals. Describe how they will decorate their houses. Spend weeks planning, minute by minute, how they will spend their first days after they are released.

She has not been able to wash since she arrived, not even her hands in cold water. So many have died because they stopped eating.

Charlotte has learned that the women who stop believing they will return are as good as dead. One has to believe, against all odds, incredible as it might seem.

SIXTEEN

THE HOUSE FELT strangely quiet. Then Claire remembered Charlie was off at the doctor's, getting her yearly physical. As far as Claire could tell, this consisted of the doctor running a half-dozen tests and then marveling that the results were those of someone half Charlie's age.

While she stretched her tight muscles, Claire leafed through the paper Charlie had left in an orderly stack of sections. The top one was folded to the back of the Metro section, where an article was circled. For the second time in a week, a man in their neighborhood had been viciously beaten by what was described as a gang of teenage boys or young men. The first man, who had a Hispanic name, had been beaten at a bus stop at Gabriel Park. The second, a white homeless man, had been attacked late at night outside an automotive shop, the Velvet Wrench. Claire's and Charlie's house lay squarely in between the two. Both were places Claire walked, ran, or drove by several times a week. Both times the gangs had yelled racial slurs, the first because the victim was perceived as Mexican, the second because they hadn't liked the idea of a white man living on the streets.

Claire didn't think there was any point in being worried. She was a white woman who had a home. And besides, both attacks had taken place late at night, not early in the morning, the time she usually went running. It was hard to imagine bad guys setting their alarms. Still, she decided to be careful for the next little while, to keep her CD player turned down low and an eye on her surroundings.

Even if the article didn't make Claire fearful for herself, it did make her fearful for her city. Portland was the most multi-

cultural place in Oregon, but even still, it was predominantly
white. Heck, in Oregon, people weren't even that tolerant of
Californians. In the small town where Claire had grown up,
there had been exactly one black family, and Hispanics had
been routinely referred to as wetbacks and goat-ropers. Skinheads had made Portland home before, and Claire hoped it
wasn't happening again.

After skimming the rest of the day's news, Claire set out,
wearing her new Nikes. Because Nikes ran small, she wore an
embarrassing size eleven. However, this particular pair was
white with a three-inch-wide swath of blue up the middle.
From her vantage point, at least, she thought they looked
smaller than most of her other shoes. It was like the shoe version of slimming stripes on a swimsuit.

As she ran, Claire thought of Elizabeth, deserted by those
she thought would help her, pregnant and so desperate that she
literally found herself at the end of a rope. Back in the days
when a woman's body wasn't her strength, but more often her
betrayer. With her thoughts to occupy her and with Mark
Knopfler singing in the buds of her headphones, Claire felt surprisingly fast. It was seven-thirty in the morning, prime com-
mute time for both workers and students, so there were no
good opportunities to cheat and walk, not when she had so
many witnesses. Following her regular route, she cut through
the business area of Multnomah Village. Everything was closed
except for Fat City. A man walked out of the alleyway and
turned toward her. Claire quickly sized him up, deciding what
kind of look to give him. Mid-fifties, polo shirt, dress pants,
briefcase in one hand. A businesslike nod, she decided.

With women, she usually added a smile to the nod. With another runner, she might mime being hot or tired, sticking her
tongue out in an exaggerated pant, not bothering to use words
since many runners wore headphones. With a teenage boy, she
would make eye contact only, a wordless acknowledgment of
each other's existence. If there were four or five boys, Claire
kept her eyes on her shoes and made sure to run past them

quickly, the way she figured a deer would sprint when it spotted a wolf pack. You didn't want to appear weak or vulnerable.

When she drew even with the businessman, he met her eyes with the briefest of glances, then quickly cut his gaze away and concentrated on the ground. Claire had done this herself more than once, the decision unconsciously made for her by her body, a mute show of submissiveness, an acknowledgment of the other's dominance. But now, for the first time she could remember, she was the dominant one. She was the one a man was careful not to make prolonged eye contact with. Claire smothered a laugh.

As she ran down their street, Claire's eyes were drawn to the Lisacs' house, or at least to where the Lisacs' house was, hidden by the hedge. Pretending to shake off a cramp in her leg, she walked halfway up their drive. The curtains had been pulled back. On a table next to the window stood a yellow vase holding several sheaves of red gladioli.

SEVENTEEN

1952—EVEN THOUGH SHE FELT most at home in a city, Charlie had chosen to live out here in the country. If she wanted to, she could drive into the city, into Portland. Although what they called a city was really a town. The tallest buildings in Portland were five or six stories. Portland felt raw and new, but she liked it that way. When she came here after a year in the refugee camp, it felt like Portland didn't have any history to forget.

Multnomah was on the city's outskirts, five blocks of small businesses and a few scattered houses surrounded by apple and cherry orchards, dairy farms, and miles of tangled woods. The woods comforted her with their wildness.

Charlie wasn't a country girl and would never be, but out here you could hear another car coming at night. You could hear the slamming of doors. If it happened, you could hear the march of stiff boots.

It wasn't rational, she knew. In America, she had been told over and over again, she was safe. But since arriving here, she had heard stories that gave her pause. Once at Elizabeth's house she had sat next to her on the front steps while Elizabeth showed her the family photo album. She had leafed through the parchment sheets covered with black and white snaps, chattering about her grandparents and cousins, as her little brothers and sisters played in the bare dirt yard at their feet. Suddenly there it was, a photo of men in hoods and white sheets, torches burning in their hands. Elizabeth flushed and turned the page, murmuring that it had all been a long time ago. She had acted as if it hadn't been her grandfather or uncle under that sheet, peering out from those eyeholes. People in America were naive.

They thought nothing truly bad could happen here. And with their thoughts they could make bad things happen. Through their ignorance. Evil was like a weed flourishing in a neglected crack, taking stubborn root.

STUMBLING OVER his own feet, Tom walked toward the black phone mounted on the cherry-paneled wall. "I'm calling Warren."

"What about a doctor?" Charlie asked. "Should you not call a doctor?"

Something like anger tightened Tom's face, deepening the tanned furrows around his eyes, and he gestured abruptly at Elizabeth. "She's dead, Charlie. You don't need to be a doctor to see that. And if we call Dr. Hannover, everyone will know. He's nothing but a drunk and a gossip. There'll be a scandal. Warren won't like that."

Elizabeth was the one who was sprawled on the floor, but Tom seemed to be more concerned about his boss. "Everyone will know no matter what you do," Charlie said. She was still sitting on the floor next to the body. "What do you suppose Warren will say? What nineteen-year-old girl who has never gotten so much as a sniffle?" With her thumb and forefinger, she reached out and closed Elizabeth's eyes, but a rim of white still showed. The girl's skin, the blue-white color of skim milk, was already losing its warmth and flexibility.

"An accident. We'll say it was an accident. She slipped and hit her head. Look at all that blood." He walked back, leaned over, and tried to pull a few strands loose, but they stuck fast. He looked shamed. "God, I wish we hadn't dropped her. Anyway, we'll say that she tripped and hit her head, and fractured her skull."

"No one will believe that." Charlie pointed at the line where the cord had bit into Elizabeth's throat. "What about her neck?"

"They can put her in a dress with a high collar. Come on, Charlie, help me out here. Her family's Catholic. If she's a suicide, they'll say her soul is damned. A priest won't officiate at the ceremony. Do you want to do that to her family?"

Before Charlie could answer, there was a scream. They had been so caught up in their argument that they hadn't heard the front door open. They turned in time to see Austrid drop her armful of Meier & Frank and Frederick & Nelson shopping bags in the entryway. Her gray eyes rolled back in her head. Suddenly graceless, her long body collapsed on the floor.

While Tom hurried to Austrid, Charlie quickly found the linen closet and then shook out a white sheet over Elizabeth's body. Her shoes crunched over slivers of glass from the broken china cabinet. Elizabeth was still in her nightgown, as if she had been unable to bear facing the day even long enough to put on her clothes. Charlie tucked one outstretched bare foot underneath the sheet, as gently as if it belonged to a sleeping child. The notion was immediately blotted out by the sight of the white sheet wicking up the rusty brown blood as it settled down over the back of her head.

Still stooped over Elizabeth, Charlie heard Austrid's trembling whisper behind her. "Oh, my God, what did you do to her?" She turned in time to see Austrid roughly push Tom away as he leaned over her. He staggered sideways, but did not fall. The older woman struggled to a sitting position, then crabbed frantically backward until her back was against the wall. Austrid only had eyes for Tom as she repeated, louder and with an edge of hysteria, "What did you do to her?"

"Elizabeth did it to herself." Charlie's voice was rougher than she had intended. She got up and then knelt by Austrid's side, blocking the terrible sight of the sheet, and took the older woman's cold hand in hers. Charlie tried to soften her voice, reminding herself that Austrid had just had a horrible shock and wasn't thinking rationally. "I found her. She hung herself. Tom helped me cut her down, but it was too late."

It was the closest contact Charlie had ever had with Austrid. She had never touched her, never even been close enough to see the careful layers of subtle makeup on her face that were obvious now that the color had drained away. Charlie had never had much use for Austrid, with her manners and her pretensions. The woman was incapable of seeing past the surface. In her eyes, Nova was a flirt and a flibbertigibbet. Charlie was a Jewess. And worst of all, Tom was a servant. It was clear from the way she stiffened whenever Tom came into the room that Austrid was scandalized that her son and future daughter-in-law were fraternizing with the help. Austrid never said any of these things in words, but you could tell she was thinking them.

Charlie's parents had taught her to consider the whole human being, but she had had a few schoolmates whose mothers were just like Austrid. They thought that servants were rightfully born into their lower positions, that they were by nature coarse, larcenous, brutal.

Tom walked away from Austrid, but his back was rigid with what Charlie knew was anger. He picked up the phone and dialed. "Mr. Lisac, you and your son need to come home right away." Mindful that it might be a party line, he continued, "There's been an—an accident." He listened for a second, his eyes closed, then answered, "It's Elizabeth." Slowly, he hung up the phone.

Austrid's eyes were no longer so wild, and Charlie let go of her hand, thankful to release those cold fingers as tight as wires.

"Why did Elizabeth do this?" she pleaded with Charlie. "Did she tell you why she did this?"

Forcing her voice to be gentle, Charlie said, "Austrid, she was dead before we cut her down."

"Did she leave a note?" The older woman's gaze roamed over the room, looking everywhere except at the body under the sheet.

"I don't know. We've only been here for a few minutes. We're having a hard time believing it's true ourselves."

Austrid's voice turned to steel. "Well, start looking. If there's a note, we need to find it. You take the guest bedroom—I'll start looking out here." She pushed herself to her feet, and Charlie was surprised to see that the older woman was no longer trembling. Her back was as straight as a fireplace poker.

"What?" Tom looked startled.

"This is a private matter, and I want it to stay that way. How this girl could be so thoughtless to break my son's heart like this—and so cruel to defile our home—I don't know. But I do know that if she wrote something I don't want anyone else to find it. I don't want the damage she has done to spread. I don't want strangers picking at this, this…scab. Now quick, start looking, before Allen comes home. This is going to kill him."

Charlie had never heard Austrid say so much at any one time.

AS SHE SEARCHED the Lisacs' house for any sign that Elizabeth had left a note, Charlie thought about the people she had seen before who had killed themselves. In Munich, the Jewish couple in the apartment below hers had done it to keep themselves out of the hands of the Nazis. After the smell of gas filtered into Charlie's apartment, she had known what was happening, and had been careful to give it another hour before she went downstairs to check. She found them in front of the stove, slumped forward on their knees, their hands still intertwined, their lips so blue they were nearly purple. On the kitchen table lay the summons.

In the camp, she had known a woman who slashed her wrists with a piece of broken glass, and another who had drunk stolen bleach. Others had taunted the guards, or their dogs, or tried to scale the walls. All of them knowing there was no way out unless they left their bodies behind.

Before the camp, she and Max had been sheltered by an old Christian landlord in a false room above his fabric shop. She and her son and two other families for a total of eleven people crowded into a single hidden room twenty paces by twelve. One of the women, Marta, had had a baby, gave birth in silence, grinding her teeth on a rag while the wives of Nazi party leaders bought silk ribbons and satins below.

Even Max, at four, had known how important it was to be quiet. The thin floor and walls carried the sounds so well, the jingle of change, the slam of the cash register drawer, the tone of people's voices, if not the words themselves. Charlie had

whispered to him that he was her "little man," but it had frightened her, how he had left his childhood behind, how quiet and
pale he was, with a pinched old man's face.

A few days after Marta's baby was born, they heard the
tromping boots of soldiers down below as they came into the
shop, their sure, strong voices. Why would men be in a fabric
shop, unless they knew the secret it held? Marta's infant, a little girl, began to make breathy, whimpering sounds. The others turned their heads toward mother and child, eyes wide,
fearful, knowing the baby would betray them all. To keep it
from crying, Marta yanked up her blouse and shoved her nipple in its mouth.

Pressed up tight against its mother's breast, the baby smothered. When the soldiers finally left, pretty ribbons for their
girlfriends in their hands, the infant was limp as a rag doll.

For three days after, Marta did not sleep, her breasts swollen with milk, her mind crazed with fever and grief and loss and
shame, her body rocking back and forth. No one blamed her,
but no one could find words of comfort, either. On the third
night, when it was late and Max was asleep and they could talk
in whispers, Marta told Charlie she didn't know if she had
meant to kill the baby all along. Later, just before dawn, when
everyone else was finally asleep, Marta had hung herself from
the water pipe with her own knotted shoelaces, hidden by the
sheet they had rigged up around a chamber pot. She died as quietly as her baby had, not making a sound. When they found her,
they stuffed their fists in their own mouths to keep from crying out.

After the war, a doctor friend of Charlie's told her that hanging oneself was a terrible way to die. Condemned prisoners had
the luxury of the platform and the drop designed to snap a
man's spine. With no fall of any distance, death came only
through strangulation. And it was much slower.

This was what Charlie thought of while they looked through
the Lisacs' house for a note from Elizabeth. She found nothing
but an empty wine bottle and glass in the kitchen, signs that

Elizabeth had had to numb herself before she stepped out into
the air. But long after Charlie had stopped looking, Austrid
continued to search, looking in ridiculous places, underneath
the couch cushions, in a desk drawer jammed full of rubber
bands and pencil stubs, tucked in the shoes Elizabeth would
never wear again. As she worked, Austrid cleaned, furiously
wielding a wet sponge as if to wipe out any lingering trace of
Elizabeth.

EIGHTEEN

"AUSTRID MUST HAVE SPENT hours looking for that note, long after it was clear it did not exist. She was not rational. She even thought Tom might have had something to do with it. She was afraid of him!" Home from the doctor, Charlie for the first time was telling Claire the whole story, from beginning to end, of how she had found Elizabeth. Her appointment had triggered the memory of what another doctor had said, long ago, about how painful a death suicide by hanging was.

Claire put up her hand. "Wait a minute, Charlie. Go back. What did you mean when you said there was a lot of blood on the back of Elizabeth's head? But I thought she died by hanging."

Charlie colored. "I told you. She fell when Tom cut her down, she fell like a sack of potatoes. I could not hold her. I tried to, but she was far heavier than I. Her head hit the china hutch."

"But Charlie—dead bodies don't bleed."

A pause hung in the air. Then Charlie grabbed one of Claire's hands between hers. Her fingers were like ice. "Are you sure?"

"Yes. The heart isn't pumping any longer."

"My God! I had seen that in the camps, but those were women who had been dead for some time." Claire tried not to imagine what her friend might have seen. "I never thought of it where Elizabeth was concerned. I felt guilty about not being able to hold on to her." She hesitated. "But then where did the blood come from? And how did it get there?"

Claire tried to think of another explanation. "Maybe Elizabeth was still alive when you found her, but unconscious?"

"No. Tom checked for a pulse. And her body was already

cooling." Charlie closed her eyes. "Tom had to cut her down quickly. He put the blade under the rope and turned it. I saw later that it had cut her neck a little." Charlie tilted her chin back and touched the side of her throat. Her eyes opened. "But the cut had not bled. It made a thin red line, no more."

"So she had to be dead when you found her. But her head—tell me more about it."

Charlie's eyelids closed again, but her eyes did not stop moving, as if she were seeing into the past. She raised her hand to the back of her head, a few inches above her nape and to the left. "Here it was"—she hesitated, her words coming slower—"soft and broken. Like when a windscreen is cracked, but it still holds together even though it is in a thousand tiny pieces. The back of Elizabeth's head was like that. And there was blood matting her hair."

"Matting?" Claire zeroed in on that one word. "You mean it was tacky? Sticky? Like drying blood?

Charlie's eyes snapped open again. "Yes. Like drying blood. So whatever happened to Elizabeth must have happened before, not after we found her. We were not to blame."

But who was? Claire wondered. A feeling like an electric shock straightened her spine. "Could Elizabeth have been…murdered?"

Charlie shook her head, but more in confusion than denial. "Elizabeth was pregnant and scared. It makes sense that she killed herself. As much sense as it ever can."

"But her death could have been convenient for other people." Claire leaned forward. "Suppose Allen Lisac didn't want everyone to know that Elizabeth was pregnant. He could have killed her in a fit of passion, and then tried to make it look like a suicide. Tried to cover everything up. And it worked. You told me his father had everything hushed up. No wonder. They were trying to cover up a lot more than a pregnancy. And that must be why Allen's mother was so intent on finding a note—because she guessed the truth—that it wasn't a suicide at all." Claire's headlong rush faltered. "Are you sure about the blood, though, Charlie? Are you sure about what you saw?"

"At my age, I am nothing but memories. I will ask Tom, but I am sure he will say the same. Which means that someone killed her. Someone killed her and walked away untouched. For fifty years, they have gone unpunished." Her eyes burned like blue flames in her otherwise colorless face. "That is not right. It is not just."

Claire faced reality. "But it's probably fifty years too late to find out the truth now. Even if Tom agrees with you, what does it matter? No one will want to open up a fifty-year-old suicide."

"You do not understand, Claire. I need to know for myself. When I found Elizabeth dead, I did not allow myself to worry and pick at it. This was my new country. I did not want to believe that here there was evil. I had learned to be good at not thinking about things. I had learned—I had had to learn—how to leave the past behind. Now I wish I had not closed my eyes. I owe it to Elizabeth to find out the truth." Charlie took the ring from the drawer and picked up her keys. There were two bright spots of color on her cheeks. "And the key is Allen. He lied about the ring. And you are right that he had a reason to kill her. But he might not be the only one. You say he and Mary are home now—come with me to return it. I want to watch him and Mary both when they see the ring, but I cannot watch two people at one time. I want to know if it was a surprise to them that the ring was in the wall, or if they knew it all along. Come with me, Claire. I knew these people well once, but it was such a long time ago. You have young, fresh eyes. Maybe you will see something that I will miss."

"I can't, Charlie." It was hard to say no in the face of her roommate's intensity. "I promised Dante."

"Then I must do it myself." Charlie turned on her heel and marched out of the room.

NINETEEN

1944—THE FRENCH GIRL does not get into line fast enough. An SS sets the dog on her. The fangs pierce the girl's throat.

A single cry hangs in the air. Charlotte does not know who has made it, the dying or the living.

After, the SS wipes the blood from the dog's muzzle with a folded white handkerchief. With the toe of his boot, he turns the girl's body over, the way he might a deer.

The other women are still and silent, watching him.

TWENTY

"You wear glasses, Ms. Montrose?" Claire turned away from the display of reading glasses at Fred Meyer. Wearing his standard dirty red flannel shirt and staring at her with undisguised curiosity was Jason Lutz, the little boy she read to once a week. Actually, Jason read to *her*—at seven he could make his way through chapter books with no problem. Claire had the feeling his teacher had enrolled him in SMART not so much to help his reading as to expose him to an adult who had her life more or less together.

"Jase—come on!" A gangly teenager, hair buzzed close to his scalp, stalked down the aisle toward them. He looked familiar, but she couldn't place him.

Jason looked at her shyly. "This is my brother, Matt. Matt, this is my reading buddy, Ms. Montrose."

"Hello."

Matt grunted in reply. From Jason, Claire knew Matt had twice run away from home, and that he had been in trouble for shooting a pellet gun into a crowd and hitting someone in the leg. Last spring his father had sent him to a boot camp in Eastern Oregon, but from what Claire had been able to gather, he had come back little changed.

While Jason's eyes were brown, Matt's were an odd, nearly startling green. He didn't look much like his brother. It was clear that one of Jason's parents was black, probably his mother, since Claire had met the dad, and he was definitely white. Jason had milk-chocolate skin and not quite nappy hair, whereas Matt's olive skin and black-stubbled head made him look Italian.

Whoever their mother or mothers had been, they were long

gone now. From what Jason had said, he'd grown up without a mom. At school, he seemed starved for female affection. He always managed to sit as close to Claire as possible, and would have happily sat in her lap to read if she had let him. Since she didn't, he had to content himself with frequent hugs.

He gave her one now, nearly knocking her off balance. "'Bye, Ms. Montrose."

Just past Jason were racks of kids' clothes, the riot of bright colors and designs a cruel contrast to the frayed ends of his sleeves. Claire was seized with a sudden inspiration.

"You know what today is, Jason? It's my birthday." Her birthday was a month away. "And in my family, we have a tradition. We always buy someone a present on our birthday. It brings you good luck the whole year."

"It does?" Wide-eyed, Jason hung on every word. Matt, standing behind him, pursed his lips and shot her a skeptical glance.

"So in order for me to have good luck this year, I need to buy you a new shirt." Claire wanted to buy him a dozen shirts, as well as pants, socks, underwear, and shoes, but she knew she would be lucky to get away with buying him a single shirt.

"Really?" Jason threw his arms around her thighs so tightly that Claire nearly toppled over.

Over his head, her eyes met Matt's. He shrugged and muttered, "Whatever."

AT FRED MEYER, besides buying Jason a long-sleeved blue shirt with a silk-screened picture of a fire-breathing dragon on the front, Claire also purchased a pair of reading glasses with heavy black plastic frames and the smallest possible correction. In the tiny mirror bolted to the top of the display, Claire looked like a gangly adolescent boy who spent a lot of time online involved in role-playing games.

The reading glasses made the air look filmy, so Claire took them off to drive home. Now she stood with Charlie on the Lisacs' doorstep, wearing the best disguise she had been able

to devise in a couple of hours. She knew she was risking
Dante's anger, but at the same time she couldn't abandon her
friend. A few years back, Charlie had saved Claire from becoming the kind of never-married woman who still lived at home
with her mother. Oh, Charlie would have claimed she had gotten the better end of the deal, gaining a roommate to help main-
tain her eighty-year-old house as well as pay the property taxes,
but Claire knew she was the one who had really benefitted.
Charlie had become more mother to her than her own had ever
been. She had expanded Claire's horizons about food, life,
love, and art. Claire owed Charlie a lot.

Which was why she was now wearing her hair in a bun so
tight it slitted her eyelids. On top she had jammed a black baseball cap so that not a single red curl—her most distinctive fea-
ture—escaped to identify her. Dressed in baggy sweatpants
and a loose sweatshirt bulked up with two sweaters underneath, she had looked in the bathroom mirror and gotten a
pretty good idea of what she would look like if she stopped running and kept eating Doritos.

The plan was that Claire would refrain from giving her
name, keep her head down, and observe Mary when the other
woman was busy looking in some other direction. Like at the
ring. There was no way Allen Lisac could connect her with
Dante. If he ever did meet her, it wouldn't be until after the museum had already made the decision about who would curate
the wing that would have Allen Lisac's name above the doors.
And once the decision was made, then it wouldn't matter much
if he recognized her.

The door to the Lisacs' house was so large that Charlie had
to stand on tiptoe to reach the knocker. Claire held her breath,
but all she heard was a lawn mower. There was no answering
sound of footsteps. A few seconds later, Howard popped out of
his door and walked across the driveway. His expression turned
from puzzlement to delight when he saw Charlie. Claire didn't
think he noticed her at all. He brought both hands up as far as
his waist, and then didn't seem to know what to do with them,

as if torn between hugging Charlie, squeezing her shoulders, or shaking her hand. He finally settled for a two-handed handshake.

"Charlie? Charlie Heidenbruch? Gosh, how long has it been since we last saw each other—five, six years? You look wonderful." He seemed so delighted that it crossed Claire's mind that Charlie had been wrong, that it hadn't been Elizabeth whom Howard had secretly longed for, all those years ago.

"You are looking well yourself, Howard," Charlie was saying. He did look like he had made an effort, and Claire guessed he might be expecting visitors other than themselves. The edge of a new-looking white T-shirt peeked through the blue cotton shirt he wore, open a single button at the neck. His jeans were even pressed. She imagined him carefully choosing each item, scrutinizing himself front and back, combing hair over his bald spot, managing to make his preparations fill up an entire morning.

"So you came to see Allen and Mary, but not me," he said in a mock-chiding tone. "I'm afraid they have gone out to lunch, but they should be back soon." Howard gave Claire an odd look, and she knew he was trying to place her. "Why, I remember you. Usually you're not wearing so many—" He stopped himself, coloring. "You're the one who wanted to know about the wall. My, it's a small world. Are you related to Charlie?"

"She is my housemate," Charlie said. "And a dear friend."

The lawn mower stilled, and then Matt appeared, pushing it from Howard's backyard to the front. His eyes were half-closed, and he had headphones in his ears. Claire realized she had seen him around the neighborhood before, mowing people's lawns. She was relieved when he didn't seem to register her presence.

Howard said, "I guess I've only seen you in your running clothes—I almost didn't recognize you in your civilian garb." He still looked a little puzzled. "I think of her as our lady of perpetual motion. Trotting up the hill day after day. And then last week she was asking questions about the Lisacs' wall, wanting to know more about it. I told her the stones came from the river. I didn't tell her your boyfriend was the one who built it." The lawn mower started up again, so loud he had to raise his voice to be heard over it. "I'm forgetting my manners. You ladies should come inside."

Charlie was already shaking her head. "No, Howard, I don't think—"

Howard's tone was wheedling. "I've got homemade brownies. No one can say no to brownies. Why don't you visit with me a little while you wait for the Lisacs to come home?"

"So it won't be long until they come back?"

Howard's smile exposed his snaggly teeth. "I expect them back any minute. Come on, come on." He opened the door. "I don't think you'll find it's changed that much, Charlie. A few more books, maybe."

Once inside the house, Claire looked around, half-expecting an old man's bachelor pad, with perhaps a painting of a reclining nude above the fireplace, or a wet bar with glasses decorated with bare-breasted Tahitian ladies. Instead, it was spick and span and suburban. The house was old enough that it must have had oak floors, but they were hidden by flat tan carpets. The living room held a beige-striped couch, a spindly-legged chair, and a wheat-colored La-Z-Boy lounger in front of a TV inside an open armoire. Next to the door, an umbrella stand held a furled golf umbrella. The only deviations were the huge built-in bookcases crammed with books.

There was no painting above the mantelpiece, just mirrored tiles. They were probably supposed to make the room look larger. Instead they just made Claire feel like she was in a funhouse, as she kept catching her reflection out of the corner of her eye.

The whole house was so small Claire could see most of it from where she stood. A hallway to the left of her, the twelve-foot-by-fourteen-foot living room in front of her, a dining room that was more suggestion than reality to her right, with a cramped kitchen jutting off it. "It's not much, but it's home." Howard said. "It actually started out as the home for the hired help. Back in those days, this place was considered to be out in the country, so the help had to live in."

Outside the dining room, a bird feeder hung from a maple tree that grew close to the house. On the windowsill were a pair of binoculars, an open narrow notebook, and *Birds of Oregon*.

"You girls want a cup of coffee? I've got instant. Or tea if you want it. And I've got those brownies I told you about." Howard squeezed past the narrow dining table, then quickly swept the red box that read "Betty Crocker" off the counter and into the garbage under the sink. He turned and Claire pretended she hadn't seen this. Then Howard caught sight of a squirrel that was trying to climb out to the bird feeder. He leaned forward and slapped the window. His fingernails were thickened and yellow. "Get away!" It hesitated, then ran down the trunk. "Like rats with fluffy tails," he muttered in disgust. Picking up the pan of brownies, Howard turned back to Charlie and Claire. "Or instead of coffee, would you girls rather have milk?"

Howard was the kind of host who wouldn't be satisfied until you had expressed a need and he had filled it, so Charlie requested tea and Claire took a chance on the instant coffee. When she had lived with her mother, it had been all she drank. She found her taste buds had changed in the past few years, though, so she had to wince her way through every bitter, sludgy swallow.

Howard and Charlie made small talk about what they had been doing for the past six years, then their conversation gradually reached further and further back into the past.

"This time of the year, I always find myself thinking about Elizabeth," Howard said as he got up to clear the dishes. "There's not many of us now who remember her. And once we're gone…" His words trailed off.

"It is about Elizabeth that we wanted to see Allen and Mary," Charlie said. "A piece of the past has turned up in the present."

"What do you mean?" Howard stopped and turned.

"It is why Claire was stopping by Allen's house last week. She found something in his wall that she wanted to return."

"In the wall?" Howard echoed.

Charlie turned to Claire. "Show him."

"I'm sorry I didn't show it to you when I met you," Claire said, as she pulled the drawstring bag from her jacket pocket. "It just seemed so valuable I was afraid to turn it over to someone I had just met." She shook out the ring onto her palm. "Of course, now that Charlie has told me how close you are with the Lisacs…"

The coffee cups and plates bounced off the carpeted floor. Legs visibly trembling, Howard sat down hard in the recliner. The color had drained from his face, except for his nose, which turned bright red. Then he fumbled a handkerchief from his breast pocket. Claire caught the glimpse of embroidered initials before he held it to his face and began to sob.

"Oh, God, oh, God." And then no words, just strangled sounds. Howard was the first person who had seen the ring and truly mourned Elizabeth, whose grief seemed as fresh as yesterday. There was nothing worse than hearing an old man sob, Claire thought, while she stared down at the ring, wishing she were anywhere but here. Old men who had been brought up not to cry, so that when they did it sounded like something irreparable was tearing inside them. The sound wasn't meant for anyone else's ears, a private grief with no calculation to it.

Charlie got up and went to him. She was so petite, and Howard so lanky, that standing she was barely taller than he was sitting. She reached out and pulled his head onto her shoulder.

There was a long, awkward silence, punctuated by the sound of Howard's ragged breathing. Claire wished she had thought of a more subtle way to show him the ring, something slower that would have given him time to brace himself for what was coming. It was clear that Howard had loved Elizabeth. Even fifty years later he had not yet come to terms with her loss.

Finally, with a heavy sigh, Howard lifted his head from Charlie's shoulder. She sat down on the arm of the recliner and rested her hand on his shoulder. Howard wiped his eyes, refolded his handkerchief, and then tucked it away in his breast pocket. From the same pocket he pulled out a pair of reading glasses and pushed them onto his nose, then slowly raised his head. Behind his glasses, his magnified wet blue eyes swam like fish in an aquarium. Without saying a word, he reached for the ring, his trembling fingers dancing across Claire's palm. His hand seemed to sink at its solid weight.

"Liz's ring." He surprised Claire by thrusting the ring back at her. "In the wall? Did you find anything else there?"

She hadn't thought about the possibility that the wall might hold anything more than the ring. "There was just a little hole. I had to get it out with a stick. I don't think there was anything else there but this ring."

"The ring being there is what I do not understand," Charlie said. "I am sure Allen said Elizabeth gave the ring back to him."

"Did he say that? I don't really remember." Howard pulled out the handkerchief again, half-turned away from them, and blew his nose. Holding the balled-up handkerchief to his bowed forehead, he spoke from behind the shelter of his forearm. The lawn mower was off again, and they could now hear Howard's ragged breathing. "Everything from that time is a blur. I don't remember her funeral, I don't even remember the rest of that year."

"You loved her," Charlie said simply.

Howard's face crumpled again. His mouth sucked into itself. He shook his head, but didn't say anything. When he finally spoke, his voice was bitter. "If I had really loved her, things would have been different. They wouldn't have turned out the way they did. People can get to the point where they feel like they don't have any choices, except the worst one." Claire suddenly knew that Elizabeth had told Howard about the pregnancy. "But if they could only lift their heads up and see, look around a little bit, then they wouldn't have to..." There was a long pause. "To do the things they do. I've spent fifty years wishing I had done something different, said something different. I've had fifty years. And Liz hasn't had a single day."

"Howard, Howard," Charlie said slowly. She gave Claire a meaningful look across Howard's bowed shoulders. "I am no longer so certain that Elizabeth killed herself."

He lifted his head, confusion twisting his features. "Of

course she did." He hesitated, a gentleman with mores fifty years out of date. "Only a few people know this, but…but Elizabeth, was, well, was pregnant."

"I know that, Howard, but there is more." Charlie explained about the blood. But the more she explained, the more confused Howard looked.

"I'm not quite following you." Howard shook his head slowly. "You think someone hurt Liz? But no one would want to hurt her. That just plain doesn't make sense."

"That," Charlie said, "is what I want to talk to Allen and Mary about." She squeezed past him and into the dining room to look out the window. "And their garage door is open, so they are home." She came back into the living room and patted him on the shoulder. "You stay here. Take some deep breaths. You have had a great shock. Claire and I will go and talk to them right now."

TWENTY-ONE

1944—MARCHING IN FORMATION is hypnotic. Charlotte keeps her gaze focused on the feet ahead of her. Rows of five women. Ten feet.

Her eyes fasten on these feet, marching, marching. Some are bare and leave bloody footprints. Even though she is lucky enough to have shoes, she has found they are never dry.

Marching, marching. There is no sense in it. They march along rutted roads, the mud frozen into ice, through flat fields, sometimes through the woods, and then back to camp again.

Yesterday she took off her socks for the first time in eighty-two days. All her toenails came off with them. She shook them out, silvery paper, then put the socks back on.

Marching, marching, marching. When she closes her eyes tonight, she knows she will march in her dreams.

Ahead of her, someone falls to her knees. Charlotte veers to the left, walks past her, so close her fingers brush the woman's bare scalp.

Her gaze does not waver from those feet, eight of them now. When the shot rings out, she does not look back.

Walking next to Charlotte, a woman SS officer, feet in leather boots, tall in her wool cape with its high black hood, laughs.

TWENTY-TWO

1952—WARREN ENTERED THE HOUSE SO QUIETLY that Charlie didn't know he was home until she heard him speak. She was in the kitchen with Tom. Her thirst had reasserted itself. The body had its needs and could not be denied for long. How many years had it been since she had first learned that lesson and been shamed by it?

"What happened here?" Warren's voice rapped out from the living room, making them both start.

Warren's tone reminded Charlie that Elizabeth had said her future father-in-law had been in the military during what had been called the Great War, back when they thought there would be no other, had served as an officer. Warren had urged his son to enlist, telling Allen that American soldiers would just need to bang a few heads together, that the "gook" problem would be settled in a week. Now things looked like they might grind on forever, and what Truman called "a simple police action" had spit out Warren's son permanently maimed. Still, Warren didn't seem to feel any guilt, or to have second thoughts.

Charlie peeked around the kitchen wall where Austrid and Warren stood only a few inches from each other. Neither of them were looking at Elizabeth's sheet-draped body.

"She's dead." Austrid drew herself up to her full height, her eyes nearly level with her husband's. She sounded like she wanted to shout, but she kept her words to a low hiss that Charlie had to strain to hear. "I never wanted her living here, never. You're the one who took her in, brought death and gossip under our roof. Our name will be dragged through the mud! She's a foolish, flighty little chippy who leaves messes for others to clean up." Charlie glanced at Tom and he raised an eyebrow.

"You're hysterical, Austrid." Warren's soft words were enough to stop his wife cold. "Where's Tom? He called me."

Tom stepped out of the kitchen, with Charlie following. "Right here, sir."

"Tell me what happened here."

"Well, sir—" he began, when Charlie interrupted. She didn't like Warren, and she didn't want to hear Tom's explanation, sure to be all larded with "sirs." Quickly, she sketched in the details of what had happened.

Warren took a deep breath, then turned to Tom. "Let me see her."

Then came the only moment when Warren seemed in anything less than perfect control. When Tom lifted the white sheet from Elizabeth's equally white face, Warren's eyes squinted reflexively, like a man blinded by the noonday sun. Elizabeth now seemed to be made of wax, a clever replica of the real girl, her skin pale and translucent next to the black of the gown she wore. Charlie watched as Warren reached out his hand and ran it lightly over Elizabeth's hair, so gently she might have been a sleeping child. When his hand reached the place where blood matted the fine strands, he jerked it back.

"What's this?" When he looked up at them, Warren's face was perfectly smooth again, without even the flicker of a muscle or a tear in his eye to reveal his feelings.

"I'm sorry, sir. She fell against the cabinet when I cut her down."

Charlie knew her anger was misplaced, but at every "sir" she wanted to shake Tom. She gritted her teeth even more when Warren ordered Tom to get a broom and sweep up the glass.

"Did you find a note?"

"We've been looking," Austrid said, raising her long slender hands in the air and then dropping them. "There's no note. Nothing. Just...her." With her chin, she indicated Elizabeth's body.

Why all this concern about a note? Charlie wondered. Were they afraid it might reveal some secret about their son?

Warren turned to Tom again. "Who else have you called? Have you called the police?"

"Just you, sir."

"Good. We don't need Allen to be hurt any more than he already will be."

"Where is he?" Austrid asked. "Why isn't he with you?"

"He's out at a job site. There's no phone there. The secretary knows to send him home the minute he gets back."

Austrid said, "You should have gone out to meet him. He'll drive home like a maniac and get in an accident."

"She doesn't know anything else than to tell him to come home, so she can't say anything else. I didn't even tell her it was about Elizabeth."

"With a message like that, he'll know enough," Austrid said. "He'll guess right away that something is wrong."

"He's going to have to know anyway, Austrid. He's not a little boy anymore. He's a man, or have you forgotten? He's going to have to figure out how to take this like a man."

Then Warren went into his den, which was just off the living room. He left the door open. Charlie could hear the sound of him dialing, of his long, rattling sigh as he waited for the phone to be answered. "Bob? This is Warren. There's been a terrible accident." A pause. "My future daughter-in-law. I don't want to discuss it over the phone. I need you to come here and help us make arrangements. And be sure to bring your bag. My wife will need something to calm her nerves."

But Austrid didn't seem distraught when Charlie looked at her. She was staring at Elizabeth's body, which was once again covered, and she seemed blazingly alive. In Charlie's experience, Austrid was normally varying shades of ash and cardboard, but now bright color stained her cheeks. Her breathing was shallow and rapid. Her head was up and her hands were tight fists. Her gray gaze met Charlie's. Austrid's chin was raised, and she stared down the bridge of her nose like a challenge. It was Charlie who finally looked away.

The next hour brought a whirlwind of activity that spun around the dead girl. Tom was sent out to buy a black wreath for the door. Without being asked, Charlie made herself useful by making tea and coffee. For anyone who looked like they could use it, she tipped in a bit of whiskey from a bottle she found in Warren's liquor cabinet. She tidied up, throwing away the empty wine bottle and rinsing out the two glasses she found in the sink. She also answered the door from time to time. The doctor was the first to arrive, coming less than twenty minutes after Warren's call. He didn't spend much time with Elizabeth, and the way he touched her, with no gentleness, as if she had never been a human being and was now nothing but a messy problem, sent Charlie back to the kitchen, where she had a swallow of whiskey without the coffee. His indifference reminded her too much of the camps.

Warren had also called Elizabeth's mother at home and her father at the factory where he was working as a floor sweeper. They arrived separately. Mr. Ellsworth was tall and gaunt and absolutely quiet when he looked upon his daughter's waxy face. Mrs. Ellsworth came with a baby on her hip and a child clinging to her dress. Her husband shouted at her for that, while she whined in a piteous way, asking what else was she to do with them. Warren took the four of them back into his den and shut the door.

Then a black hearse pulled up, and the doctor and Tom helped the two men inside bundle Elizabeth away, still covered by the sheet. At the sight of one of her linen sheets being wheeled out the door, Austrid finally did become distraught, bringing to life Warren's earlier accusation. She protested that the sheet had been imported from Ireland, until Warren and the doctor hustled her back to her bedroom. Charlie couldn't make out her words behind the closed door, just the sound of her voice rising and falling like a siren, even as the hearse slid away.

Charlie sent Tom to Lynches Market to buy more coffee, as well as to the liquor store. Without bothering Warren, she gave him money from her own pocketbook. She really wanted to tell

Tom to go home, but she didn't want to get him in trouble. At the same time, she had no desire to listen to Warren ordering him about and Tom's polite replies.

After Tom left, Charlie was surprised when she looked at her watch to see that it was only three in the afternoon. She longed for night to fall, for the chance to leave this place and try to sleep without dreams.

A few minutes later, there was another knock on the door. Charlie opened it cautiously. She'd already turned away one inquiring neighbor, blocking the door so he couldn't see Elizabeth's body, but this time it was Howard, fresh home from teaching. His face was drained of color, and he was shaking so much that it was hard for him to even speak. "Elizabeth?" he said, his tone rising.

Charlie drew him inside to hide him from prying eyes. She placed a hand on his arm and found it already trembling.

"She's dead, Howard."

He let out a long low moan, and she was reminded of a dog she had seen once, thrown to the side of the road by a car, making a noise just like that, trying to crawl forward on two front legs, dragging its broken body behind it.

"I...she... Do the police have any suspects?"

Charlie had to tell him, he would find out sooner or later, although she dreaded it, somehow already knowing he would blame himself.

"Howard—she hung herself."

His mouth fell open, and she saw that he had a tooth missing in the back. The teeth on either side of the space were brown. "No! That's not true! No!"

The force of the denial brought Warren out from the bedroom, where he had been murmuring with the doctor. "Howard, I'm sorry. I know Elizabeth considered you a good friend."

Howard was still blank with shock. "But how—who?"

"Charlie here found her," Warren said, leaving Tom out.

"And she was"—his mouth worked as he tried to say the word—"hanging? I don't understand. This doesn't make any sense. Are you sure?"

"Tom and I cut her down." Charlie put her hand on his arm, but he turned away from her and her hand fell away.

"When was this?"

"A few hours ago. A little after one o'clock."

"But—she hung herself? Where? How?"

Charlie pointed to the great beam. "She stood on a kitchen chair and threw the rope over."

"It was a cord," Warren corrected. "I found the place where she cut it off the curtains."

Howard swiveled his head, scanning the room. "Where is she? I need to see her. I won't believe this until I see Elizabeth."

"They've taken her away," Charlie said quietly.

"So the police have been here?"

"No." Warren bit the word off. "This is a private, family matter, Howard, and we are keeping it that way. She's at Finter's Mortuary. We're just waiting for Allen to come home now."

"He doesn't know?"

"Not yet."

"Doesn't know what?" The quiet voice behind them made them all jump. Allen stood there, one hand on the doorknob, the other on his cane. "What doesn't Allen know?" Each word was carefully enunciated.

For once, Warren seemed at a loss for words. "Son, um, Elizabeth is…"

"Dead," Allen finished for him. "The woman two doors down was kind enough to tell me that she had seen the hearse. And that she had caught a glimpse of long blond hair falling out from underneath the sheet that covered the body." He swayed and would have fallen if it weren't for his cane.

"Oh, Allen," Howard said, and stretched out his hand toward the other man, but then stopped short.

"You've been drinking." Warren seemed more surprised than anything.

"After I heard that bit of news, I went down to Renner's and had a couple of shots."

"You mean you were outside and didn't come in? Your mother and I have been waiting for you."

"I know. The secretary said I was to come home immediately. Do not pass Go. Do not collect two hundred dollars." Allen's words had a terrible lilt to them, and his eyes never left Warren's face.

Warren looked shocked. "Now is not the time for jokes, son."

"What do you want me to do, then, cry? Oh, I forget, a man never cries. A man knows how not to cry." Allen put on an English accent. "Stiff upper lip and all that." He resumed his normal tone. "A man knows how to clean up the mess like it never happened. Isn't that what you think, Father? So is that what you did—cleaned up the mess, got everything back to normal? So I couldn't even see her? I couldn't even see what she had done to herself?"

TWENTY-THREE

FROM BEHIND THE big house came the drone of the lawn mower, which had muffled the sound of Allen's and Mary's return. The garage doors were open, revealing a new chartreuse VW Bug and a miniature blue and white BMW convertible. The convertible was the kind of car guys always wanted when they were young, but could only afford when they were old. Next to the garage, a dark-skinned woman with dirty bare feet was working in the flower garden, her face shaded by a straw hat with a broken brim. A basket dangled over one meaty forearm, and with the other hand she expertly wielded a pair of scissors, discarding dead blooms into a waiting wheelbarrow and placing perfect ones into the basket. How strange it must be to have hired help, Claire thought, nodding at the gardener as she and Charlie hurried by. The hat dipped in return. They were always there, but not there, rendered invisible by their role. And that made her think of Charlie's old friend, Tom. What might he have seen or overheard on those long days while he carefully pieced the wall together, just a few yards away from this house?

Charlie let the knocker fall. There was a pause, and then the sound of slow footsteps, punctuated by an added thump Claire realized must be coming from Allen's cane.

The door was pulled back to reveal a man a few inches taller than Claire. Like Charlie, Allen Lisac had kept his good looks even as he aged. His black eyes were accented by his silver hair, which had been combed back into tiny waves that reminded Claire of the inside of corrugated cardboard. He wore an expensively tailored suit, a crisp white shirt and a plain dark tie. Standing very erect, he held a silver-handled wooden cane loose in his left hand, like an affectation, a stage prop, and not a necessity.

"Yes?" he said. His tone was cool, as though he believed they might be soliciting for Little League or selling magazine subscriptions.

"Hello, Allen. It's Charlie. Charlie Heidenbruch." Charlie deliberately didn't introduce Claire, who stood two steps behind her.

If Allen was surprised at Charlie's appearing on his doorstep, he didn't show it except by the faintest narrowing of the eyes. "It's been a long time. To what do I owe this honor?"

Charlie didn't answer him with words, just opened her palm to display the ring.

Claire watched the color leach from Allen's face. He put his free hand to his mouth and then turned and walked away, his cane stabbing the floor. The door was still open, so the two women followed him into the entryway.

Ten steps in, the entryway opened up into a long living room that ran the length of the house. The room was decorated in Mission-style oak furniture that Claire thought might be the real thing. A huge mahogany beam marked where the entryway merged into the living room. Claire looked up at it, and then at Charlie, who nodded almost imperceptibly. Claire couldn't help but shiver. No matter how Elizabeth had died, whether by her own hand or someone else's, it seemed like such a death would echo forever after. Did she simply imagine the air was colder here, where Elizabeth had danced in midair?

Allen Lisac fell more than sat on a long leather couch. Claire was suddenly afraid he was going to have a stroke. In a hoarse whisper, he demanded, "Where did you find it?"

Charlie walked toward him to set the ring down on the oak coffee table. Allen stared at it, his upper lip pulled back to expose long yellow teeth. He didn't look attractive or the least bit young now.

Seeing the ring had definitely stunned him. But Claire couldn't name the emotion on the old man's face. Was it fear? Grief? Surprise? Guilt? Shock? A little bit of everything?

A voice spoke from behind Claire and Charlie.

"Allen? Honey, what's wrong?"

It was the woman they had seen outside, the woman Claire had thought must be a Hispanic gardener. Now she took off her broken straw hat.

Claire started. She recognized the woman, and did a rapid recalculation. Not the gardener, then, but Mary Lisac. Without knowing who it was, Claire had seen Mary many times in the neighborhood, shopping at Nature's, browsing the new fiction shelf at the Hillsdale Branch Library, carrying a bag of cinnamon rolls out the door of Fat City. When Claire had looked at Charlie's long-ago photographs, she had thought the horse-faced woman on the plaid blanket had looked familiar. But now Claire realized it been more than the way Mary's face had resembled her sister Elizabeth's. She must also have recognized some trace of Mary before she gained one hundred pounds and started dressing like the world's oldest free spirit.

As always when Claire had seen her, Mary wore loose colorful cotton layers—an ankle-length purple skirt, a red scoop-neck top that showed her ample and wrinkled cleavage, and a faded smock, printed with flowers in unlikely color combinations. She had slipped her feet into Birkenstock sandals. She wasn't fat so much as sturdy. Her skin had been tanned to leather, her eyes were silver-gray, and she wore her white hair close-cropped as an elf's.

"Allen? What's wrong?" Mary repeated with an edge to her voice. He didn't answer, and she followed his gaze. Claire watched as Mary took in the ring, and then lifted her head to look at the wooden crossbeam. She sat down heavily on the same couch as Allen, but at the other end. She made no move to touch the ring. "Is that what I think it is?"

Allen and Charlie nodded, while Claire kept still and watched Mary. They had decided it made more sense for Charlie to watch Allen, who, Charlie had said, would be better at disguising his emotions. Mary looked as stunned as Allen had. Her mouth hung open and her chin trembled. Her breathing was labored and loud.

"Why do you have Elizabeth's ring, Charlie?" To Claire's ears, it sounded as if Mary truly didn't know the answer.

"My friend here found it in your wall," Charlie said. "She found it where a chink of mortar had fallen out." To Claire's relief, neither Mary nor Allen spared a glance or a question for her. They had eyes only for the ring. "When she showed it to me, I recognized it immediately. What I do not understand is why it was there at all. I thought Elizabeth broke the engagement off and returned the ring. Is that not what you told us, Allen?"

There was a long silence, and then a heavy sigh. "When I said what I did, I was still in shock over Liz's death," Allen said. "I was too...too ashamed to tell people the truth."

"And what was the truth?" Charlie's tone was gentle.

Claire kept her eyes on Mary's face. Mary, who had looked surprised by the ring, but not by her husband's words.

"Elizabeth never broke off the engagement," Allen said. "Just before she killed herself, she came to me and told me she was pregnant, begged me to move up the wedding. She was crying and clinging and hysterical. And instead I gave her money to get an abortion. I was..." He sighed and looked down at his clasped hands. "I was afraid of what people would say. Especially my mother." Another sigh, so deep that it rattled. "I know it sounds terrible, as if I deliberately seduced and abandoned Liz. In truth, she was the one who had come to me after I was released from the hospital. She wanted it far more than I did. As if she sensed how far apart we had grown." He smiled a bitter smile.

Mary gazed at Allen with her lips parted and pulled down at the corners, a look of such sadness for the boy he had been and the man he had been forced to become.

"Why did you not simply move up the wedding?" Charlie asked.

"Because I had decided I could not marry her, although I hadn't yet worked up the courage to tell my folks. What I had seen and done during the war and afterward had changed me.

Elizabeth had stayed the same. We were children when we got engaged, pretending we were really grown-ups. She was right out of high school and I wasn't through with college. When I gave her the money for the abortion, she became very upset. Otherwise, she wouldn't have done what she did."

"But you allowed people to think that Elizabeth broke up with you because of your war injuries?" Charlie crossed her arms.

"People came to that verdict themselves." Allen straightened up, and two spots of color appeared in his cheeks. "What did you want me to do, drag her name even further through the mud, tell everyone she was pregnant? I kept silent, and people drew their own conclusions. Then, after Liz…did what she did, the ring wasn't on her finger in the funeral home. My father questioned the workers, but they denied knowing anything. But I figured one of them had pocketed it. A single stone from this ring was worth more than they would earn in a year."

"But in truth they did not steal it. It wasn't on her hand when I found her," Charlie said. "Instead it was here on the grounds. I do not understand why."

"Maybe Liz hid it herself," Mary said flatly.

"Why would she do that?" Claire found herself asking the question before she remembered she was supposed to be silent.

"This ring has been in Allen's family for generations. Liz knew how important it was to him, and she wanted to hurt him. Maybe she wanted him to go to sleep every night just fifty feet from it, but never knowing it was there."

There was something strange about Mary's face, and it took Claire a moment to figure out what it was. All the other times she had seen Mary in the neighborhood, the older woman had been smiling. Now her expression was shuttered, but Claire could see the muscles working in her jaw. How much strength would it have taken to haul a slender girl up with a slip-knotted cord? Mary looked like the task would have been easy for her, even when she had been the thinner version of herself sitting on the blanket beside her sister, the ugly duckling to Elizabeth's swan. Had Mary secretly coveted this man who could never be hers? Had Mary killed her sister, faked a suicide, and then made sure she was the one to console the newly bereaved fiancé?

"Are you sure Elizabeth died by her own hand?" Charlie asked.

"What is that supposed to mean?" Allen demanded. "You're the one who found her—you should know exactly how she died."

Allen's answer was oddly elliptical, Claire thought, as she kept her eyes on Mary, but the other woman's face was blank, her eyes shuttered.

"After this ring turned up, I remembered something. There was a wound on Elizabeth's head, Allen. The blood was old and nearly dry. I believe it happened before we ever cut her down. I am thinking someone may have hurt her, then tried to cover it up by hanging her."

"Puh!" Allen made a sound of disparagement. "Elizabeth didn't have an enemy in the world. You're imagining things, Charlie. She killed herself because she was pregnant and knew I didn't love her anymore. When you cut her down, her head hit the china cabinet. I remember that we were still sweeping up broken glass weeks later."

"That does not explain the blood. Dead people do not bleed. Nor does it explain the ring."

Allen opened his mouth to say something when the doorbell rang. Mary made a sound of impatience, then got up to answer it. Howard came in the door and went straight to Allen, who crossed his arms across his chest.

"They showed me the ring, Allen. They wanted to be the ones who told you, or I would have told you myself."

"Then you wouldn't have had a chance to hear Charlie's little theory."

"Theory?"

"Charlie now thinks Elizabeth was murdered. Fifty years ago she didn't say a thing, but now she is sure of it." He waved his hand. "Something about how there was blood on her head, and that it was old. And she keeps talking about how it doesn't make any sense that the ring was in the wall. As if that is any kind of proof. Who knows what a person will do before they commit suicide? Obviously they are not of sound mind, by definition."

"Show me," Howard said, turning to Claire and Charlie. "Show me where it was found."

They walked back to the street. Allen trailed behind them, stabbing his way down the driveway with his cane. Claire pointed out the small niche, and Howard probed it with one long finger. His face was rapt with concentration as he leaned against the wall. "It feels like there's something else inside. I can just—just touch it."

"Go get the boy," Allen told Mary. "And tell him to bring the pickaxe from the garage."

"The pickaxe?" Mary eyed the wall dubiously. "Won't the whole thing fall down?"

"This wall is stronger than that. And if it leaves a gap, we can patch it up later."

Mary reappeared a few minutes later with Matt. A rusty pickaxe was slung over his shoulder. Surrounded by this many adults, he had lost the swaggering assurance he had had in Fred Meyer.

He had to hold the pickaxe awkwardly, about a foot away, in order to aim at the hole. But with each jab, some more of the gray, sandy mortar crumbled. Every few strokes, Matt would stop and probe the growing hole.

And finally the wall gave up its second secret: a small clasp purse reduced to nothing but its metal frame, filagreed with verdigris. Carefully, Matt freed it and handed it to Allen. They all crowded around to look. Trapped inside the framework was a brass lipstick tube that was also green with age. A white rectangle of paper that still showed the ghost of a Social Security number. A single photograph that had been reduced to a gray wash of moiré patterns. But Claire noted that despite what Allen had said about giving Elizabeth money for an abortion, there was no money at all.

The purse seemed as much a surprise to Mary and Allen as it was to Charlie. Charlie's and Claire's eyes met. What was Elizabeth's purse doing in the wall?

They all started when Howard spoke. He stood with his hand on his chest. "Oh, my God," he said slowly. "Her purse was there, too?" His mouth was open, his chin trembled. "Maybe Charlie's right. Do you think some thief robbed her?" His eyes widened. "Robbed her and…and killed her?"

Mary slowly nodded her head. "It could be, it could be. What happened to all that money you gave her, Allen? The money to"—she seemed mindful of Matt's presence—"take care of things? Did you ever find it after she died?"

Looking dazed, Allen shook his head. "I didn't think about it for a long time afterward, and then I realized it had disappeared after I gave it to Elizabeth. It didn't matter to me, though. Losing the money was nothing."

"But a thief?" Charlie protested. "Who would have stolen from Elizabeth?"

"There were workmen in and out of that house," Howard said. "The men who delivered the rock for the wall, the guy who built it, Warren's employees. Even her old friends from high school sometimes came over."

"That does not explain the ring…." Charlie's voice trailed off. "Why would the ring be there? Why would someone steal it only to hide it?"

Howard said, "Maybe they hid it for a moment, thinking they could come back and get it, and then the next layer of stones was laid down over it. Or maybe they took both the money and the ring, then realized that the ring was too unusual, that they couldn't sell it without it being recognized. So they hid it with the rest of the evidence."

Charlie only shook her head, looking confused.

TWENTY-FOUR

"DO YOU THINK a thief killed her?" Claire asked as soon as she closed her car door. "Five hundred dollars would have been a lot in those days, wouldn't it?" Using one hand to drive, she pulled off the baseball cap with the other, and then tugged the rubber band from her hair.

"It was a great deal, but I am not sure it was enough to kill someone over," Charlie said in a troubled voice. She made a humming noise as another thought struck her. "And there is no possibility Elizabeth would have entertained a stranger, dressed in a peignoir. She was very modest."

"Thieves don't usually call ahead. Maybe someone had watched Austrid leave after Allen and his father had gone to work, and thought no one else was left at home. If it was a stranger who did it, then you'll never figure out what really happened." Claire didn't add that the odds were good that they wouldn't anyway. "And why would Allen want to kill her? Since she had agreed to have an abortion, that took away the most powerful reason he might have had to kill her."

"Ah, but we only have his word for that. What if the reason there was no money in her purse is that there was never any to begin with? What if she never agreed to his demands? If Elizabeth protested that she would go to his parents, make them force Allen to marry her, he may have lost control. Then perhaps, once he was himself again, he set about fixing it so that no one would know."

Claire said, "It seemed to me that Allen may have been telling the truth, at least about not wanting to marry her. He didn't have to tell us about the pregnancy, but he did. And when he told us about how he got her pregnant and then planned to wash his hands of her, it made him look bad. If he was going to lie, wouldn't he have made up a lie that put him in a better light?"

Charlie shrugged. "Or he may have guessed that someone else might know about the pregnancy—and hoped that no one knew about the murder."

They were only a few blocks from their home when Claire was forced to slow the Mazda. A small crowd had gathered in the street, their eyes on three emergency vehicles parked in front of a modest house with weathered cedar shakes the color of the overcast sky.

Charlie craned her neck, finally back in the here and now. "My goodness. I think that may be Frank's house."

Even though Claire had run down this street hundreds of times, she had never really noticed the house hidden behind a huge fir tree. It was impossible not to notice it now, what with a fire engine idling at the curb, a police car parked behind it, and another cop car parked in the driveway. Claire pulled her car over to the curb on the other side of the street. For a moment, she and Charlie watched what was happening, as did a half-dozen neighbors who had gathered in the street. Two cops stood at the door of the house, knocking and calling, but the door didn't open and the curtains didn't twitch.

Claire and Charlie got out of the car and walked over to the knot of watchers. A couple of them held coffee mugs and even though it wasn't yet lunchtime, one man with a potbelly was sipping from a beer bottle. It was as if real life had gratifyingly merged with entertainment.

"That's Frank Ellsworth's house, right?" Claire ventured. Nods all around, but the neighbors' eyes didn't leave the thrilling sight of the idling emergency vehicles and the two cops who were now discussing things in voices too soft to carry. "Do you know what's happening?"

Everyone looked to an old woman with long gray hair that reached the middle of her back. After taking a sip from a mug reading WORLD'S BEST GRANDMA, she said, "His son called me a couple of hours ago because he's been phoning Frank since late yesterday afternoon and no one's answered. So I went and looked through the garage window and saw that Frank's car was still there, but no one answered the door when I knocked and it was dead silent inside. I went home and called his son back. He said Frank has diabetes and a heart condition, and I should call 911 because he's probably lying on the floor sick or worse. And so I did and all this happened." She gestured with her free hand, but she didn't seem worried. Maybe death was close enough to her that she took its threat in stride.

Claire had another thought. What if, after talking to Claire, Frank had begun nosing around, asking questions about his sister's death? What if Charlie was right, and Elizabeth had been murdered? Could whoever had killed her all those years before reached out yesterday to silence her meddlesome brother?

The two policemen had been joined by one of the firemen. After a brief huddle, they broke apart. It was clear a decision had been reached. The fireman walked back to his truck, said something to the other men, and they all began opening doors and pulling out equipment. The group clustered on the street watched closely as one of the policemen took a step back, then kicked high and hard at a spot just to the side of the doorknob. On the second kick, the door flew open. The firemen had readied a wheeled gurney and now they pulled it into within a few feet of the front door. After a pause, while they shouted Frank's name a few times, the two cops slowly walked inside. Claire noticed that both of them were resting their hands on the butts of their guns.

They were gone long enough for the crowd to grow restive and for the man with the beer to finish it and go back for another. When the cops finally emerged, they were empty-handed.

"Frank's dead, then," the guy with the beer said flatly, knowledgeably, and there was a kind of sigh of agreement.

One of cops went over to talk to the firemen. Although the little group on the sidewalk couldn't hear his words, they could see him shaking his head. The firemen began to put their equipment away, collapsing the gurney.

"If he's dead, why aren't they taking his body with them?" said a young girl with a baby on her hip and a ring through her eyebrow. Claire couldn't decide if she was the baby-sitter or the baby's mother.

"They need to get the medical examiner in, don't they?" said a man in a gray sweat suit who looked like he had been napping. "Haven't you ever watched a cop show? They'll need to do an autopsy to make sure the death isn't suspicious."

Another car pulled to the curb and parked behind Claire's Mazda. She took a quick look behind her, then did a double-take. It was her mother. And in the seat beside her was—Frank. Very much alive.

Claire put her hand over her face.

"What's going on?" Frank said behind them. Claire's mother stood beside him. Oh, God, Claire thought, was that a hickey on her neck?

At the sound of Frank's voice, everyone turned. The woman with the grandma mug spoke first.

"Your son has been trying to call you since last night. He was worried that you might have had a heart attack or stroke or something."

Frank's voice was more of a purr. "Let me assure you, I am very much to be numbered among the living." He gave Jean's ample waist a squeeze. "Wait here a moment while I ascertain if I can straighten this out." He strolled off, rather slowly, Claire thought, given the circumstances. He seemed to be enjoying all the attention. His shirt was rumpled, his collar unbuttoned, and something trailed from his pants pocket. It took Claire a second to identify it. The flapping ends of a yellow bow tie.

Claire turned to look at her mother, as did everyone else. Jean's raccoon eyes made it clear she had gone to bed with her makeup on. If she had gone to bed at all. She wore a black dress that seemed to contain a large percentage of Lycra, the offspring of an unholy union between a dress and a girdle. Her jutting freckled bosom had assumed the dimensions of a ship's prow. The baby-sitter, or whoever she was, giggled. There was definitely a purple suck mark on the side of Jean's neck. Claire grabbed her mother's hand and yanked her to one side. Only with an effort did she keep her voice low enough for the craning spectators not to hear.

"He was with you! Mother, he must be eighty! You are only fifty-five! He's old enough to be your father!"

Jean pulled herself up to her full height of five-foot-three. Her chest swelled dangerously. "Frank is not eighty! He is seventy-seven."

"Well, that's still plenty old." Claire could feel the heat rising in her face. "And women live longer. If anything, you should be looking the other way."

"Don't tell me you wouldn't have your nose out of joint if I came home with someone your age, missy. You're just jealous that I'm in a new relationship." Across the street, the firemen had finished packing up and now drove away. One of them gave a salute to Frank, who was standing in the doorway talking to the two cops. He waved and winked broadly in return.

In the past few days, Claire had learned more about older people's sex lives than she really wanted to know. "Don't tell me you're…" she couldn't think of the right word. Having sex? Making love? Or, to be more time-appropriate, making whoopee? "Aren't you worried about giving him a heart attack?"

"He's not an invalid! All that dancing has kept Frank in better shape than Zed ever was."

"But, Mom, he is just so much older!" Claire could feel herself starting to calm down. "I guess I just don't understand the attraction."

"You think I don't know what those other women at River-walk are saying about me? That I'm a gold digger, just after Frank's money? It's not like that at all. This is about love." Jean's eyes pleaded with Claire. "They're just jealous because I'm younger." She sagged, suddenly looking deflated. Frank exchanged a laugh with the two policemen, who then got back into their cars. Except for the woman with the long gray hair, who was now talking to Charlie, the neighbors were dispersing, talking in low voices, shooting Jean sidelong glances. Occasionally, one of them would laugh.

Claire thought of smarmy Frank, pulling her close on the dance floor while she looked down at his lipsticked ear. "True love? Oh, Mother, please, don't give me that."

"I didn't say true love." Jean straightened up. "I said love. Because that's what it is."

Frank waved at them. "Come on over, ladies!" His grin was wide, his banty chest puffed out.

With a sigh, Claire trailed Jean and Charlie. She knew she was being too judgmental, but her mother had the worst taste in men. Claire's father had been gone before Jean even figured out she was pregnant. Susie's dad had been a long-haul trucker, as had Jean's last boyfriend, Zed. In between had been a series of sleazy used car salesmen, meth-using carpet installers, drinking drywall workers. One guy, Tim, had spent more than forty hours a week trying to outwit the insurance fraud investigator who was following him with a video camera, convinced that Tim wasn't truly permanently disabled. Tim got caught when he slipped up and took Jean bowling. Jean's typical boyfriend smoked, drank, and liked risky pursuits such as raising pit bulls or driving motorcycles ninety miles an hour. Most of them moved in with Jean but somehow never could quite afford to help pay rent. And now there was Frank. Claire was fairly sure that half of Frank's attraction for Jean had been the way the women at Riverwalk had been vying for him.

Rather than being embarrassed by all the attention, Frank seemed invigorated. He put his arm around Jean's waist and gave her a squeeze, then turned to Claire and Charlie with a smile. "What are you two ladies out and about on such a lovely day?" He tilted his head to one side. "Are you going incognito today, Claire? I almost didn't recognize you."

"We have just been to see Allen Lisac to return the ring," Charlie said.

"And?"

"He kept it, if that is what you are asking. But there is something else you need to know about your sister's death." Charlie hesitated, and Frank's expression turned serious as he waited for her next words. "I am wondering if Elizabeth may have been murdered."

Jean sucked in her breath.

Frank just looked bewildered. "Murdered? No, no. Of course she killed herself."

"You knew, then," Charlie said.

"Knew what?" Jean looked impatient at being left out.

Frank hesitated, and then said, "That my sister was pregnant? Yes. Or at least I guessed she was carrying a child. What the French call *enceinte*." Claire was fairly certain Frank had mispronounced the word. "One time she was here visiting when she suddenly ran to the facilities with her hand over her mouth. When she came out I asked her what was going on, but she refused to admit anything was wrong. I always figured Liz was afraid everyone would count on their fingers and then point them at her. When the world is full of ten-pound premature babies, including yours truly. Or at least it was then, when everyone thought if you made your bed you had to lie in it. Once you got a girl pregnant, the only way out was to stick her in a white dress while it still fit and have her walk down the aisle."

"I no longer think she killed herself." Charlie explained about the blood on the back of Elizabeth's head, and about how she now thought Elizabeth had been struck and then strung up.

"That bastard!" Frank's voice was bitter. He remembered Jean and turned toward her. "Excuse my French."

"Who are you talking about?" Claire asked. "Allen Lisac?"

"The man always blames the woman when you turn up pregnant," Jean said, speaking from experience. "They forget it takes two to tango."

Claire said, "Allen says he insisted your sister get an abortion, and that he gave her the money for it. While we were there just now, he had this kid break open the wall where I found the

ring. We found what must have been the remains of your sister's purse. There was a lipstick, an old Social Security card,
and what used to be a photograph. Only there was no money.
Howard thinks a thief must have killed her."

"How much money was it?" Frank asked.

Charlie said, "Five hundred."

He let out a low whistle. "That was a lot of money in those
days. I guess that might have been enough to make somebody
do something stupid and then try to cover it up."

"There could be many reasons Elizabeth was killed," Charlie said. "Anger. Lust. Envy. Greed. Fear."

"You really think someone could have been afraid of Elizabeth?" Claire asked. "She doesn't seem like she could have
been much of a threat."

"I was thinking of the fear of secrets to be revealed."

Frank said, "I'd bet anything that Allen was afraid she was
going to go running to his parents. Allen was still like a little
boy around them, especially Mrs. Lisac. I mean Austrid. She
was a battleax. Maybe he couldn't stand to face up to her and
admit what had been going on under her very own roof."

Claire thought of what Allen Lisac had said. She wanted it
far more than I did. Had he been embarrassed by his own se-
duction, and the proof that had begun to swell Elizabeth's body?

TWENTY-FIVE

"PRACTICE RANDOM ACTS of kindness and senseless acts of beauty," said the bumper sticker on the car ahead of Claire's as they edged toward the Portland Airport. It took Claire such a long time to make her way into the parking garage that she started seriously considering the bumper sticker's advice. Maybe the world really would be a better place if everyone just did a few random acts of kindness. She imagined herself picking up the lunch tab for a trio of old ladies, going door to door raising money for the rain forest, throwing a hundred-dollar bill into the red Salvation Army kettle at Christmastime.

When she made her way into the terminal, she found that Dante's flight was delayed. She settled down to wait. Two hours later she was still waiting.

"Can you watch my spot?" she asked the woman sitting on the carpet next to her. The only response was a grunt. Claire spread her *New York Times* over her place, hoping it would still be there when she came back, then walked over to one of the ubiquitous Starbucks. Maybe a double latte would keep her awake. Behind her stood a mother with a girl who looked about seven. The child was begging for a cookie, but her mother seemed too tired to even answer her. As Claire handed over a ten-dollar bill, she said impulsively, "And can you give me one of those chocolate chip cookies, too?" She pushed a dollar in the tip jar, then turned and handed the cookie to the girl. "Here you go, sweetie."

The mother snatched it out of her daughter's hand. The kid promptly began wailing. "What have I told you about accepting food from strangers?" She turned her tiny, reddened eyes on Claire. "What do I look like? A charity case?" She stuffed the cookie in the trash can, then stormed out without ordering anything, dragging her daughter by the arm. Now the guy behind the counter was glaring at her, too.

She came back to find that half her spot had been taken, but that didn't stop her from squeezing in to sit down again, not after seeing on the reader board that Dante's flight had been delayed yet again. The effects of a band of thunderstorms in the Midwest had rippled out until it seemed that nearly every flight was now canceled or delayed.

Three hours later, Claire shifted for the millionth time on the thin carpet on the floor outside the security checkpoint. Judging by the way her butt was aching, the carpet provided a barrier less than one-sixteenth of an inch thick between her and the cold, hard concrete. Why, oh, why had she chosen to wear a skirt? Sure, it had seemed like a good idea six hours ago, when she was dressing to come to the airport to pick up Dante. She had been imagining the drive home, and the way his slightly callused hand would slowly run up her leg, parting the wrapped edges of the skirt before it, while she tried to concentrate on staying in her lane.

Now she was stuck with the skirt and no Dante to appreciate it. If Claire had known how long she would have ended up waiting, she would have gone back home, or at least worn her old Levi's. The skirt parted at every opportunity, leaving her few options for sitting modestly, and none of them comfortable.

She read an article in the Arts and Leisure section, the kind of thing she would have skipped over before she met Dante. (She would probably never have read the New York Times at all if she hadn't met Charlie.)

A woman threw two eggs at a work of art that won Britain's Turner Prize, but it wasn't damaged, the Tate Britain Gallery in London said. Martin Creed's prize-winner—a large empty room with lights that turn on and off every five seconds—was closed briefly so gallery

staff could clean up the mess. The attacker was another
artist who had dismissed the minimalist construction, ti-
tled "227: The Lights Going On and Off," as "electrical
work" rather than art. The egg thrower was immediately
escorted from the gallery and banned indefinitely from
returning. The works of other Turner winners and final-
ists have been vandalized in recent years. Tracey Emin's
installation of her unmade bed, a 1999 Turner finalist,
was disturbed when two visual artists staged a pillow
fight on it.

Finally, the crowd began to stir. The PA system crackled.
"Ladies and gentlemen, we are pleased to announce the arrival
of Flight 207." A cheer went up.

Claire suddenly became aware of the two lattes she had
drunk. It would be at least ten minutes before the passengers
began to deplane, as they called it in airline-speak. And she
couldn't wait the additional forty minutes it would take to get
back to her car and drive home. Like a fish swimming up-
stream, she wiggled her way through the people who were already beginning to crowd around the security checkpoint, and
found her way to a restroom.

As she stood up from the toilet, Claire heard it begin to
flush itself. Even though she had run into these all-knowing toilets before, the sound still startled her. And why was there a sliding, breezy sensation on her thighs? Too late, she realized that
one of the ties of her skirt must have fallen into the bowl.

Now the toilet was sucking off her skirt.

She turned and grabbed for the swiftly disappearing fabric.
Most of it had already disappeared, but there was still a foot or
two of blue and green paisley material. Claire tightened her
grasp, but even this remnant was yanked from her hands. From
the bottom of the bowl, now empty of anything but water, came
a sound nearly like a swallow. The toilet had won.

Claire was left standing, empty-handed, wearing sandals, a
blue silk short-sleeve sweater, and nothing in between but her

nicest pair of lace panties. Sheer, white, and delicate, they were basically meant for nothing more than being taken off.

"Um, hello?" she called out from behind the stall door. Silence. Not even the sound of other toilets flushing or of hands being washed. Her voice was tentative, too soft. Claire made it louder, so that it echoed off the walls. "Is anyone in here?" It was absolutely still. She pushed the latch to the side and peeped out the door. No one.

She had to wait five minutes before anyone else entered the restroom. Finally, a tiny elderly Asian woman bustled in. "Excuse me," Claire called to her. The woman started and looked all around, not seeing her. Claire let the door open a little wider. The woman gasped at the sight of a half-naked stranger, muttered what sounded like an admonition in a foreign language, and scuttled out the door. Once again, Claire was alone.

Only thirty feet and a doorway away were people with luggage. Luggage filled with clothes. Maybe she could shield the front of herself with her wallet on a string and beg the first person she saw to donate something to the cause. She walked over to the mirrors above the sinks, her thighs very conscious of the sensation of eddying air. *Ulp.* That lace was pretty see-through. Even if she clutched her clutch to her crotch, everyone would be able to tell she was a natural redhead.

Overhead, the speaker crackled. "Claire Montrose. Claire Montrose. Please proceed to a white courtesy phone."

Damn. It must be Dante, checking to see if she was still waiting for him. If she didn't get to a phone soon, then he might take a taxi back to her house, figuring she hadn't hung around. Or call home and scare Charlie, who would wonder what had happened to her.

The page was repeated. This was it. Her chance to connect with Dante was going down for the count. Claire began madly pumping the paper towel handle, spinning the roll around, until she had about six feet of rough brown Kraft paper. She wound it around her hips, clamped her arms to the side, and then took tiny mincing steps into the concourse hall. There, standing with his back to her, was Dante, holding his cell phone and looking around expectantly. Claire felt like she was walking in a cone of silence. Was it her imagination, or had all activity within twenty feet of her suddenly come to a halt? Dante turned his head, then did a double-take, and said something to the person on the other end of the line before snapping his phone closed. He was already slipping out of his sport jacket while he walked up to her.

"Well, don't ever let them say you don't know how to make an entrance."

He wrapped the jacket around her waist and tied the arms over her hip. She let the paper fall to the floor. One thigh was still bare, but at least the essentials were covered. A few Japanese tourists began to laugh and clap, as if this were all part of some elaborate American mating ritual they had been lucky enough to catch sight of. Dante tilted his roll-aboard on its side and knelt down in front of it, then offered Claire a pair of Nike running shorts. She considered stepping into the restroom to put them on, but figured it was a little too late to be modest. She stepped into the shorts right there instead, then handed Dante back his jacket.

"I COULD GET USED to this," Dante said, looking at the blue sky dotted with white puffy clouds. His window was rolled down because Claire's 1988 Mazda 323 econobox didn't have air-conditioning.

"This is the time of year we Oregonians try not to let anyone know about," Claire said. "September and October. Hot days with plenty of sun, but the nights are cool so it's easy to sleep. And then right around Halloween it starts to rain and you forget that there ever was a sun. Where the sun used to be, there's just a paler spot in the cloud cover."

She spoke lightly, not sure how she really felt. If Dante got this job and moved out here, it would be a big step. It would mean leaving his entire world behind—friends, family, and an excellent job—for her. Sure, the position at the Oregon Art Mu-

seum was a good one, probably one of the best, but could anything be better than working at the Met if you were a curator
specializing in Old Masters?

Claire and Dante had only talked around the edges of what
would happen if he was offered this job. Would he definitely
take it? And if he did, what would happen then? Would they
marry, move in together, or live separately? The only success-
ful married couple Claire knew was her sister Susie and J.B.,
and they weren't even technically married. And how could she
leave Charlie alone?

But even though she could think of a million reasons to be
wary, every time she looked at Dante, with his dark eyes, brown
curly hair, and the single gold hoop in one ear that made him look
like a pirate, she found herself forgetting her reasons. She glanced
over at him now, and he gave her a smile. One of his front teeth
had been broken and then mended with a flash of white.

"If you came here, wouldn't you miss the Met?" Suddenly
Claire felt apologetic about her city. She could have added, *The
theater, the restaurants, the music, the bookstores, the museums*...but didn't.

"Of course. But at the Met I will always be one of several
dozen curators. Even when you just narrow it down to those
who specialize in Old Masters there are still eleven of us. If I
took this job at the Oregon Art Museum, it would give me a
chance to be head curator. The only way I'll get a position like
that at the Met would be if someone died."

"Or retired," Claire added.

"Hah. These are the kind of people who love their jobs and
are quite capable of working into their mid-eighties." Dante
pushed down the sun visor as they crossed the Marquam Bridge
and drove into the setting sun. "And I'm intrigued by the collection. Old Masters drawings are quite rare, and here you have
seven of them."

Claire had been wavering, but for now she decided not to
tell Dante about meeting the owner of these particular Old
Masters. "So why are Old Masters drawings rare?"

"Because they were never meant to be the end product. They were usually done before the artist turned to the true medium—paintings, carvings, sometimes even sculptures."

"So they're like preliminary sketches?"

"Exactly. It's rare for a drawing to survive, because an artist would be much less likely to keep what was simply a draft. And paper is inherently more fragile than a canvas. And God knows, that's fragile enough." Dante was gesturing with his hands now, flicking one to show how ephemeral art was. "We put a price on them, but really, they are priceless. They are like road maps to a great artist's creative process. It's the nexus between an initial idea and its finished state. These men didn't leave behind diaries, and of course there weren't any newspaper articles or videotapes made about them back then. So often, the only thing we know about them is that they left behind these marvelous works of art."

"Like Vermeer," Claire said softly, then realized Dante couldn't hear her over the rush of wind from the open windows. She repeated her remark with a little more volume, thinking of the painting that had originally brought them together. Then she said, "But these sketches weren't even meant to be the final product. Isn't it odd to lavish a huge amount of time, attention, and money on something the artist dashed off in a couple of hours?" She merged onto I-5, then put her signal on and moved over to the right lane. Despite the posted speed limit of fifty miles an hour, people were blowing past her as she did sixty, which was about the top end for the Mazda. The speedometer dial was marked up to 110, which she had always figured was some Japanese idea of a joke, unless perhaps they had thought it was kilometers.

"I'm interested in anything the Old Masters created. And in some cases, the end result has gone missing, and the preliminary sketch is all we have left to guide us. These people were geniuses."

"And we don't have geniuses in our day?" Dante was so passionate about his work that it was sometimes fun just to say something that would tap deeper into that passion.

"Is someone five hundred years from now going to spend hours ruminating on a Jeff Koons sketch for a larger-than-life-size gold-leaf Michael Jackson? I don't think so." He saw the expression on Claire's face. "All right, I'm being facetious. But I don't care for modern art the way I do for things that have stood the test of time."

"Well, at least you know no one's going to be staging a pillow fight on one of your paintings." Claire told him about the article she had seen in the *New York Times*.

Dante laughed. "It sounds like they gave that installation what it deserved. I was at the Museum of Modern Art last year. There was one display everyone was really talking about. They were standing around it three deep. It was a battered metal cart with some rubber gloves and cleaning products and a garbage can on it. Some people were saying it was such a clever comment on our society and its obsession with cleanliness and the way we dispose of anything worn or old."

"And?" Claire said, knowing there was a punch line.

"And then the janitor came and pushed it away." Dante rolled his shoulders, then stretched his arms as much as the cramped quarters of the car would allow. "With these works by Old Masters, it's more than just being the creation of a genius. Part of it, too, is the scarcity. Time takes its toll. Things get worn down, burned up, thrown away, looted, flood-damaged. Touched up by some painter one hundred years down the road when the owner hires him to make the subject's dress match the new drapes. A painting or drawing that is several centuries old is a rare thing, and it's only getting rarer. Many, many things that intrinsically have no value in themselves are worth millions because there are only a few of them. There are people who are willing to pay any amount to own a Mickey Mantle baseball card, which is just a little square of cardboard with a picture on it. Looking at it doesn't make someone's life any better. It doesn't give them a lift, like a painting can. It doesn't have any deeper meaning. It's just a piece of paper."

"Just like Beanie Babies," Claire said as she signaled for the

Multnomah exit. "They got all these people to buy into something because they only made so many of each one and then stopped."

"Right." Dante nodded. "When it's a little lump of polyester plush filled with plastic beads. And people were willing to pay thousands of dollars for one of the rare ones. At least an Old Masters sketch has some intrinsic beauty."

TWENTY-SIX

IT WAS NEARLY nine o'clock at night when Amit Patel looked up from the computer at the young man walking up to the counter of the Bridge City Motel. His hair was military-short, his shoulders squared off like a soldier's, but to Amit's eyes he looked barely old enough to shave.

"Can I help you, sir?"

The young man half-turned to look behind him, as if he thought Amit might be talking to someone else, then turned back.

"Do you have a lost and found? I think I may have left an umbrella here a few weeks ago."

Amit didn't remember the young man, but that didn't mean anything. Every night, a couple of dozen people stayed in one of the twelve shabby rooms, strung like chipped beads on a frayed string, in the old motel on Barbur Boulevard. Only a fraction of the people who stayed at the Bridge City actually came into the office. Despite the postings in each room that declared there should be no more than two people in a bed, or four people in a room, Amit had found it was better never to inquire too closely as to how many occupants he had or how they passed their time.

"What color was the umbrella, sir?"

"Black."

In Amit's experience, men in this country did not carry umbrellas, especially young men, but a customer was a customer, and at least this one was sober and neatly dressed. Amit thought of the cardboard box in the back room filled with a jumble of children's toys, pilled sweaters, romance paperbacks, items of women's clothing that had been meant more for show than for coverage. And two or three umbrellas, he was fairly certain.

"Just a minute, sir, and I'll check."

Amit turned the key in the cash drawer and slipped it unobtrusively into his pocket. If someone else came in, a buzzer would sound. He opened the unlocked room behind him. The narrow space was filled with shelves of clean sheets and towels, bins full of tiny shampoo bottles and bars of soap, stacks of toilet paper rolls. With a sigh, Amit leaned over the big cardboard box in the corner.

The first clue Amit had that the young man had vaulted the counter was the small grunt the man made as he landed. The second clue was a fist hitting the side of his neck. Pain bloomed in Amit's throat, choking off his air. He went down to his knees, then toppled over sideways, spilling the box. Opening his eyes, he found himself nose to nose with a purple Care Bear, faded to gray. There was a buzzing sound, but Amit wasn't sure if it was in or outside his own head.

A kick to the small of his back made his eyes widen. Amit turned his head and saw three pairs of feet. One boot-shod foot was drawing back to kick him.

"Terrorist!" one voice shouted as the kick jarred his spine. "We're going to clean up this town!"

Another voice, this one pitched a little higher: "Hey, Mohammed, where's Bin Laden?" Another kick, this one landing just below his rib cage. Pain knifed through him as the man's toe connected with some organ hidden inside his belly.

Amit realized two things. The first was that these men thought he was a Muslim. And the second was that if he didn't get back on his feet, he was a dead man.

Next to the Care Bear was a black umbrella, the one he had planned to show to the young man. Amit curled his fingers around it and rolled to his hands and knees. Another kick made him skid forward, but still he managed to stand and get his shoulder blades against the back wall.

There were three of them, he saw now. All of them young, fit, shaven-headed. The one with dark stubble barely flecking his scalp jabbed at Amit, but Amit ducked left. He pressed the button on the umbrella, and it popped open, the flimsy black fabric providing him with a second's surprise.

"Vimla!" he shouted. Or tried to. All that came out was a croak. One of the men batted the umbrella away from him. Amit found he was too weak even to hold on to it.

But Vimla heard him, even if he no longer had a voice. Nineteen years together in a strange country, nineteen years of working side by side eighty hours a week, nineteen years of trying to bring up their children in one country by the principles of another.

The door buzzed as Vimla came into the office. Amit heard her suck in her breath. Then he saw her startled face. She opened her mouth and began to scream. The three men froze, their attention split. One turned and ran toward her, and it was only then that Amit saw the gun in his hand. Vimla must have seen it, too, because she stopped screaming and began saying frantically, "Let me open the cash drawer, sirs. Please let me open the cash drawer for you."

A second had gone to the counter and was yanking on the locked drawer. "Come on, bitch, open it up!" Then his attention was caught by the switchboard display, the one that showed each room's telephone activity.

"What is this!" he yelled, slamming down his fist. "Someone's calling 911! We gotta book it!"

The third just stared at Amit for a moment, before turning and running. The last thing Amit thought, just before his legs folded underneath him, was how green the young man's eyes had been.

TWENTY-SEVEN

CLAIRE GOT UP from the breakfast table and picked up her own and Dante's plates, bare except for a slight sheen. Charlie had made German pancakes, waving away all offers of help as she mixed up the batter and then poured it into the well-seasoned cast-iron frying pans. Fresh from the oven, the puffed-up pancakes had been topped with melted butter, powdered sugar, and juice squeezed from wedges of lemon. The three of them had eaten until every bite was gone.

"Here, let me help," Dante said, starting to get up.

Claire handed him the *Oregonian* and the *New York Times* and pushed him in the direction of the living room instead. "Sit. Read the newspaper. Relax while you still can."

In just two hours, the director of the Oregon Art Museum would be giving Dante a personal tour of all the exhibits, as well as a behind-the-scenes look at what was in storage or undergoing restoration in the museum's workrooms. The final stop of the morning would be the collection of drawings and paintings donated by Allen Lisac and destined for the new wing.

The afternoon would be taken up with meeting the various board members for a series of interviews. Dante had told her that each would bring his or her own personal and professional biases to the meeting. Some would want to know Dante's take on how to improve the museum's financial future. Others would want to discuss how to make the museum more appealing to people who didn't traditionally go to museums. And some would be interested in how his connections in the art world might lead to blockbuster exhibitions.

Claire went back to the kitchen and began to dry and put away the dishes Charlie was washing.

"Tom's coming over at seven, right? Do you want us to stay around and meet him, or would you rather it be more private?"

Tom had invited Charlie out to dinner, but she had insisted he come over to the house, that it would be her pleasure to cook for him. He had compromised by offering to bring dessert. Claire was dying to see what he looked like, but she wanted to respect Charlie's privacy.

"Perhaps it would be better if we were this first time alone. Not so overwhelming." Charlie's pink sponge paused in mid-swipe. "Claire-le"—the German diminutive was one of very few traces of Charlie's past—"Claire-le, could you perhaps help me pick out something to wear for tonight?"

"Of course I can." Claire couldn't think of another time when she had heard Charlie ask for help of any kind. She hoped her friend wasn't getting her hopes up too much. Tom must be well over eighty by now, and from what Claire had seen, time did not treat men as kindly as women. She imagined a fat, bald man using a walker or even one of those motorized scooters, maybe with a green canister of oxygen tucked between his legs.

Dante called to her from the living room. "Hey, isn't this in your neighborhood?" When she came out, he pointed at an article in the Oregonian, and Claire read over his shoulder.

Hotel Owner Attacked in Southwest Portland:
Police Fear Hate Crime Spree

A motel owner and his wife may have been victims of a hate crime, according to police. This is the third seemingly racially motivated attack in Southwest Portland in the past two weeks. After forcing their way into a storage room, attackers kicked and struck Amit Patel, 48, owner of the Bridge City Motel, and called him "terrorist" and "Mohammed," evidently taking him for a Muslim.

Tuesday's attack on Patel, a native of India who is in

fact a Hindu, appears to be the most serious of a spate of hate crimes motivated by anti-Arab sentiment in Oregon since the September 11 terrorist attacks. Police departments across the state recorded 29 such crimes between September 11, 2001, and the end of 2001, the last year for which complete crime statistics are available.

The attack on Patel also appears to be linked to a series of attacks that have left a Hispanic man with neurological and facial injuries, and a white homeless man with several broken bones. Victims have said their attackers appeared to be skinheads.

"Skinheads?" Dante looked shocked. "You have skinheads in Portland?"

"We did twenty years ago," Claire said. "I haven't heard anything about them for a long, long time, though." Twenty years before, an Ethiopian immigrant had been beaten to death in Portland by baseball-bat-wielding skinheads. They had been part of a loose-knit group urged to violence by a toupee-wearing former appliance salesman who had turned to selling hate. For months, the skinheads had stalked the city by night, beating up immigrants or people of color, attacking even those who innocently questioned their shaven heads and motorcycle boots. But the city had rallied against them, and over time the group had splintered and fallen apart. "Since nine-eleven, there's been more bias crimes, not just in Oregon. Although it doesn't help that we've got one of the highest unemployment rates in the country, and the highest hunger rate. Or that there aren't that many minorities here anyway. In bad times, people tend to turn on outsiders."

"Then how are they going to feel about a guy from New Yawk?" Dante deliberately exaggerated his accent.

"You?" Claire said. "You, of course, they're going to love."

EVEN THOUGH IT WAS only three in the afternoon, the house was filled with the mouthwatering smells of tomatoes and garlic.

Charlie was making a long-simmering pasta sauce that had everything from pork ribs to bite-size pieces of steak to chunks of pepperoni imported from Italy. Claire didn't know if Charlie had ever kept a kosher kitchen, but for her roommate it seemed being a Jew was more a matter of race than religion.

Charlie and Claire had just decided on the perfect outfit—a rose-colored wool tunic top and pants that brought out the color in Charlie's face—when the phone rang. They both hurried to answer it. The caller ID display showed the number for Dante's cell phone, so Claire was the one who answered.

Dante explained that some people at the museum had invited him out to dinner. "And they want you there as well. A place called Mercury in Northwest Portland. At eight. I told them I'd call and check with you, but that's okay, isn't it?"

Even Claire, with her low-key lifestyle, had heard of Mercury. The restaurant had been open for only a couple of months, but was already rumored to be Portland's hottest restaurant. Claire had gathered Mercury was as much about scene as cuisine. Mercury sounded like the place to go to prove you could eat and dress and drink the way you imagined the rich and famous did in New York or Los Angeles.

"Sure," Claire said. "This must be a good sign. Taking you out to dinner."

"I think it went well. But they might be taking every candidate to dinner. They made a point of how difficult it is to get dinner reservations at Mercury, and it sounded like they booked them weeks ago."

"From what I hear, if they had decided you weren't worth feeding, they could have scalped the reservations on the sidewalk outside the restaurant and made a nice profit." Claire hesitated. "So do you think you might get this job?"

"It's hard to say. I'll tell you more about it when I get back. You'll have to help me decide what to wear. I brought interview suits and jeans, but not much in between."

"That's my job for the day, it seems," Claire said, thinking of Charlie. "You'll have to help me, too. I don't know too much about Mercury, but I do know it's not the kind of place I can wear my Nikes, even the cool ones with no laces." Something else occurred to Claire. "I guess I hadn't thought about that," she said slowly.

"Hadn't thought about what?"

"If you get this job, then I'll probably be expected to go out to dinner a lot. Or dinner parties. You know, because I'm your girlfriend or spouse-equivalent." She used the term lightly, but if Dante got the job, it seemed possible they might actually marry. Claire imagined herself trying to make small talk with a West Hills matron with a helmet of dyed blond hair. "Not to mention cocktail parties and show openings." In her mind's eye, she saw white-coated men holding out trays filled with foods she couldn't name and wasn't even sure she wanted to eat. Who was she kidding? She had grown up on wiener wraps, not foie gras. "I never know what to do with olive pits," she said, almost to herself.

If Dante was impatient to get back to their would-be hosts, he didn't show it. "You put them on the edge of your plate. The rule is, you use the same method to take something out of your mouth that got it there in the first place. Fingers or fork, depending. Then the olive pit or the fish bone goes on the side of your plate. And no spitting in your napkin unless it's something really unappetizing."

An even more panic-inducing thought gripped Claire. "If you get this job, will I have to entertain?" She couldn't imagine the art crowd, even the Portland art crowd, which was presumably less formal than New York's, would get too excited at the prospect of Chex mix, Jean's party standby.

"Of course. While wearing a tiara and elbow-length gloves." She could hear Dante's smile through the telephone. "Let's not get too far ahead of ourselves. How about when I come home I give you a back rub, get some of the kinks out?"

Claire tried to rein in her anxieties. Dante was right. No sense worrying about more than the here and now. "If I know you, you'll try to get some of the kinks in."

"Can't blame a guy for trying. Oh, and Claire?"

"Yes?"

"There is one thing I forgot to mention. Our hosts tonight are Allen Lisac and his wife."

How DID YOU DRESS for dinner with a man you had last seen while you were wearing a disguise? A man who could possibly be a killer? And a man who was treating you to a meal at the most talked-about restaurant in town?

Claire finally picked out a scoop-necked black dress that set off her red hair and pale skin, in the hopes that her hair and the tops of her breasts might draw attention away from her face. It was certainly a far cry from the frumpy and fat figure she had last presented them with. Dante looked gorgeous and slightly dangerous in a charcoal suit and eggplant-colored shirt worn without a tie. He had exchanged the small gold hoop he usually wore in his left ear for an even larger one.

At twenty to seven they stopped in the kitchen to show themselves off to Charlie before Tom showed up. All set to preen, they found Charlie distracted. She held out a wooden spoon toward Dante. "Do you think this salad dressing is tasting too much of vinegar?" Behind her, the oven timer buzzed. Charlie started and put a hand over her heart. It was Claire who slipped on the oven mitts and pulled the homemade loaf of French bread from the oven. The hot, yeasty scent made her mouth water. Seeing how distracted Charlie was, Claire and Dante settled for quick good-byes. When Claire kissed Charlie's cheek, it was as warm as if the older woman were running a fever.

Claire opened the front door, then stepped back in surprise. A white-haired man stood on the porch, juggling a bottle of wine, a bouquet of red tulips wrapped in green florist's paper, and a round, covered silver pan.

"Oh! You must be Tom!" So much for worrying he might be a fat old guy driving a motorized scooter. He was a slightly stooped six feet tall and his rolled-up shirtsleeves exposed wiry, corded arms. His beak of a nose made him look as fierce as an eagle. His full head of silver hair had receded just a bit at the temples. Only his face truly showed the years. It was tanned and as creased as a baseball mitt.

His face crinkled into a smile. "And you must be Claire. Charlie told me about you. I'm Tom. Tom Bonfiglio." He tried to shift things to free up his right hand, nearly dropping the bouquet in the process. "I know I'm early, but at my age you don't like to wait too long."

"Come in, come in. And here, let me take something from you." Claire relieved him of the covered pan. It was surprisingly heavy. If she hadn't stiffened her wrist it would have dropped from her grasp. She set it on the end table.

"Dante Bonner," Dante said, offering his hand.

"Dante, eh? That's a good name." He tipped Dante an insider's wink, as he set down the bouquet and the wine next to the tart pan.

"My mother's name was Pieruccini."

Claire wished for the dozenth time that she were more than just a mongrel with no tradition, no heritage, no native dress, and no special holidays. What would it be like to belong to a tribe?

Charlie hurried into the living room. She had taken off her apron and pushed down the sleeves of her sweater, but her hair still sprang up in untamed tendrils around her flushed face. She stopped when she was about ten feet away and her hand fluttered up to her chest again. "Tom." Her voice was quiet, as if pitched only for his ears. "I can't believe how long it's been."

"Too long," he said simply, and held out his arms "Too long." Charlie walked straight into them, tucked her head under his chin, and gave him a hug. It was suddenly clear there were two people too many in the room.

"Well, we better get going if we want to make that dinner reservation," Claire said loudly, but only Dante was listening. Tom and Charlie were still in each other's arms when Claire softly closed the front door.

TWENTY-EIGHT

HE GAVE THE KID fifty dollars, thirty more than it cost to get the lawn mowed.

"I don't have any change." The kid looked up at him with eyes the same color as the grass behind him.

"That's okay. Maybe I can think of some other stuff that needs doing so you can earn it."

"Maybe."

They exchanged a look, and the look was a promise.

He thought so, anyway. He hoped so. After he watched the kid push the mower down the street until turning the corner, he went back into the house and to the locked drawer on the bottom of his desk, the drawer filled with magazines he had bought off the Internet.

TWENTY-NINE

CLAIRE PRESSED the bottom of her beer glass on the wooden table, leaving behind a ring of condensation. She added another one to it, then a faint third, but there wasn't enough condensation to allow her to form the five rings of the Olympic symbol. Before they were due at Mercury, she and Dante were killing time by splitting a pitcher of India Pale Ale at the Hillsdale Pub. Like all the other pubs owned by Portland's McMenamin brothers, the Hillsdale Pub featured beer brewed on site, signs from other countries and/or times, and funky paintings that looked like the artist had eaten a lot of acid before picking up his paintbrush. They were filled with smiling suns, dancing hammers, leaping rabbits, and lots of psychedelic colors.

"Allen Lisac's collection is truly fabulous. It's going to be the Oregon Art Museum's crown jewel, that's for sure. The Met would be happy to have it," Dante was saying. "Nineteen paintings and seven drawings. The paintings aren't that distinguished, but the drawings are exceptional. They told me he paid nearly seven million for the lot, and I'm thinking he got a bargain. There is a black chalk study of an infant's head that's just enchanting. And a beautiful pen and ink study of a seated female figure. And a sketch that I think may have been for an altarpiece that's now in Frankfurt. I wish I would have had more time to really look at them. What the director and Allen really wanted to talk about wasn't the art itself, but how to market it."

Claire flinched inwardly at every mention of Allen Lisac's name. "Market it? Isn't this supposed to be about the art?"

"I think they've moved beyond that. They kept asking me about how I would display them, what the initial marketing plan would be, what interactive events we could stage, et cetera, et cetera. When this wing opens, they want it to feel like the one must-see event of the year, not just for people in Oregon, but for art lovers all over America. The idea is to have something so crowded that only a limited number of tickets can be sold every hour. Something people will actually camp in line for. So that simply getting in to the new wing will be an event in itself, you know, with the TV cameras panning over the long lines, so that even people who normally never go to art museums will know they have to see this."

Doubt nibbled at Claire. "But is that the kind of thing you want, Dante?"

"I don't know if it matters what I want. That's what everyone wants now, a marketing plan, not a discussion of the scholarship. Museums are hurting for money like everyone else. Without money, they say they can't afford scholarship. Big museums today aren't necessarily about study. It's just as much about entertainment and politics. Spectacle has overwhelmed serious scholarship. Take the Jackie O. exhibit we had. It was ostensibly about her style, but it was more about the woman. And how much of it was about art at all? A blockbuster exhibition can underwrite a lot of scholarship, just like a blockbuster potboiler can underwrite the same publisher's putting out more scholarly works."

Claire said, "In some ways, don't you have to give people what they want? Or in the case of the Jackie O. exhibit, you just know someone is going to do it, so it might as well be you. I mean, there's a place for both things, isn't there?"

"I think most museums are afraid they are in danger of being forgotten. So they court attention any way they can. Do you think anyone was really sorry when Guiliani denounced the Virgin Mary painted in elephant dung at that Brooklyn show a while back? Far from it. When he started talking about obscenity and an outrage and threatening bans, a whole lot more people were suddenly willing to line up for three hours to see it. A scandal can be the icing on the cake."

Claire looked at her watch. In less than half an hour, she would be face-to-face again with the Lisacs—and she didn't know whether they would recognize her or not. Should she just keep quiet and hope that she went unrecognized? Or should she confess now, before she got into even worse trouble? Dante had asked her not to go with Charlie, and she had gone. Claire knew that he would consider her betrayal compounded if he learned about it from the Lisacs over dinner.

She interrupted him in midsentence. "There's something I need to tell you about before we go to Mercury."

Dante looked at her for a long moment, then sat back in his chair and folded his arms.

Deciding this was a bad sign, Claire poured herself a fresh glass of beer before she began. "It's about the Lisacs," she said, after taking a long sip.

He pressed his lips together, then opened them only wide enough to say, "You didn't."

It wasn't really a question, so Claire didn't answer it. Instead, she took another swallow of beer and tried to make a fourth ring on the table even as the others faded away.

Dante leaned forward. "You went to their house? Claire, this is the man whose collection I'm hoping to oversee. Are you trying to throw a wrench in the works? This is going to be very awkward."

"But I never gave my name. And I wore a disguise."

"A disguise! You sound like a child who thinks if she closes her eyes no one else can see her."

"They didn't even talk to me, just Charlie." Claire tried to sound innocent. "Are you saying you didn't want me to return Allen Lisac's ex-fiancée's ring, one that had been in the family for generations?"

"I'm not saying that, and you know it." Dante's tone was exasperated. "But Charlie could have gone over by herself. You should have just stayed out of it."

"Charlie asked me to go along. It was very important to her. She wanted me to be with her to see how they reacted when they saw the ring." Claire leaned forward. "Dante, there was a lot of blood on Elizabeth's head. Even though she fell after they cut her down, dead people don't bleed. That means whatever happened to Elizabeth must have happened *before* she died, not after. Maybe she didn't kill herself at all. Maybe someone strung up Elizabeth's body after she was already dead."

Dante's arms were still crossed. "Claire, are you sure it's really possible for Charlie to remember a little detail about something that happened decades ago? And I'm sure the whole event was very confusing and upsetting for her. I can't even remember what happened last week."

"Charlie's memory is probably better than both yours and mine together. And she remembers things that happened decades ago as if they were yesterday."

"Yeah, but how do you know her memory is exact? This was more than fifty years ago." With exaggerated enunciation, he added, "Five-zero. If it was a murder, why didn't they pick up on it then?"

"Charlie says the police were never called, just the funeral home. Allen Lisac's father called in a few favors and had it all hushed up." Without quite remembering how it had gotten that way, Claire realized her beer was gone. She reached for the pitcher and poured another glass.

"It's still been fifty years. What can anyone prove now? It's not like there's a crime scene anyone can investigate. You've got no clues, beyond this ring showing up in the wall and Charlie's brand-new hunches."

"That's not true!" Claire set her glass down with a thump that was harder than she had intended. "Nova says Elizabeth was pregnant! That might have given Allen Lisac a reason to kill her."

"Who's Nova? And how does she know Elizabeth was pregnant? And why would that make Allen Lisac the killer? You said she was his fiancée."

"One possibility is that Allen Lisac got mad at Elizabeth when she turned up pregnant. But Howard's theory is that the killer was a thief."

"Who's How—" Dante started to ask, then stopped in mid-sentence. "Claire, listen to yourself. You're not making sense. Are these little bits of fifty-year-old hearsay enough to mess up my one chance to live in the same city as you? Is it that you don't want me to come to Portland, but you can't think of a way to tell me, is that it?" His expression was no longer angry, but pained.

Claire didn't want to screw up the chance for Dante to get this job. Or did she? Her thoughts were about as clear as creamed corn. What would happen to them if Dante did move here? Dante had told her it was common for curators to move from museum to museum to climb the ladder, but still, Claire was sure he wouldn't have looked twice at this job if it weren't for her. If he came here, would he grow to resent her for taking him away from his home? For his moving from a bustling city to one where the streets of downtown were deserted after ten at night? Was part of her secretly hoping that he wouldn't get this position, that they could continue their long-distance romance, not put it to a test she wasn't sure they could pass? If she had to choose between Dante in New York and no Dante at all, Claire knew which she would pick.

She didn't answer Dante's question, just reached forward and hooked the plastic handle of the beer pitcher instead. When she tilted it, she was surprised to find it held only enough beer to fill her glass halfway.

Dante heaved an exasperated sigh. "So, did Charlie lose any more contemporaries back during the Korean War? Were there any more suspicious deaths? Or just this Elizabeth's?"

It wasn't a matter of "just," Dante knew that. "Only her," Claire muttered. She knew she sounded sullen, but she couldn't help it.

"So it's not like you're hot on the trail of a serial killer. My guess would be that whoever did it—if someone did it, which I still think is questionable—has probably already paid the price. I can't imagine that you could kill someone and just forget all about it and go on to live a happy life." Dante shook his head. "And more than likely, whoever did this—if anyone did—is dead themselves after all this time."

"Let the dead bury the dead, is that what you're saying?" Claire drained the last of her glass and then looked longingly at Dante's, which was still three-quarters full.

"I'm just saying that sometimes a cigar is just a cigar. You're letting your imagination run away with you. I just don't understand how you could put some dead girl above everything we've talked about."

Claire found herself becoming angry, even though part of her knew she was over-reacting. It wasn't loyalty to a dead woman she would never know, could never know. "It's not Elizabeth I owe something to. It's Charlie. And if you don't understand that, you don't understand me."

THIRTY

AFTER SHE GOT behind the wheel of the Mazda, Claire belatedly realized that maybe she shouldn't be driving. She compromised by taking surface streets rather than the freeway, but even still she had the sense she was floating rather than steering the car. It felt as if the car were navigating itself. Dante was quiet, and she wasn't sure if it was because he was lost in thought, mad at her, afraid of distracting her, or some combination.

Claire was used to hunting for parking in northwest Portland, where parking spaces were as scarce as sunny days in an Oregon winter, but on her second pass by Mercury she saw that they had valet service, a rarity in Portland. The valet managed to keep a straight face when Claire handed over the keys to her Mazda 323, which was probably only a couple of years younger than he was. He pretended not to notice the Snickers wrappers on the backseat or the long crease in the front fender that Claire had decided to ignore after she found out how much the body shop wanted to fix it. The income from a small trust provided Claire with just enough money to live on if she bought most of her clothes on eBay, lived with Charlie, and managed to keep her car running forever.

Mercury was hot, as predicted. Not just full of hotties dressed in black, but also too warm. Although the atmosphere was open and uncluttered, the thirty-foot-high ceiling seemed to amplify the noise rather than absorb it. Several of the tables had pairs of blood-red velvet curtains that could be drawn for privacy. The room was dimly lit, with most of the light provided by dozens of flickering candles.

The maître d' held up a finger to show that he would be with them in a second. A few feet away, a waitress in a black thigh-high miniskirt walked past, a tray balanced on one shoulder. Instead of nylons, she wore a black garter belt fastened to hose that ended a few inches below the hem of her skirt. Claire saw Dante eyeing the dark shadowed space between the woman's thighs and elbowed him in the side. Hard. And then almost lost her balance. Dante might be mad at her, but she didn't think that gave him license to gawk.

Behind Claire and Dante, the door opened and Allen and Mary Lisac came in. Allen was dressed formally in a navy-blue suit, whereas Mary was wearing a bright red flowered dress with Birkenstock sandals and what looked like lumpy hand-knit forest-green socks. Among all the black-clad diners, she stood out like a parrot loosed in a flock of ravens.

After introductions all around, Claire braced herself, waiting for either Mary or Allen to look more closely at her, for recognition to dawn, but it didn't.

Mary said, "Taking all you folks out to eat has given me an excuse to drag Allen to some of the best restaurants in the city. Of course, I'm sure they don't hold a candle to the ones you have in New York." Good, Claire thought. Maybe Mary thought Claire lived in New York with Dante.

The maître d' returned and led them to their table, which was covered with a white starched cloth and six or seven white candles flickering in cut-glass holders in the colors of emerald, topaz, and ruby. The miniskirted waitress came back with menus, and this time Dante was careful to look at nothing but her face, even though they were now sitting eye level with her laced-up bustier that seemed about two sizes too small for her breasts. Claire had the depressing thought that with her big thighs and B-cup she could never be hired here.

Instead of appetizers and entrées, Mercury's menu offered what it described as small plates and large plates. Small plates started at twenty-five dollars, which Claire figured placed Mercury firmly in the stratosphere of Portland's most expensive restaurants. The food was billed as fusion cuisine, with

French, Caribbean, Asian, and Italian spices, terms, and flavors commingling, complementing, and—in some cases, if Claire's imagination was any guide—colliding.

Looking up from the menu, Mary said, "How come there's never fusion cuisine that takes in the English? No banger sausages, no pickled hard-boiled eggs, no ploughman's lunches?"

No one answered Mary's question, but she didn't seem to expect anyone to. Claire smiled to herself. She didn't know if it was just the alcohol, but she was beginning to like Mary, who seemed as warm as her husband was cold. Pretending to look around the restaurant, Claire let her glance glide over Allen Lisac. He certainly didn't look happy. His lips were pressed together in what was either disapproval or pain. What would the prospect of a lifetime of unrelenting pain do to a man?

She was so lost in her own thoughts that it took her a minute to notice the smell of smoke. It didn't smell like cigarettes, exactly. More like…

"Claire! Your menu is on fire!" Dante said. A flame about two inches high was moving from the left-hand corner—which listed the appetizers—and down toward the main courses. With his bare hand, Allen slapped her menu down on the table, extinguishing the fire with a half-dozen rapid-fire smacks. He moved so quickly that the only evidence was a smudge of ash on the white tablecloth and the remains of Claire's menu. Dante shot Claire a horrified glance before saying to Allen, "Is your hand okay?"

"Fine!" He held it up, although in the candlelight it was hard to see if his palm looked any redder than normal. "The trick is to move quickly."

"Your hand was definitely quicker than my eye. Or my nose," Claire said, then tried to change the subject. "What do you guys think you'll order?"

"Definitely the oysters. We'll have to get them, for starters," Mary said decisively. "There is nothing better than a fresh oyster."

Did fresh mean raw? Claire wondered. The Montroses had

never been much on eating food in its natural state. In her family, the delicacy of choice had been Spam. Before the war, Claire's grandmother had been one of the Hormel Girls. She had traveled around America, marching in parades and singing about the wonders of canned meat products. Ever since, no Montrose family gathering had been complete without a Spam casserole.

There was certainly no Spam on Mercury's menu. In addition to the Willapa Bay oysters and the bottle of white wine ordered as a starter, Allen requested steak skewers, Dante chose ravioli with fillings never before wrapped in a ravioli dough, and Mary ordered steamed baby vegetables and something described as pumpkin-stuffed roasted ravioli. Claire settled on bite-size pieces of pan-seared Chilean sea bass with a vermouth cream-reduction dipping sauce.

The wine steward appeared, carrying a silver stand with a chilled bottle of wine. With a flourish, he opened the bottle, offered Allen the cork to sniff, and then poured out the first sip. After Allen nodded his acceptance, the wine steward poured glasses for each of them. Claire was glad it was a white wine. If her clumsy streak continued and she sloshed a little out of her glass, it probably wouldn't leave as bad a stain as a red wine. Telling herself it was better to be on the safe side, she gulped down the contents of her glass in one go. The wine steward had already walked away from their table, but when he saw Claire toss back her glass, he pivoted and refilled it. When Allen wasn't looking, Mary gave Claire a conspiring wink. Claire found herself winking back.

The waitress brought them a loaf of fresh bread. She pointed at the carafe filled with gray crystals that sat next to a tall bottle of pale green liquid. "That's Fleur de Sel salt, from the coastal area of Brittany. It's collected by hand using traditional Celtic methods. And the olive oil comes from a small estate near Lucca. The owner picks her olives by hand and cold-presses them within a day." Her delivery was flat, as if she had memorized the words without any thought for their meaning. "This fruity oil has the purity, clarity, and balance of a Renaissance masterpiece." She seemed startled when everyone at the table laughed.

Allen spooned some salt and drizzled some olive oil across a small white plate, then tore off a piece of bread. "Speaking of Renaissance masterpieces, Dante, what did you think of the collection?"

"The paintings as a group are good. Very solid." Allen's expression seemed to freeze, and Claire guessed he was worried his paintings were being damned with faint praise. But at Dante's next words, Allen's features relaxed. "The drawings, though, are exceptional. It's rare to have so many in one place."

Allen nodded, a small, unexpected smile flitting across his face. "People think Portland's a little backwater hick town. They can't even pronounce the name of the state right. Everyone says Ory-*gone* instead of Ory-gun. Wait until they see we've got something to rival the Louvre and the Met."

"Craig Larson—that's the museum head," Dante explained in an aside to Claire, "tells me that you have designed the wing, Allen."

Allen took a small notepad and a gold Cross pen from his shirt pocket. "After forty years in the business, I've worked with enough architects to know what I want." He sketched rapidly as he spoke. "Outside, there will be stone steps leading to big pillars. But once you step inside the entryway it will be narrow and dark. And there's a low ceiling, so it's like a tunnel, like birth." Even though she had been listening to every word, Claire jumped when he slapped his hand on the pad. "Then, boom, you're out in the hall, and the ceiling's so far overhead, you can't even tell where it begins, and there's no overhead lights, just indirect lighting on each of the drawings or paintings, so it feels as if you are walking into a dream." He leaned forward and extended the notebook to Dante.

Claire nodded as she looked at the sketch over Dante's shoulder, picturing the drama of it. Then she noticed a few drops of wine beaded the tops of her breasts. When Allen slapped his notepad, she must have jerked her wineglass. Trying not to draw attention to herself, she crumpled her napkin in her fist and swiped them up.

Allen said, "We break ground this month, and we'll be finished by next June, in time for the summer travel season and the tourists."

"Nine months—that's fast for a building, isn't it?" Claire asked. Her cheeks, she noticed suddenly, felt numb. She reached up and pinched one. It felt like it had been deadened with novocaine.

"Not if you've been in this business as long as I have. There won't be any surprises on this job. I personally handpicked all the subcontractors. They all have the schedule and they're all committed to meeting it." He took a sip of his wine, looking satisfied, then reached for the bottle in its silver holder. "Would you like another glass, my dear?"

Both Claire and Mary said yes, so he poured out the last of the wine and then waved down the steward and ordered another bottle.

While they waited, Dante said, "Tell me more about how you acquired the artworks. Have they been in your family?"

Claire thought she heard a certain inflection in Dante's voice. She wondered if Mary did, too, because the other woman had cocked her head and was regarding him curiously.

Allen didn't seem to notice anything. "They've been in a family, just not *my* family. We travel in Europe quite a bit. A few years back I met a man, an English fellow, and we got to be friends. He began inviting us to out-of-the-way museums, even to a few private galleries. I've always appreciated art, not as a professional, of course, but as an amateur. An aficionado. Last year, this fellow told me about a family he knew who had fallen on hard times. Their great-grandfather had been a collector, with a special love for drawings. They could have put the whole lot up for auction, but they knew what that meant. One piece in the British National, one at the Guggenheim in LA, one at the Louvre, and half a dozen disappearing into pri-

vate hands, never to be seen again. They didn't want to see their
great-grandfather's collection parceled out a piece at a time.
When I bought it, I had to agree to buy all of it."

Dante said carefully, "And this Englishman, why didn't he
buy them himself if he could see how valuable they were?"

Claire was afraid Allen would take affront, but the expression on his face didn't change. "He didn't have the money for
them himself. Few people would." Allen stated this fact calmly,
without gloating. "But it was an opportunity I could take advantage of."

"Did you have them appraised before you bought them?"

"Of course. I'm not stupid. But not by someone from
Christie's or Sotheby's. I didn't want them getting wind of it,
cutting some deal. No. I found somebody private and swore
them to secrecy. You should have seen his expression when he
saw what there was. Nineteen paintings and seven Old Masters
drawings. When I first laid eyes on them, I hardly believed what
I was seeing. I knew enough not to touch, that even your fingers have oils that would degrade the paper, but I couldn't stop
staring. I knew how rare some of the pieces were. And now all
of Portland will be able to see them. People from all over the
state, all over the country, heck, all over the world, will come
to see the Allen Lisac Wing. I'm betting the unveiling of this
collection will set the art world back on its heels. But it won't
just be for the rich. We'll let in grade-school tours for free. We'll
have family days, senior citizen days. We'll hold classes for kids
from North Portland, teach them how to draw, maybe frame the
best pieces every year and hang them side by side."

Dante leaned forward. "You are absolutely right about the
collection. I only had a few minutes to spend with it, but I found
it hard to tear myself away. You know what I would like?"

He answered his own question. "To have a little more time—
a few hours—to spend with the pieces. Drawings are like people. It takes time to get to know them. Some of those pieces
seem similar to ones we have at the Met. In a few cases, we
may even have other preliminary sketches that were done for

the same finished piece, or even the finished painting or sculpture itself. I'm thinking"—he took a sip of wine—"that it might make sense to see if the two museums could put together a joint show. Such a show could play up the similarities and the contrasts. We could mount a show that would open here and then travel to New York, instead of the other way around. Of course, I need more time to look at them and think about what could be done."

Allen Lisac looked enormously pleased. "Certainly. Why don't you come by tomorrow morning? I'll talk to the museum to let them know you're coming. Would you like me to meet you there?"

Dante shook his head. "I think it would be better if I were alone to think about all the possibilities."

Mary leaned forward, her cleavage threatening to spill out of her dress. "Can I ask a dumb question? What exactly does a curator do?"

Dante smiled. "That's not a dumb question. There are a lot of areas a curator is responsible for: highly detailed cataloging, advising on potential acquisitions, scholarship, and lecturing. But basically, a curator is almost like a writer. Only instead of using words, he—or she—uses art to get his point across. Look at all the people in this room." He swept his free hand to one side and then the other. "Imagine they are works of art and I need to curate an exhibition. Curators never get to include all the art they find, so I would begin by selecting three or four of the people to create my thematic show." He smiled at Mary. "I'm not going to tell you what my theme is, other than it's concrete. I'll choose them because they all have something in common. See if you can guess what it is." He turned his head and slowly scanned the room. Then he said, "I choose that man in the corner eating by himself, the woman to my immediate right, and the man who led us to our table. What is the theme?"

"They're all wearing purple," Claire said after a second. It was only after Dante frowned at her that she remembered that this was Mary's game.

"That's not what I was thinking of," Dante said. "But it's common for curators to choose one theme and for viewers to see another. Both are equally valid. Mary, can you think of the theme I was trying to express?"

Mary pushed herself back into a sitting position and was quiet for a long moment. "Is it that they are all wearing glasses?"

"Very astute!" Dante said.

Just then the harried-looking waitress finally appeared with two plates of oysters, which she placed in the middle of the table. Each plate held a ring of oysters arranged on a bed of crushed ice. Netting-wrapped lemon halves nestled in the center.

Dante pulled one of the plates toward him and Claire, while Mary reached for the other plate. From a foot away, Claire regarded the oysters dubiously. They were a grayish color tinged with green, darker around the edges. They smelled like the sea, but that wasn't a smell she associated with hunger. She had another thought, a worse one. Could raw mean alive? Dante answered her question by squeezing lemon juice over the oysters. When the droplets landed, she distinctly saw one of slimy-looking blobs quiver.

With thoughts of teenagers in the fifties gulping down wiggling goldfish, Claire quickly drank the rest of her third glass of wine, hoping it might further numb her tongue. What if she threw up instead of swallowed? That certainly wouldn't bode well for Dante's getting the job.

"There's nothing better than oysters in their liquor," Mary said.

Dante must have seen the confused look on Claire's face. "It's just another name for their own juices," he murmured sideways. He was good at murmuring, Claire thought hazily. It was probably the kind of thing you learned when you worked in a museum, where the galleries were filled with visitors talking in hushed voices.

Mary lifted the shell to her lips, tilted her plump neck, and slurped back the oyster with lustful abandon. With a click, she set the now-empty shell back on the plate.

Figuring that she who hesitated was lost, Claire picked up one of the blue-black shells.

"Don't chew. Aim for the back of the throat and swallow," Dante whispered.

Claire closed her eyes, tipped back her head, and tilted the shell, trying to ignore the briny scent. The combination of her position, coupled with closing her eyes, screwed up her eye-hand coordination, which had never been very good to begin with. Rather than plopping on her tongue, the oyster landed with a slap between her breasts. Then it promptly slid, cool, wet, and disgustingly slippery, until it lodged somewhere in the region of her belly button. It felt like a giant slug trailing slime—and it was moving ever lower.

Squealing, Claire lurched forward, trying to claw the oyster out of her scooped neckline. By this point, however, her balance wasn't very good. Trying to catch herself, she dropped her wineglass, which splashed Mary's long skirt before bouncing twice and then shattering on the flagstone floor. Despite her mad scramble, Claire still managed to tip over her chair and land flat on her ass.

She leapt up, her face burning and her eyes nearly squeezed shut with humiliation. How could she have done something so stupid, so—she searched for the right word—gauche? The oyster was still skating ever lower on her belly, but she no longer cared. Everyone in the room seemed to be staring at her, from the waitresses to a too-cool couple in their sunglasses. Claire ran toward Mercury's bathroom, half-hoping there might be a window she could crawl through.

In the stall, she pulled up her skirt, peeled the oyster off her skin, and let it fall into the toilet with a plop. Suddenly feeling the pressure of all the beer and wine she had drunk, she sat down on the toilet. While she peed, she blearily regarded the paintings on the inside of the stall. The extremely detailed and realistic depictions of spiders, beetles, and other insects didn't seem conducive to a relaxed bladder. Maybe the Mercury's owners secretly hated women. After all, it wasn't kind to make your waitresses dress up like bondage babes. By the end of the night, their feet must ache from the sky-high heels.

Claire realized she couldn't put off making a reappearance much longer. With a sigh, she stood up, then stumbled sideways when she stood on one foot to flush the toilet. Great. She was clearly both drunk and stupid.

Until she came out of the stall and saw Mary standing at the sink, Claire hadn't realized the other woman had followed her into the restroom. With a handful of wet paper towels, Mary was swabbing at the wine on her skirt, making it even wetter and leaving behind little shreds of white paper.

Claire met the other woman's eyes in the mirror.

"I'm really, really sorry. Oh, God, that was so embarrassing."

With a smile, Mary said, "Go back and laugh at yourself. Better that than wasting time apologizing. Everyone does something stupid now and then. There's no point in taking this all too seriously."

"But I wanted Dante to get this job!" Claire wailed. Now that she could feel it slipping away, she was suddenly certain that was what she did want.

Mary said calmly, "Allen's very interested in your boyfriend's idea for a joint show, especially with the Met. And Dante will get the job or not get it on his own merits, not yours."

"Sometimes I think I'm a detriment to him. He doesn't need me. He needs one of those trophy wives, you know, someone who's a size four with a trust fund and perfect hair and capped teeth. I'm too messy, I grew up in Minor, and nobody in my family ever went to college." With effort, Claire made herself stop babbling. She thought of the Latin saying Charlie had taught her, *In vino veritas,* which translated into something like, "In wine lies truth." Claire hoped the truth wasn't that she was a clumsy, unsophisticated idiot.

"I'm sure if Dante really wanted someone like that he would already be with her. He's smart, he's funny, and he's the kind of guy that every woman in this restaurant has already noticed.

If I were you, I would just figure he has made his choice and stop second-guessing it." Mary pushed the air dryer button and then held the folds of her skirt up to it. She had to raise her voice to be heard over the whooshing sound. "Besides, if you are so worried that what just happened might cost him his job, then why did you return the ring to us?"

"Of course I returned it. It's not mine." A heartbeat later she realized it was too late to protest that she didn't know what the other woman was talking about. "So you recognized me."

In the mirror, Mary eyed her shrewdly. "Those black-framed glasses looked so out of place, I took a good look at the face that was underneath. Your face."

"What about your husband? Does he know?"

Mary shrugged. "Who knows what Allen knows? He holds his cards close to the vest, even around me."

"The reason I did that was it was just a coincidence that I found the ring. I didn't want to screw up things for Dante by telling you who I was. This is probably the only opportunity we'll have to live in the same city."

"Why don't you move to New York? To me, it seems like a position at the Metropolitan Museum of Art would be a curator's dream job." The blower shut off, but Mary's skirt was still wet. She pushed the button again.

"I don't want to move because of Charlie. She's been more than a friend to me, more like a mother. After all she's done for me, I couldn't just go off and leave her. She doesn't have anyone else in the world." She changed the subject. "You can tell your husband loves art. His face really lit up when he talked about it."

Mary nodded. "He loves the idea of a building with his name on it even more. Just the same way people say there are going to the Schnitz when they mean the Arlene Schnitzer Auditorium, Allen wants people to say that they are going to the Lisac. We weren't blessed with children, so this is his bid for immortality."

Talking about immortality made Claire think of the long line of Lisac women, stretching back a century or two, who had worn the ring she had found. "Will you wear the ring now that it's turned up?"

Mary shuddered. "No. Allen and I are in agreement about that. I don't know what we'll do with it, but I'm not putting it on my finger. Not when Elizabeth might have been killed for it." The blower shut off again, and Mary left it off even though her skirt still had a dark stain. "I was always surprised that Warren, Allen's father, didn't make a fuss about the ring when it turned up missing. He had been the one who insisted that Austrid give it to Allen to present to Elizabeth. Austrid had been loath to part with it, but Warren said it was time to hand it down to a new generation. Maybe Warren just figured it was cheaper than Allen buying an engagement ring. Warren was a mean, mean man, with a calculator for a brain. It served him well when it came to making estimates at job sites, but he was a terrible human being. Nothing Allen ever did was good enough for him. And Warren was manipulative, and he was vain. He used to fancy himself a real stud, eyeing all his son's female friends. And some of them reciprocated." She pressed her lips together and shook her head, as if thinking better of adding anything more.

Nova, Claire guessed. Charlie had said that Nova was a wild one, with a taste for married men. Had that taste extended to her best friend's future father-in-law?

"Allen only came to terms with his father after Warren died, a year after Liz did. It's a lot easier to forgive someone if they aren't still around, acting like an asshole. But since you brought the ring back I don't think Allen has slept for more than a couple of hours. I'm not sure he really believes that Elizabeth didn't commit suicide, but I know he keeps thinking about it. It stirred up memories that he had tried to forget. I used to be able to jolly him out of a bad mood, but now he won't let me. It's like he's punishing himself all over again for Liz's death. He suffered so much after she died."

Had he really? Claire wondered. Or could Allen's suffering have been the pangs of a guilty conscience?

"Come on," Mary said, tucking her hand companionably under Claire's arm. "I don't think we can hide out in here any longer. Let's go see if they've finally brought dinner."

THIRTY-ONE

CLAIRE MANAGED to make it through the rest of the meal without any more mishaps. She had expected Allen to regard her disdainfully when she and Mary returned from the bathroom, but instead it was Dante who sat stony-faced and Allen who seemed to view her escapade with the oyster with amusement. Desperate to leave as soon as possible, Claire ate her main course as quickly and neatly as she could. Despite Allen's offers to pour more wine for her, she drank nothing, and then refused all offers of dessert.

Dante kept silent while they waited outside the restaurant for the valet. When he offered up the keys, it was Dante who put out his hand.

In the car, Claire said, "I am so, so sorry for the way I acted tonight. I promise to never have more than two drinks at any one time again." She tried out a laugh that sounded false, even to her own ears. "In any one week again!"

Dante kept silent.

"How long are you going to be mad at me for?" Closing her eyes, Claire rested the side of her head against the chill of the window. She was beginning to feel more and more sober now, as well as more and more stupid. Like a beginning skier so afraid of falling that she sits down in the snow, Claire had sabotaged herself. She had worried that if Dante moved here, their relationship might fracture and break. So instead she had done her best to break it herself.

Dante sighed heavily. "I don't understand, Claire. I wish you hadn't gone to the Lisacs after you told me you wouldn't." He sighed, and signaled for the Multnomah exit. "And now I'm starting to get cold feet about the Oregon Art Museum."

Claire felt even sicker. "Why?"

"Something Allen said tonight raised a red flag for me. What do you bet his 'friend' helped him find the person who evaluated the collection?"

"But he's got a reputation as a savvy businessman. Wouldn't he realize that was suspicious?"

"Does Allen Lisac strike you as a modest man? They appealed to his vanity. When people get greedy, they stop thinking clearly. Maybe I'm wrong and the works were even genuinely appraised. There's just something too...too good about the whole thing."

When she got out of the car, Claire put her key in the lock and opened the front door without knocking, forgetting that Tom might still be there. The flames of two tall white candles guttered in the sudden breeze. Charlie and Tom hastily pulled their hands from each other's grasp, while Claire and Dante pretended to notice nothing.

"How was dinner?" Charlie said with what was clearly feigned interest.

"I'm certain it wasn't as good as yours, Charlie," Dante said.

Tom got up from the table. "You're just in time to sample some of my dessert."

While Charlie got plates and forks from the buffet, Tom set the pan in the middle of the table, and took off the lid to reveal a tart. It looked like something from an upscale restaurant's pastry chef. The cream-colored filling was decorated with alternating circles of regular red raspberries and golden ones. He carefully cut four slices.

"My God, it's so beautiful I wouldn't feel right eating it," Dante said, then picked up his fork as the others did the same.

The buttery crust crumbled at the touch of the tines. The rich, creamy filling had a tang that was nearly grassy, a flavor Claire couldn't quite place.

"Can you guess what's in it?" Tom said, looking proud.

"Sugar, butter, eggs…" said Charlie. "And something else."

"Ground pine nuts." He sat back with a satisfied smile.

"This is delicious." Claire used her finger to maneuver the last bite on her fork. "I've never seen yellow raspberries before."

"I think they actually have better flavor than the reds. They're sweeter. I swapped them with the guy at the next stall over."

"You have a stall?" Claire asked.

"I've got a little stand at the Hillsboro farmer's market. It's called Toms-atoes. My kids thought of that."

Kids, Claire noted. So there must have been a wife once. She hoped for Charlie's sake there still wasn't one.

Tom went on. "I sell mostly organic tomatoes, as well as other produce. I swap cuttings and seeds with people. I like all the old varietal vegetables, Five Color Silverbeet chard, Golden Sweet pea pods, but I concentrate on tomatoes. I like the heirloom stuff, a lot of it, although some of it is just plain 'bite and spit.'"

"'Bite and spit'?" Dante repeated.

"One bite and you'll spit it out. Some of the old stuff wasn't grown because it tasted all that darn good. It might just have been hardy. But most of them are pretty flavorful. I've got the traditional tomatoes, you know, Early Girl, Mortgage Lifter, Yellow Pears, but what I really like are the unusual ones." He reeled off the names. "Amana Orange. Black Krim. Cotoluto Genovese. Cherokee Purple—which even when they're ripe are really pink, brown, or green."

"Are those the green tomatoes, you know, like in that movie?" Claire asked. Feeling more sober, she was alert to the way Charlie looked at Tom whenever he spoke. She'd never seen Charlie look like that before. Underneath the table, Claire crossed her fingers that it would turn out all right.

"No, Cherokees are ripe even if they're green. The movie green tomatoes are basically just plain old red tomatoes picked before they are ripe. If you haven't ever had them, you should try some. Fried up in bacon grease and finished off with some cream gravy—it's worth what it will do to your cholesterol."

His smile was contagious. "And now that I know you like raspberries, Claire, I should bring over some of my green tomato and raspberry cobbler." So Tom was planning on returning.

"Where do you get all these different kinds of tomatoes?" Dante asked. "Can you just buy the seeds or the plants at the store?"

Tom shook his head. "You can get some through heirloom seed catalogs, but mostly I get mine from people who come to the stall. Old people stop to talk to me because they've got plenty of time on their hands. If they tell me they've got something unusual in their garden at home, I ask if they can bring me a cutting. The old guys—the Italians, the Russians, the Mexicans—they've got some of the best-kept secrets. It's only been in the last few years that people have even realized that the agribusiness produce they've been buying is not grown for the taste. The big boys are more worried about yield and shipping endurance than flavor."

"If your stall is in Hillsboro, do you live there, too?" Claire asked. Hillsboro was a good thirty minutes away, and the light was fading. She hoped Tom had what Nova seemed to deem the most unusual of qualities in an old man: the ability to drive at night.

"I've been out there for fifteen years now. My children are always after me to come live near them. Gregg is in Los Angeles, and Betsy finally settled down in Dallas. Those aren't the kinds of places I want to live. Of course, Hillsboro's changed a lot since I moved there. A lot of Mexicans have moved in, and it makes some of the old-timers nervous. Me, I kind of like it. I like their food. They appreciate fresh," he said, waving his hand in a half-circle to take in their bare dessert plates, which shone as if they had been licked clean. "They don't always run to the cupboard to get out a can."

"Where did you learn to cook?" Dante asked.

"From this girl right here." It took Claire a half-second to realize he meant Charlie.

"Charlie showed me some pictures of when you all used to

be friends," Claire said. "Do you still keep up with anyone from the old days?"

Tom shook his head. "They weren't really my friends. They were more Charlie's."

Charlie's expression was serious now, aging her back into the eighty-one-year-old she was. "I told Tom about Elizabeth's head, and about how the blood on her head must have been from something that happened before she died. And about her pregnancy. Go on, Tom, tell them what you told me then."

Tom took a long sip of coffee before he spoke. "I remember the blood, too. Her scalp there was all soft and…pulpy. She might have had a skull fracture. I didn't dwell on it because I was so ashamed that we had maimed her even further. But now Charlie tells me that must have been there before we even found her. And there is…something. Something I told Charlie about tonight."

"What?" Dante asked, leaning forward. He didn't seem nearly so skeptical now.

Tom rolled his coffee mug in his hands. "I hadn't thought about this for years until Charlie started asking me questions tonight. There was something I overheard while I was working on the wall. I remember it was a warm afternoon, maybe two weeks before Elizabeth was killed—I mean, died. Austrid had gone downtown, shopping the way she always did. Elizabeth was the only one in the house. At least that was what I thought. Then I heard noises through the bedroom window—the guest bedroom Elizabeth had been staying in. The window had been left half-open. Probably she had opened it up at night to let the cool air in, then forgot to close it when the day began to heat up. And what I heard was, you know"—he dipped his head—"noises. The sounds of two people making love. I figured Allen had snuck home in the middle of the day to do what he couldn't while his parents slept under the same roof."

"Did you hear the man's voice?"

Red stained Tom's cheeks, visible beneath his tan. "Not saying words, anyway. I was trying not to listen."

"But?" Charlie prompted.

"But," Tom continued, "Charlie asked me tonight. She asked me whose voice it was I heard. And now that I think about it, I don't think it was Allen's."

THIRTY-TWO

CHARLIE KNEW she should be tired, but she wasn't. She hadn't touched a drop of coffee, either. Three hours of sleep, and still she had managed several backward figure eights. On skates, no less. She smiled to herself. If youth only knew, if age only could. Well, Tom had proved that age still could, and without any help despite all those commercials they had now for Viagra.

Charlie had so many memories of them together, back when they were both young. They hadn't felt young, though, they had felt old. And next to the others, next to everyone except perhaps Allen, they had been old. Until Elizabeth died and forced everyone else to grow up in a hurry.

That year was the turning point for the Lisacs. Allen came back from Korea maimed and quiet. Elizabeth had died, young and desperate. Warren—he was a big bear of a man, with a barrel chest and a pipe (how long has it been since you saw a man with a pipe!) Warren started to dwindle away that fall, and by the next spring he was gone. Cancer eating him up inside. And a few months later, Austrid was dead, too, of a stroke.

Charlie had loved everything about Tom then, except for the way he acted around Warren. In the intervening years, Tom seemed to have grown surer of himself. He was his own man now, no one else's.

Yesterday, when Tom came over for dinner, he had made it clear from the start that he wanted her. Wanted not just her body underneath him in bed, but her lips, her hands, her heart, her stories, her humors. They had scarcely touched their meal for talking. And then Claire and Dante came home, Claire oddly off balance, Dante withdrawn, but Charlie hadn't had time to think about what it might all mean. After dessert, they made coffee, and then Tom insisted on helping Charlie with the dishes. Every time he reached for a plate, her skin tingled at the slightest brush of his hand.

Was he an old man, she wondered, passions spent? Then they heard Claire and Dante going up the stairs. Without a word, Tom had taken her in his arms, not minding her wet hands at his neck, in his hair, on the small of his back.

She needn't have worried. They were still themselves, still true inside the slightly shabbier clothes of their bodies. Later she was glad her room was a floor away from Claire's.

Before she had left this morning, she kissed Tom full on the mouth on her own porch, not caring who saw. "I'll come by tomorrow as soon as the market closes," he told her when they finally broke apart. "I'll bring you some of my fresh tomatoes and we can cook dinner together."

Finding herself without the breath to speak, Charlie only nodded.

Tom grinned at her, his eyes caught in a web of wrinkles. "I can't believe how lucky I am." For an answer, Charlie had kissed him again.

THIRTY-THREE

1944—THEY ARE COMING back from the day's work when the command comes to run. Why? They don't ask why. There is no time. Already the cudgel is descending on shoulders, arms, heads. One SS giggles as he hooks anyone who comes too close, his cane around the neck.

Schneller, schneller. Faster, faster.

Some maneuver to be in front of another who is weaker, to take her blows. Some get behind a woman no longer able to run, to hold her up if she begins to fall.

Some women fall.

Run. Keep running. No slowing down. No stopping. Do not even look at those who fall. Try to stay with one woman from your tier. It is impossible to look after the others.

Run, the guards and the kapos and the SS say, run.

So they do. Those who fall are not allowed to get up again. Those who turn to help die also.

THIRTY-FOUR

DANTE WAS STILL ASLEEP—or pretending to be—when Claire slipped out of bed. Her teeth seemed to be wearing little mittens. With every beat of her heart, someone hammered a nail into her right temple. When would she ever learn that she couldn't handle more than two drinks? She grabbed her workout bag and went downstairs. Dante's breathing didn't change, but she thought he might be awake.

Her regular five-mile run, even if she ended up walking the majority of it, would clear her head. At least Claire hoped so. At a minimum, it would get her out of the house and give her a chance to pull her thoughts together before she had to talk to Dante. Yesterday she had screwed up, big time, and now she had to figure out what to do about it.

The house was quiet. Claire knew that Charlie must have already left for one of her twice-weekly ice-skating sessions at Valley Ice. Claire pictured Charlie stroking calmly around the rink. Her hands would be clasped behind her back, the sound of her blades like knives on a whetstone. Claire was sorry the older woman was gone. She would have welcomed Charlie's insights and advice.

As she ran, Claire thought about what Tom had said the night before. Had Elizabeth really been having sex with someone else besides Allen? And if so, whose child had she been carrying? As beautiful as Elizabeth had been, she probably could have had her pick of lovers. But everyone had agreed that she was also an innocent. Or had that been a facade?

In addition to puzzling out the past, Claire also had the problems of the present to keep her occupied. What was she going to do to clean up the mess she had made with Dante? Or for Dante? Would Mary Lisac end up telling her husband who Claire really was? And if she did, would it cause Allen to look at Dante in a new light? As far as Claire could tell, Allen had truly liked Dante, and he had liked Dante's connections to the world's finest museums even more. And Dante seemed very interested in Allen's collection, and not nearly as interested in what had happened to its donor's dead fiancée.

Claire crested the hill and began the long gradual descent. A block away, a group of kids waited at a school bus stop. One child stood apart from all the rest, a black boy who looked about ten. The other half-dozen kids clustered together, silent and staring, watching the lone boy. His hands were balled into fists and his face was empty. Claire could feel the tension stretching between them. Had she interrupted teasing, taunting, the beginnings of a fight? There were so few black kids in this section of Portland that she wouldn't be surprised if he were subject to trouble. She slowed down, ready to jump in to help.

The boy took one step back, another, his eyes never leaving the faces of his tormentors. Then he leapt up in the air, his body twisting like a fish. Almost quicker than Claire's eye could follow, he flipped once, twice, three times, his feet barely touching the sidewalk before his hands followed after. After his third flip, the other kids crowded around, laughing and slugging him on the shoulder in admiration, not even taking notice of Claire as she ran by.

What other things had she seen and not understood? Claire wondered as she automatically turned and ran up the street where the Lisacs and Howard Backus lived, side by side. Had she been too quick to pass judgment on Allen Lisac?

In his driveway, Howard was polishing his car, which looked more like an inflated balloon than an aerodynamic machine. Would such a beast require leaded gasoline? And where would you get it?

He smiled and waved at her. When she waved back, he motioned her to come over. She pulled her headphones down until they circled her throat like a necklace. She looked over at the Lisacs', but the curtains were drawn, the garage doors closed.

"Out for a run?" His big eyes gave her the once-over.

Claire stifled a groan at the way his gaze oozed over her. "Yes, so I can only stop for a minute."

"Is everything okay at your house? I've been worried about Charlie because of those hate crimes."

"Charlie? The only thing she's worried about is me going running, but I don't think skinheads are the type to get up early."

Howard ran his hand through his hair and straightened up. "But she's Jewish. Who knows who they'll target next?"

Claire hadn't even thought that Charlie's being Jewish would put her at risk. Although, come to think of it, when she had last lifted weights, there had been more security guards than usual at the Mittleman Jewish Community Center. But Jews were so used to being targets that they tended to err on the side of caution.

"Oh, I think we'll be fine. These seem more like crimes of opportunity, kids who get drunk and go out looking for someone who looks different and is by themselves. I can't imagine anyone attacking a little old Jewish lady who never leaves the house at night."

Howard nodded, but he didn't seem convinced. "I hope you're right." His mouth was still twisted with worry, reminding Claire of how distraught he had been talking about Elizabeth's death. An idea occurred to her—could Howard have been Elizabeth's secret lover? With his job as a teacher, Howard would have been free during the afternoons and summer months, free to press his suit with Elizabeth. Maybe the reason Tom hadn't seen a car the day he heard someone making love to Elizabeth was because her lover had simply walked next door. She could imagine Howard as Elizabeth's lover, but she found it hard to believe, face-to-face with this frail old man in the clear morning light, that he could be a killer.

"Charlie was telling me how much you liked Elizabeth," Claire ventured. "Really liked her. It must have been hard on you when she got engaged to Allen."

"That was a long time ago." Howard's face went still and expressionless. "Elizabeth and I were never more than just friends." He looked at her sharply, and she knew he had guessed what she had been thinking. "I didn't know if she could be happy with Allen, that's all. Their personalities were very different. It was Warren Lisac who thought it up. Getting married to Elizabeth was a lot more his idea than Allen's."

In the tree above them, a bird sang, the pure, piercing notes temporarily louder than the tinny music floating up from Claire's headphones. Howard's expression lightened into a smile. He cocked his head, turning in a small circle until he spotted the source of the sound. "A western tanager," he announced. Claire finally saw what he was focused on, a small bird with a red head and black and yellow body.

"Are you a what-do-you-call-it, a birder?" Claire asked. "I saw the bird book in your house." And binoculars, she realized. And a clear view of the Lisacs' house. Had Howard ever been tempted to train those lenses a little lower, to watch the woman he claimed had never been more than his friend? Or had he perhaps been like Tom, an unseen observer as someone made love to Elizabeth?

Howard's face brightened. "Yes, I belong to the Audubon Society. This weekend we went on a field trip and I spotted an ibis at Bingen Pond in Klickitat County. They said it was the first record for an ibis for that county. The trip put me up to the three hundred species mark on my lifetime birding list."

Claire nodded absently, not really hearing the details of what he said. She was still turning over all the possible ways Howard's and Elizabeth's lives might have intersected fifty years ago. Finally, she realized Howard had stopped speaking and was regarding her curiously. "I'm sorry, what were you saying?"

"That's all right. I was just saying you and Charlie should come over for a visit again. I've got some marvelous illustrations of native birds that were drawn around the turn of the century. And don't just think I'm some randy old guy asking you to look at his etchings. You haven't lived until you've seen a painted bunting. And you can bring your boyfriend. I hear he likes old drawings. Mary tells me he is up for a job at the Oregon Art Museum."

Claire realized she had been thinking of Howard and Allen and Mary as if they led separate lives, when really they lived cheek by jowl. "You must talk to her and Allen a lot, being neighbors and all."

An expression she couldn't quite interpret crossed Howard's face. "Not really. Not as much as you might think. You know. They're busy. Allen and Mary have their own lives."

He looked so lonely and pathetic standing there that Claire began to doubt all her previous speculation. Howard with his birds and his notebooks suddenly struck Claire as more of a voyeur, the kind of guy who would rather watch than risk making a move. All these years of flirting with women, yet he had never married. Or had his heart been broken when Elizabeth died?

On the way home, Claire had to detour around the body of a crow. It had been run over so many times that the flesh had been stripped from the carcass. All that was left were black feathers and white bones, the wings outstretched as if a taxidermist had wired it for some two-dimensional display.

THIRTY-FIVE

THAT FIRST YEAR AFTER, Charlie bathed twice, sometimes three times a day. She would scrub her body with a nail brush and fine French-milled soap scented with lilacs.

And still she could smell it on her skin, the odor of the camp, of sewage and carrion.

THIRTY-SIX

As SHE RAN ACROSS the imaginary finish line made up of the edge of her driveway, Claire hit the stop button on the built-in stopwatch on her wristwatch. Forty-one minutes, seven seconds—an excellent time for a five-mile run, especially considering she had a hangover. While stopping to talk to Howard had probably let her catch a second wind, she decided not to let the idea detract from the pride she felt. Hands on hips, Claire began to walk in circles, cooling down.

As she did, a car came up the street. The driver looked like a leftover hippie, with a gray ponytail. His mouth fell open as he stared at the side of Claire's and Charlie's house. He slowed nearly to a stop, rolling down his window. His face was a mask of shock. Claire's heart was already beating faster, as she guessed that in the next few moments everything would change, even if she didn't know how. Was the house on fire? Her thoughts flashed to Dante, still asleep.

"I am so sorry!"

"Sorry? About what?" Claire felt off balance.

"Those words!" He must have seen how blank she was. "Don't you know? Someone spray-painted your house!"

She ran to the other side of the house. The whole side of the house was defaced with black dripping spray-paint letters a foot high. "Die Jew!" "Christien Nation!" "Go back to Izreal!"

In shock, Claire found herself focusing on the misspelling rather than the sentiments they represented. Did the mistakes make the words less dangerous—or more?

The skating rink lay in the other direction, and Claire guessed that Charlie hadn't yet seen how the house had been defaced. For that she was grateful. Was there any extra house paint in the basement? Could she cover the slogan up before Charlie got home? Every word would wound her friend.

Four or five more drivers went past, each of them gawking. A young woman with pink hair walking a yellow lab crossed the street and hugged Claire, not seeming to mind that she was covered in sweat. A dozen rings went around the rim of each ear. Claire had never seen the woman before in her life.

"Oh, my God! That's just awful. Do you know who did this? What do the police say?"

"The police?" Claire realized how sluggishly her thoughts were moving, shocked into near immobility. "I just found out about this myself. I need to go call."

When she saw a strange man in the kitchen, Claire came to a dead stop, her hand still on the doorknob. The man had his back to her and a knife in his hand. Then she realized it was only Tom, dressed in the same clothes he had worn the night before, and she let out her breath in a pent-up rush. He started and turned, his hand still gripping the knife, a neat hill of sliced mushrooms on the cutting board behind him.

"Tom, where's Dante?"

Tom must have read something in her face. "He left a note saying he'd taken a taxi to the museum. Why? What's wrong?"

"I have to call the police. Someone spray-painted our house last night."

"What?" He looked more puzzled than afraid.

"Threats about Charlie being a Jew."

Tom put down the knife and made for the door while Claire dialed 911.

GRAFFITI, IT TURNED OUT, was not a high-priority crime. Claire had the feeling it might have fallen off the list completely if it had been a simple tag or two. But the words themselves elevated it to a hate crime. They sent a beat cop to look at it, who in turned called for a criminologist to gather what little evidence there was.

While they waited for the criminologist or Charlie to come, Claire and Tom went back in the house, seeking a reprieve from the stares and the questions and comments of passersby, however kind.

"I hope that evidence guy hurries up," Claire said. "I'm hoping I can paint over those words before she sees them."

"Charlie's a strong woman. Words are only words."

Claire wasn't so sure. "But will it stop with just words? There have been three racially motivated attacks around here." She sketched out for Tom what else had happened.

"Those sound more like crimes of opportunity." Tom sounded as if he were trying to convince himself as well as Claire. "Gang of skinheads see a white homeless guy, or a Hispanic guy waiting at a lonely bus stop, then they lay into him."

"What about the Indian hotel owner? It's not like they were just driving down the street and had X-ray vision to see that he had dark skin."

Tom squared his shoulders. "Then we'll make sure that Charlie is never alone until they've caught these guys." He managed a smile. "It will give me a good excuse to spend as much time as possible with her."

Claire wondered if Charlie shared the same desire. Things seemed to be moving pretty fast. Then again, in your eighties you wouldn't want to waste any time. And the two of them had already been a couple, even if it was a long time ago. As Claire herself got older, she had already noticed time speeding up. Maybe when you were in your eighties, fifty years didn't seem like that long.

"What happened between you two, anyway?" Claire would never have asked the question if Charlie were there. It wasn't a matter of Charlie not answering. With Charlie, you just didn't ask the question in the first place. Charlie was closemouthed about her heart. Only once had Claire heard Charlie say the name of her husband, who had died in the camps.

"We fought over money. Warren gave me a five-hundred-dollar bonus for finishing the wall, and told me he could count on my discretion. In those days, that was a lot of money." Tom had been cracking eggs into a bowl, finishing the omelet he had started earlier, but now he paused. "Charlie thought I should give it back. She said Warren was just paying me to keep quiet. She didn't realize I was doing it for her. In my mind, it was like I felt like I needed to bring something to her, like there was no way I could marry her without some money of my own. Here I was, this day laborer with nothing but his back and his hands and an old pickup to offer. And there she was. Charlie had traveled all over Europe before the war, she spoke three languages, and even after everything she still had enough of her family's money to live on and to buy this house. To me, Charlie was all money and class. And I didn't have either."

"And what did Warren want you to say? Or not to say?"

"That Elizabeth must have slipped and fallen and hit her head. Nothing about her killing herself. Of course, now Charlie has got me thinking that Warren's version was closer to the truth. For sure, somebody or something hit her head." Tom cracked the last egg and then picked up the whisk. "It didn't work, though. Everyone knew very quickly what had really happened, or I guess they knew what we thought had happened. I don't know who talked, if it was the people at the funeral home, or the nurse at the doctor's office who took the call, or maybe someone from Elizabeth's huge family. Her dad spent most of his time on a barstool at Renner's. There were just too many people involved to keep it quiet."

They both started at the sound of a knock on the door. It was the criminologist, a compact man with a short black crew cut, gray at the temples. He carried a digital camera and a black plastic toolbox. Working in silence, he took pictures of the words, both close up and from a distance.

"What are you looking for?" Claire asked.

"For one, how many people were responsible for this." He spoke without taking his eyes off his work. "I'm looking at the letter shapes, the spelling, how close the assailants stood, how they crossed their t's or dotted their i's. It's like handwriting analysis, only it's complicated by the fact that it's spray paint, not ballpoint. The height of the letters from the ground also gives me a clue to the height of the perps, assuming they didn't stand on anything."

With an X-Acto knife, he cut a swath of paint from each of the three hateful slogans, then slid them into glassine envelopes. "We'll try and identify the paint, but it's probably something common you can pick up at any Ace Hardware or Fred Meyer. I'm hoping, though, that we can match it to paint used in the other incidents."

"Other incidents?"

"Those beatings. We're keeping it kind of quiet, but in two of the three cases, we found spray paint next to them. Very similar to this. With that white homeless guy, for example, we found the words 'Race Traitor' spray-painted on the wall next to him."

"The people can't have had much education," Tom said. "Half the words are spelled wrong."

"Sometimes people do stuff like that deliberately. To make you look in one place instead of another." He shrugged. "Although in these cases, I don't think the guys involved are that smart."

"Do you think my roommate is in any danger?" Claire asked.

He turned from his work and his gray eyes appraised her. "I would be careful, if I were you. Both of you, even though I was told it was your roommate who was Jewish. These are probably just young bored kids cruising around, looking for someone who's different. In the three previous cases, either the victims were robbed or there was an attempted robbery. So this"—he swept his hand out to indicate the words—"no physical attack, no robbery, is new. But maybe robbery has always been a secondary motive, a little bonus after they had kicked the victim's teeth in. Until we've caught these punks, I'd advise you to both to be careful whenever you enter or exit the house. Call 911 if you see or hear anything out of the ordinary." He shrugged. "Of course, they've more than likely moved on to other victims. Why come back when someone's on alert? They'll probably pick on someone who has no idea what's coming."

CLAIRE CALLED DANTE'S cell phone. "Did you look at the outside of the house when you were leaving? The side by the English walnut?"

"No—the cab picked me up in the driveway and when we drove past I didn't pay any attention. Why? Did someone break a window?"

Claire explained what had happened. "I don't know whether we should be scared or not, and the police can't tell us, either. There was a criminologist here taking samples, but he doesn't seem to think it will lead to them immediately catching anybody."

"What about Charlie? How's she taking it?"

"She's still at the ice rink. Tom's here, though, and he's vowing to stay for the duration. It sounds like he's not planning to leave her alone. They seem to have picked up where they left off and then some."

"Since he's there, do you think it will be all right if you left for a couple of hours?"

"I guess so," Claire said uncertainly. "Why?"

"It would really help me if you could come down here and talk to me. Something's really bothering me, and I need to talk to you about it."

"Is this about last night?" Her stomach suddenly hurt.

"In a way. But it's not really the kind of conversation I want to have on the phone."

Was this why Dante had left without even talking to her this morning? "I'll give Tom your cell phone number, and then I'll be there as soon as I can take a shower."

Had she ruined things to such an extent that he was rethinking everything? Claire thought as she turned the shower spray until it was as fine and sharp as needles. Was Dante longing for his old girlfriend, with her monied charm? She would never have made a scene or a fool of herself. Claire had only met her a couple of times, but she had been smooth, sophisticated, and polished from the tips of her Prada mules to the top of her casually sexy tousled hair that probably cost two hundred fifty dollars to get trimmed and highlighted.

Claire pulled on some simple black cotton pants and a black silk jacket hand-embroidered with colorful flowers. She ran a mascara wand over her lashes, then pushed out her lips and quickly coated them in tinted Blistex. Real lipstick made her look too much like Mick Jagger.

She was so lost in thought, in imagined conversations, that she hardly noticed the drive to the Oregon Art Museum. She had to hunt for a parking space, and by the time she found one, it had begun to rain. Her feet trudged up the marble steps and in through the tall glass doors bound in brass that gleamed like gold.

"I'm here to meet Dante Bonner," she told the elderly woman at the desk.

"He asked that you meet him in the work area downstairs." The woman stood up and pointed to her right. "Go through that doorway, down the stairs, and he'll be behind the second doorway on your left."

Claire knocked softly. After a few seconds, Dante opened the door. In addition to a black turtleneck and slacks, he was wearing white cotton gloves and an anxious expression. The small room was crowded with easels, each of them holding a painting or drawing. The rest of the space was taken up by a long table where more art was lined up, side by side.

"This is so hard for me to explain, Claire. There's something I've been pushing away, trying not to think about it, but I can't keep doing it. There's something wrong here. That's what my gut is telling me, anyway. But I don't know if I can get you to see what I'm seeing."

"Wrong?" Claire echoed. It was like something inside of her was shrinking, smaller and smaller. How could she have been so stupid last night?

"I need to talk to someone, Claire, and you're the only one I can think of. Even if it's just to hear myself talk."

Relief washed over Claire. So it wasn't about her, then. It must be the art that filled the room. "You mean there's something wrong with the paintings?"

"It's the drawings. The paintings, at least on first blush, are solid, if unspectacular." Dante was agitated, pacing back and forth on the narrow strip of unencumbered carpet. He picked up one of the drawings, his white-gloved hands contrasting strangely with his swarthy skin and untamed curls. The drawing was set in a gold-leaf frame, at least six inches wide, that threatened to overpower the plain pen-and-ink sketch it held. "This one was the first that caught my eye. It's part of the reason I asked to come back here today."

Claire looked over his shoulder, trying to see what Dante was seeing. The sketch was about twelve by sixteen inches, done on fading yellowed paper. She could see how fragile it was, appreciate the miracle that it had survived five hundred years. The drawing was of a seated woman, shown from the waist up. Her full, rounded shoulders were bared by a richly embroidered dress. Around her thick neck, which rose from the swell of her shoulders, was a string of jet beads. The pendant ended in a pearl as big as a thumb nestled in the beginning of her cleavage. Even her hands, with rings on most of the fingers, looked wide and plump. She was a woman, Claire thought, who would be forced to shop for plus sizes today. But hundreds of years ago, when only the rich could afford to be fat, she must have worn her flesh like an expensive fur mantle. The left side of her face had been lightly crosshatched to suggest shadows. In the background, a few puffy clouds and a single tall tree had been limned with quick, sure strokes.

Dante said, "At the Met, we had a beautiful little pen-and-ink study, very similar to this one. A seated portrait of a female figure, circa 1498. Same pendant, same rings, same woman without a discernible mood."

Claire bent closer to it, as tentatively as if her breath might somehow injure it. The woman's expression, while less ambiguous than Mona Lisa's, still seemed to be open to interpretation. The full lips neither rose in a smile nor were pulled down into a frown. She looked—Claire sought the right word—pensive. Her wavy hair was worn loose down her back, caught back by a circlet just visible at the top of her high forehead. Her eyes were large and round, her nose straight, long, and narrow.

Claire wondered what the final painting had looked like, or even if it still existed. What color had the woman's dress been? Had her face been as pale as milk, or had her complexion been ruddy?

"So is this one of the drawings you were talking about last night, you know, the ones you thought you could use to build a joint show? Would you display this one side by side with the one from the Met? Are they both signed or just from the same school?" She had learned that it wasn't uncommon to find artists reworking their own or others' subjects, or the pupil aping the master.

"Both are unsigned. Originally, the Met's drawing was attributed to Raphael."

Claire's knowledge of art didn't extend to knowing whether this was a clue to Dante's discomfort. "And?"

"And a few months ago I decided the one the Met has is probably a forgery."

"A forgery!" Claire thought for a minute. "Do you mean this could be the original and the one the Met has is a copy of it? Or do you think they are both forgeries?"

"To me, this one just isn't…right. Just like the other one wasn't. And after spending the last four hours looking at these drawings, I'm beginning to wonder if three of them might be the work of a forger who was very active a few years back. In fact, I'm pretty sure Troy Nowell of Avery's was working with him. You remember Troy, don't you?"

This was a little dig directed at Claire, who had dated Troy exactly twice before she figured out he was pursuing her simply as a means to get his hands on her great-aunt's painting. Claire narrowed her eyes and then gave Dante a nod.

"I was never able to prove it, but I think Troy was working

with a partner, a man named John Maxwell. John had a certain...gift for taking previously undistinguished canvases and making them more marketable."

Dante explained how, under the delicate touch of John's brush, older women lost their wrinkles and were revealed as young and beautiful. Soldiers in an unknown military campaign gained a general's rank and fought on a storied battlefield. Every previously empty field of grass was now grazed by a thoroughbred. Some of his best forgeries required the smallest amount of effort—a squiggle of paint that turned an unsigned canvas by an unknown painter into something much more valuable.

"I think some of these drawings of Allen Lisac's are genuine," Dante continued. "You'd have to have balls of brass to sell a whole passel of fakes. So some of these are real, if undistinguished. But I believe they've been salted. John was killed in a car accident last year. Rumor has it that toward the end of his career, he moved on by moving backward."

"Backward?" Claire asked.

"What he did was to take real works of art and then invent the sketches, drafts, and preparatory studies that must have come before. In the past two years, suddenly all these wonderful Old Masters drawings have been turning up. Including the so-called Raphael the Met bought."

"And how did you know the Met's was faked?"

"That's the problem. I still don't have proof."

"Aren't there tests you can run?"

"And I did. The ink was made from authentic ingredients, primarily oak gall. But a good forger, and a patient one, can whip up his own inks. Then there's the matter of the paper. It was carbon-dated to the time period Raphael was working."

"So does that mean it didn't begin life as a fake? Maybe it's something one of his pupils did that's now been passed off as the master's." Claire had learned that this was common, sometimes done deliberately, sometimes just the result of a collector's or a museum's wishful thinking. "That would explain the carbon dating."

Dante shook his head. "Forgers know about carbon dating, too. Not only did John Maxwell scrape paint off old canvases, but he also laid out a lot of money buying Renaissance-era books and manuscripts. Not for what was written in them—he didn't care about that—but only if they had blank pages he could harvest. He studied paintings and worked backward. First he might do a careful rendering, then a study, then the barest of sketches. He created evidence of artistic processes that never took place, all in preparation for finished masterpieces that in some cases never even existed."

Claire looked at the drawing of the seated woman with more interest, trying to see what Dante saw, lines and shapes that didn't look right. Were her thick fingers drawn clumsily? Or was that simply the artist's style? After all, a painting wasn't supposed to be a photo. "What do you see that makes you doubt it?"

"That's the tricky part. It's more art than science. Authentic works are…" Dante hesitated while he tried to find the right word. "Are true all the way through. They hang together and make a single statement. There's nothing odd that nags at you. It doesn't matter what angle you look at it, or whether the lighting is strong or indirect, or if your mood is good or bad. With a fake, on the other hand, the more you go back to it, the more it reveals its weaknesses. To me, this paper seems to be over-washed and unnaturally aged. The ink looks tired, as though the fading has been accelerated. And then there is the work itself. This is supposed to be just a sketch. But it seems, too…well, too complete. Too detailed. It's got all the impeccable motifs of the finished paintings."

Claire, of course, could see none of this. The drawing still showed what it had before, when she had thought it had been drawn five hundred years ago, and not five.

"Let me show you in a different way." Delicately, Dante reached out and turned the sketch upside down. Everything shifted. Claire had always thought a person's eyes were in the top third of the face, but upside down, it was clear they were set in the middle. The woman's plump body, rich clothes, and half-dozen pieces of jewelry became an abstract jumble of line and shape.

Softly, Dante said, "When a fake is right side up, we anticipate the whole, and our brains automatically correct subtle problems. It's called the principle of closure. But once you turn a fake upside down, mistakes begin to pour off the page. Look at her hands. They look stumpy. And the shading on her face seems exaggerated." His voice strengthened. "Her hair is lifeless, her arms grow out of her ribs, and she has hands like flippers. To my eye, this woman is so awkward that there is no way she was drawn from life. But Renaissance artists almost always drew from life. Forgers tend to draw from other paintings."

"But couldn't you be wrong?" Claire hesitated, then risked saying what she was thinking. "You thought Great-Aunt Cady's painting was a fake at first, too." She had met Dante when he had evaluated a little oil painting she had inherited, a painting of a woman holding a letter. In the end, it had turned out to be a priceless Vermeer, something he was always a little defensive about.

"That's why I have to be careful. With the wrong word, you can tar something forever. The whispers will follow it, even if it turns out to be clean." He set the framed sketch back down, then waved his hand to indicate the other pieces. "I'm just suspicious about the quality and even the quantity of the work here. I should have heard at least some rumors about these being in existence. But I've never heard anything."

"Didn't Allen Lisac say they were from someone's private collection, you know, in a private family for years?"

"I didn't say anything when Allen told us that last night, but that's the oldest dodge in the world." Dante adopted a fake British accent. "Noble family, come upon hard times. Forced to sell what they've owned for generations, but they want to keep it hush-hush, all very embarrassing, you know."

"But if people know John Maxwell was faking drawings, why aren't they more cautious? I can understand why Allen Lisac might be taken in—but the Metropolitan Museum of Art?"

"It all stems from desire." Suddenly looking exhausted, Dante sat down in the only available chair. "If you want a particular kind of something, and then you finally find one, you might not look at it too closely. Even the best curator can be fooled if he thinks with his heart and not with his head. Forgers find a need and fill it. And right now, this type of drawing is very hot. We're obsessed with authenticity, but we have no idea how to assess it. Not with absolute certainty."

"But what if this drawing is real?" Claire asked. "What if the awkwardness you see is just because the artist was having a bad day? Or because it was only a preparatory sketch and not the final piece?"

"There are two sins a curator can commit. One is to authenticate a forgery. In the art world, buying a forgery is seen as a very embarrassing lapse in judgment. The other is to accuse a genuine work of art of being a fake. And to me, the second is much worse. It's…" He searched for the right word "It's heinous, because you've condemned something that a great artist labored over. His last surviving message to us, and you say it should be crumpled up and thrown away. You can't rush to judgment, or you will condemn yourself as well as the art. I'm afraid some people are already thinking that about me. In the past year, I've identified one more drawing in the museum I am nearly certain is a forgery. It's supposed to be the only surviving drawing by Desiderio da Settignano. It's an invaluable historical relic. Or it would be if it were real."

Dante was pacing again, his long strides brought up short by the little free space left that wasn't crowded with art. "Desiderio was an Italian sculptor who lived in the mid-1500s. We acquired a sketch for an altarpiece. Madonna and child and cherubs. However, the Virgin Mary in this sketch is nearly identical to one in a known Desiderio sculpture—except in the other one, she's facing left."

"So part of it was the same as something else, only in reverse?" Claire said.

"Exactly. That's a typical forger's trick—flipping an existing picture and hoping no one notices. The problem with any forged work of art is, if it looks like something we already have, then it's easy to condemn it as a simple knockoff. Any innovation is likely to be anachronistic. So the forger tries to mix or match elements from different existing compositions to make what looks like a new piece of art."

"But you thought that painting I had was like that," Claire pointed out. "You thought it had to be a forgery because it used all the typical elements of a Vermeer painting, like the windows, the light, the woman holding a letter, the chair with the lion's-head finials."

"That's exactly why this is driving me crazy. If I bring up my doubts, I'm sure I won't get this job at the Oregon Art Museum. Even at the Met, no one wants to hear about any doubts I have. Not really. Not when it means we have to take something down off the wall, not when it means the gossip will spread that we've hung fakes side by side with the real thing. I've got my doctorate, I've got my experience, but in the end, in some cases it all comes down to your gut." He waved his hand. "And my gut said two drawings we have at the Met are wrong. And my gut's telling me the same thing about at least a couple of these."

"You never said anything about having troubles at the Met." Claire had thought Dante told her everything. Their phone bills were astronomical. "Are you afraid they are going to…get rid of you?"

"Not that baldly, no. And there are only a couple of people who feel that way. They content themselves with hints. My guess is they would be more than happy to give me a glowing recommendation for this position in an unspoken quid pro quo for my silence. And then I would become someone else's problem." He sighed. "I wanted to tell you, Claire, but it seemed too hard to put into words. I've started to question everything I see. Can my eye be right and the eyes of all the other experts be wrong? That Desiderio altarpiece I told you about? X-ray fluorescence tests confirmed that the chalk and ink were consistent with the time period."

"So it's not a fake?"

"It doesn't prove anything!" Claire found herself shrinking back, even though she knew Dante's anger wasn't directed at her. "I told you that everyone knows Maxwell only ever used the real materials. You have to look for his signature flaws. The hair he draws is too curly, the hands are awkward, and sometimes he even bordered his works with doodles."

Claire hesitated before she spoke, knowing that her next question would be heresy to Dante. "But if you can't tell if something is a forgery, then does it really make any difference if it is or not?"

Dante snorted. "Come on, Claire, you know it does. A forgery tells us nothing about a great artist. Worse, what it does is make us think what we see revealed about the forger is really a truth about the artist. In my opinion, museums have to hold the line. People rely on us to show them what's true, what's real. Every year, millions of people pay to get into the Met. They never consider the possibility of having to decide for themselves the authenticity of what they have come to see. But how do you know that what you see in the museum isn't a fake? How do you know that the Met doesn't have a clever team of forgers stashed down in the basement making statues and then chipping their noses and arms off? Or maybe copying a masterpiece and then reversing a vacuum cleaner on it so that in ten seconds you get the layers of dust a real painting would get in five hundred years?"

Dante was looking at Claire as if he truly expected an answer.

"I—I don't know. People just take it on faith." She thought of her nonexistent dog. You saw a dog dish filled with kibble, you believed in the dog. You walked into a museum, you were already willing to believe that whatever you saw was art. "I guess they figure you guys are supposed to be the experts."

"But what if we're not, Claire? Think of all the layers and layers that are designed to tell you that we know what we're talking about. When you come into a museum, there are uniformed guards, there are sensors that buzz when you get too close, spotlights trained just so, Plexiglas shields protecting the most important pieces. You get handed a glossy four-color guide. And mounted on the wall next to every piece is a caption with the name of the artist and the year it was created and the name of the benefactor who donated it. The whole thing creates a kind of institutional authority. Of course what you're seeing is real. All these experts have authenticated it, cataloged it, and then set out to display it."

He paused. "But what if we're wrong, Claire? What if we're wrong?"

THIRTY-SEVEN

IT WAS ANOTHER HOUR before Dante managed to tear himself away from the drawings. Claire had to finally insist that she was leaving whether Dante came or not. She was worried about Charlie. She imagined the older woman shaking, afraid, maybe even crying, although Claire had never seen her cry.

Multnomah Boulevard was clogged with cars, but it wasn't until she turned down her own street that Claire realized the reason. The road was already narrow, but it had effectively been turned into a one-way street by dozens of cars and two satellite TV trucks parked along both sides of the road. One truck's tires were squarely on top of what had once been a rosebush of Charlie's. As she drove past her house, Claire saw the yard was filled with people. The impact of the spray-painted words hit Claire afresh, and she heard Dante moan under his breath, as if he had been struck. She finally found a spot to park two blocks away.

They had walked half a block when Dante touched her sleeve and then pointed at the windows of the houses next to them. Taped up in the front window of each house was a white paper menorah. Claire's eyes prickled with the beginning of tears. Most of the people in these houses were strangers to her, yet they were trying to present a united front to the world.

Someone had set up a card table in their driveway, and people were waiting in line to sign what seemed to be some kind of petition and pick up a paper menorah. Two eight- or nine-year-old girls sat on the ground next to a table, one tracing and the other cutting out more menorahs. Adults knelt next to them scrawling messages on big pieces of cardboard. The one closest to Claire read, "Hate," with a circle and slash through it. Knots of people stood talking earnestly. Three men in white coveralls with "Miller Paint" stenciled on the back were running their fingers across the paint of an undamaged section of the house.

Claire had seen some of these people before—at Fred Meyer or the library or walking down a driveway to pick up the newspaper in the morning—but many of them were strangers.

In the middle of all the action was Charlie, standing directly in front of the hateful words on the side of the house. Charlie was being interviewed by a woman Claire recognized as Tara Patten from Channel 8. Another crew from Channel 2 was packing up. Dante and Claire found a place next to Tom on the sidelines. He took Claire's hand and gave it a brief squeeze. Along with a dozen other people Claire had never seen before, they listened in.

"When you saw these slogans, how did they make you feel?" Tara asked earnestly from beneath her blond hair, which hung in a perfect, unmoving pageboy.

"These words do not hurt me," Charlie said with her face set and stern. "I lived through things far worse in Nazi Germany. America is a big country, big enough for many different types of people. I have found so many good, caring people here. Why should I pay attention to the few—the very few—bad ones?"

The cameraman swung his lens around to focus on Tara. With a cheerleader's smile, she said, "The community has really rallied around this brave senior. Nearly every house in this neighborhood is displaying a paper menorah, and a candlelight rally is being planned tonight at seven p.m. in nearby Custer Park. Local businesses have offered security guards, to repaint the house, and many other services."

There was a pause while Tara pressed her hand against the side of her head, listening to her flesh-colored earpiece. Then she turned solemn. "Jeff, police say they are investigating any possible links between this incident and the recent racially motivated attacks in this neighborhood. There were no witnesses to this crime, but suspects in the previous assaults have all been described as white young men with shaved heads. Have Neo-Nazi skinheads returned to Portland? Only time will tell. Back to you, Jeff."

As soon as the cameraman turned off his camera, Claire, Dante, and Tom hurried over to Charlie. Claire gave Charlie a hug, and she thought she felt the older woman tremble at her touch. Tom wrapped his arm around her shoulder and pulled her close. "How are you holding up?" Dante asked. "I'm so sorry this happened."

"Evil has sewn the seeds of good," Charlie told them. "Go look in the kitchen. There are enough donuts and pizza to feed an army. Instead I am offering them to all the people who come wanting to start a petition or put up lawn signs or"—she gestured at the men in coveralls—"paint over the wall. One of them took a chip back to their shop to match it, but I am thinking now perhaps we should leave the words where they are for a day or two. Let hate show its face so everyone knows it has not yet disappeared from the world."

Charlie's words were defiant, but there was also something about her that seemed fragile, as if she were holding herself up by force of will, pretending that she wasn't wounded when she could barely stand.

"I'm glad you two are back," Tom said. "I don't want to leave her alone. I'm going home to get a suitcase, and then I'll be back in time to make dinner."

"Tom, I do not need to be protected."

"Ah, but there's want, and that's another matter," he said, kissing the top of her head.

Claire waited for Charlie to protest, but she was silent. Her silence told Claire more about how Charlie was doing than any words could have.

Tom squeezed Charlie's shoulder while he found his car keys with his other hand. "I'll see you guys in a couple of hours." He took Claire aside, with Dante following. "Maybe you could get her away from this for a while, Claire. Why don't you take her over to Nova's? Charlie called her last night and told her that they needed to talk. She was going to tell her about how Elizabeth died and ask her who the real father of the baby was. It would be good for her to get away and get her mind off this. Everyone wants to talk about it, everyone wants to help—but each conversation is taking it out of her."

"I can stay here and hold down the fort," Dante said. "I want to make a couple of calls, but I can still keep an eye on things."

THIRTY-EIGHT

IT TOOK A LITTLE BIT of doing, but Claire finally persuaded Charlie to go with her. The weather matched Claire's unsettled mood—the smell of ozone hung in the air, and black clouds were beginning to mass on the horizon. As they walked to the car, she deliberately turned the topic to Elizabeth. Better old dusty troubles than ones so new, the paint was barely dry.

"Tom says you want to ask Nova who the father of the baby really was. But why would she tell us that if she didn't when we first talked with her?" They reached the car and got in.

"She did not know then that Elizabeth was murdered. She was covering up for her old friend. But now there is a reason to tell us the truth." Charlie buckled her seatbelt. "Do not tell her about the…incident…would you? I am already tired of talking about it."

Then she fell uncharacteristically silent. Claire was worried about her, but when she looked over, despite what had happened, Charlie was staring out the window with a Mona Lisa smile on her face.

There was only one reason Charlie could be smiling after such a day. "So…how are things with Tom?"

Charlie gave a one-shouldered shrug. "It is one date only, Claire-le."

"And one night! He gave me a start this morning when I came into the kitchen."

"You cannot make a life out of one night. I certainly do not need any more excitement. I am only letting him stay again to-night because he insisted that he needed to protect me."

"Uh-huh," Claire said. From the corner of her eye, she could see the private smile that curled Charlie's lips. Maybe it wouldn't be so bad to be eighty-one, after all.

Without the throng of visitors, Riverwalk looked somehow lonelier. The only person visible on the sprawling campus was an old lady in a walker, valiantly inching along the sidewalk. Slowing down, Claire leaned out and offered her a ride. She motioned at the sky, which looked ready to crack from the weight of the rain, but the elderly woman just waved her on.

Nova lived in one of a series of townhouses that ringed the sprawling complex. She answered the door in a white lacy slip, worn over a bra with conical stitching that to Claire's eyes, at least, contained more padding than Nova. Sheer purple nylons dangled from her hand. Under the already teased and sprayed helmet of resolutely blond hair, there was something strangely naked and expressionless about Nova's face. Claire chalked it up to a lack of makeup.

"I can't talk to you for long," Nova said. "I'm meeting someone at the Burger King, and I have to get ready. I don't want to jinx it by saying too much, but this one might be a keeper." She sat down on the edge of one of the two couches and began to gather up one leg of the nylons. The compact townhouse was overfilled with furniture, as if she had been reluctant to part with the contents of a much larger home. "I know I probably look foolish at my age, trying to get a man. God knows I've had enough of them. I don't want to live with someone. I have no desire to cook three meals a day for a man again. I like my independence too much."

Nova stood up to pull the nylons into place, and Claire looked away from her slack belly, covered by the kind of giant white cotton panties that Jean always bought at Sears.

"But there's more to life than going out to lunch with my friends, or volunteering at the Red Cross once a week and handing out cookies. I just want someone to talk to, someone to bring me flowers and tell me I look pretty. You'd be surprised how hard it is to find that at my age. Well, you probably know a little something about it, Charlie."

Nova sat back down, took a flowered makeup case from an end table, and upended it in her lap. Without waiting for an answer, she kept talking, fingers picking through two dozen tiny bottles and tubes, pausing every now and then to take a quick puff on the cigarette slowly smoldering in the ashtray next to a round makeup mirror standing on wire legs.

"But I'm hoping this will turn out different. It's like they say: Better the devil you know…I've decided I'm not going out anymore with men I meet through the ads in *Seniors' World*. People shade the truth or flat out lie." Nova looked up from her mirror as if reading from the air, while her fingers unerringly smoothed thick, tan-colored foundation over her face. "'Widowed male, mid-seventies, wants companion who likes bingo and short trips.' He told me later he got fifty-seven answers. So we're out having coffee at the IHOP and he breaks down crying, saying he feels like he is cheating on his wife. When she's been in the ground for four years! I should have gotten up and left right there, but instead I stuck around for another three dates." When Nova picked up a brown eye pencil, Claire realized what was wrong with the older woman's face. Her eyebrows had been completely plucked out. She began to pencil short arcs in what was presumably a better location than nature had originally given her.

"So one advertises for men as one would for a used bicycle?" Charlie's tone was dry.

Nova heard the unspoken rebuke. "I guess you don't know what it's like. You could always take men or leave them, so of course they were interested. It's that reverse whadaucallit."

"Psychology?" Claire supplied.

"Right. They want Charlie because she doesn't particularly want them. Now, me, I want a man. So I have to hunt around a little bit. But I take all the precautions." Nova stared into the mirror, talking to her own image as she tilted her head down and began applying black mascara to her sparse eyelashes. "My rule is that for the first date you meet in neutral territory for coffee only. And I won't go out with anyone twice if they're rude to the waitress, wear a toupee, or talk too much about their late, sainted wife. On the second date, each of you still brings your own car. But if someone makes it through the second date, well, all bets are off. If they want to follow me back to my place, fine. At my age, you're living on borrowed time, anyway. The doctor here is always nagging at me, telling me I should give up smoking, cut out butter and red meat, and do more exercise. Well, I do like my time in the pool, but I'm not going to do the rest of that crap. Life is for living. Who wants to live if you can't enjoy a rare steak or a bottle of wine, or a cigarette after sex? My sister says I should get some condoms. I said okay, but I haven't yet. I'm seventy-six years old. I mean, what's going to happen to me? Am I going to die at one hundred and forty?" Nova whooped with laughter, then picked up a purple lip pencil and began to line her bottom lip well past where it really ended.

"Nova—" Charlie began, but the other woman cut her off and continued talking.

"I have all these friends who are brand-new widows and they come to me for advice. They were married to the same man for fifty, sixty years, and now they don't know what to do." Nova's laugh sounded more like a bark. "Now, there's a problem I've never had. They want to know how to go out on a date with someone new after being with the same man for half a century. They ask me what should they say, how should they act, when should they sleep together. Like I know the answers."

As Nova took a second to draw a breath, Charlie was quick to fit her words into the pause. "Nova, Nova, wait a minute. Please. I want to ask you something." Outside, rain began to patter against the windows.

Nova paused with her lip liner in midair. Claire noticed that one of the newly drawn eyebrows seemed lower than the other. "About what?"

"Whose baby was Elizabeth carrying?" When Nova didn't answer, Charlie said, "No one can be hurt by the truth fifty years later." She managed to utter the sentence as if she really believed it. "There is something you must know. I do not believe Elizabeth killed herself." Charlie explained about what they now believed. "Someone hit Elizabeth over the head, then tried to make it look like a suicide. Nova, Elizabeth was murdered. She didn't kill herself."

"Someone killed Liz? Strung her up like she was a piece of washing?"

"That is what I believe. So she did not kill herself over lack of money for an abortion. There is no reason to feel guilty."

Nova's skin had lost all color, so the makeup stood out like paint. "Aren't I still just as guilty, then? If I had found a way to get her the money, do you think she would still have been killed? Whoever put that baby in her belly didn't care—but I was her best friend. I should have figured out a way."

"Whoever?" Claire echoed. "Nova, who was the father of her baby? Was it Allen?"

Nova sighed, then shook her head. "That's why I didn't want to tell you. I don't care, but Liz did. Very much. Even after she was dead, I didn't want to see her name dragged through the mud. I thought Liz killed herself rather than have anyone find out the truth. I didn't see it as my place to tell." Nova ground out her cigarette, then lit another. "When Liz came to me and told me she was pregnant, I told her she should just move up the wedding. See, I figured Allen would go along with it because it was his baby, right? But then she told me it wasn't his. She said he had wanted them to sleep together before he went to Korea, but she had been too scared to. And that he hadn't pressed her since he had come back."

"Whose baby was it, then?"

Nova shook her head. "She wouldn't tell me. I tried every way I could think of to get her to say, but she just clammed up. Then I asked her if she wanted to marry this other man. Liz was horrified by the idea. Said it was impossible. She was so ashamed, she wouldn't look me in the eye. That girl was about as innocent as a new-laid egg. She just kept saying she had sinned and that the baby would probably be a monster. Damned

Catholics and their guilt. As if Liz were the only one responsible. As if nobody had ever done what she had done. As if it
was even a baby yet, instead of just a little lump of flesh. I told
her she should try and get the money from the guy who made
her pregnant. She said she had asked him, but he refused to
help. He told her that Allen wasn't that smart, that if Liz gave
herself to him, Allen would never be able to figure out it wasn't
really his baby."

"Wasn't this man afraid that Elizabeth would make a big
stink about it being his baby?" Claire asked.

"What good would that have done her? In the long run, Liz
would have just been labeled a slut and been left with nothing
to show for it. Poor thing. She was desperate, scared, and sob-
bing. The best plan we could come up with was the one the real
father of the baby had suggested. So she borrowed the sexiest
nightgown I owned, black and long and clingy, with a matching fur-trimmed peignoir." Nova ran her fingers down her sides,
miming the way it had fit. "She was the palest blond, with
white skin, so on her the contrast was stunning. Allen's parents were going to be at the symphony that night, so they
would have the whole house to themselves. The whole thing
might have worked, too, except she didn't know Allen wasn't
capable."

"Was not capable?" Charlie echoed.

"Mary and I went to the same ob/gyn for a long time. Years
after Liz died I found out from this nurse who liked to gossip
that there was a reason Allen and Mary never had any children."
Nova took another puff on her cigarette. "It wasn't just his leg
that got mangled in Korea."

"So he was impotent?" Claire asked, picturing Elizabeth
desperately trying to be sexy—and failing miserably.

"He couldn't make a baby, if that's what you mean. I'll always remember the way Liz looked in that silk gown. That was
the last time I saw her alive. And when you found her body,
Charlie, she was still wearing that peignoir."

Claire and Charlie looked at each other, and Claire knew

they were both remembering Allen's bitter murmur, *She wanted it far more than I did.*

Nova said, "I always knew Allen was lying when he said Liz was the one who broke the engagement. He was her only hope of remaining a respectable woman. Liz would never have broken up with him. What else was there for her? If she had gone home to her family, her father would have kicked her out on the street once he realized she was pregnant. He was a drunk, in and out of work—mostly out—but his word was law. Liz had been desperate to be an adult, to be on her own and away from her father. That was why she was so grateful to Allen's parents for putting her up when he was off in Korea. That was why she was willing to undergo Austrid's little lessons on etiquette and how to be a proper lady. How to be a proper Lisac."

Claire said, "If you guessed Allen was lying about Liz breaking up with him, why didn't you call him on it?"

"What good would it have done? Sure, I figured Allen was the one who broke up with her. But I also thought he hadn't expected her to kill herself over it. Once she was dead, he made up a story that put him in the best light. I just figured Allen had to live with what he had done, just like I had to live with not finding a way to give Liz the money for an abortion. But I guess he's probably had to live with a lot more than a sin of omission."

"What do you mean?" Claire asked. "Do you think he's the one who killed her?"

"It makes sense, doesn't it?" Nova said. "Here he begged her to sleep with him before he shipped out, and she turns him down. Then as soon as he's gone, she starts putting out. And then tries to trick him when he comes back. Men are territorial, you know." Nova sighed, then shrugged. "But nothing we do will bring her back."

"Howard thinks a thief must have killed Elizabeth, a thief who took the money Allen had given her for the abortion."

"And you only have Allen's word that there ever even was money, don't you? Howard's just saying that just because he wants to distract you from focusing on Allen. He's always been impressed by Allen's money and charm and success. No, no matter what wild theories Howard comes up with, my money is on Allen. The army made him a killer, and when he was under stress, he reverted back to his training."

"You believe Allen killed her and yet you will not do anything about it?" Charlie rapped out the words, her back stiff and straight.

Nova shrugged. "You have to be practical, Charlie. Allen's a big shot now, just like his father was. You mess with somebody like that, you'd better know what you're doing. At the first sign of trouble, he'll have twenty lawyers and hot-and-cold-running politicians. And the easiest thing to do would be to call us two dotty old ladies with no proof."

"Couldn't we exhume her body?" Claire asked. "My mom's dating Frank now, and he might agree to it. We could prove Liz's skull was fractured."

"So? Liz is nothing but bones now. Even if they dig her up, then what? Even if her head is broken, well, Charlie has already said that Liz's head hit the china cabinet. They'll just say that happened after she was dead—not before."

"But there must be something we could do to find out who killed her," Charlie insisted. "There is no time limit on justice."

"I'll put on my thinking cap," Nova said. Then she caught sight of the clock on the wall. "Ohmigawd, I'd better put on my dress, too. I'm already ten minutes late for my date!" She hurried them out the door and into the driving rain.

Before she started the car, Claire said, "Charlie, I'm afraid Nova's right. Even though we know she was pregnant and that it wasn't Allen's baby, we've got no proof that he or anyone else killed her." She had to raise her voice to be heard over the sound of rain drumming on the roof. "We don't even have any proof that she was murdered. We've got nothing."

Charlie shook her head without replying.

THIRTY-NINE

As she drove away from the Riverwalk campus, Claire tried again. "Let's start from the beginning. What do we know? Someone killed Elizabeth and then went to the trouble to make it look like she hung herself. And someone—presumably the same someone—hid her ring and her purse, minus the money, in the rock wall Tom was building. Elizabeth was pregnant, and Allen wasn't the father, but we don't know who was. Allen lied about breaking up with Elizabeth, and let us believe that he was the father of the baby. To me, a big piece of the puzzle is still missing. Who was the real father of Elizabeth's baby? Wouldn't he have just as much reason as Allen—if not more—to kill her? Maybe he was afraid Elizabeth would cause him trouble and decided to take care of it—by taking care of her."

"But Nova said he refused to give Elizabeth money for an abortion. If this man really wanted to keep it secret, why did he not simply give her the money? That is certainly an easier solution than killing her."

"Five hundred dollars was a lot of money back then. Maybe he just didn't have that kind of money. Maybe he was afraid she would break down and tell someone."

Charlie only shrugged, but Claire could tell she was listening.

"And I don't buy the idea of a thief, either," Claire continued. "A thief would have kept the ring and found a buyer who didn't ask too many questions. Or pried the diamonds out and sold them loose. And if a stranger had killed her, then he probably wouldn't have bothered to make it look like a suicide." The car hydroplaned for a second, and she lifted her foot off the accelerator. "Maybe what we need to figure out is, who were the men in her world? I would guess there were dozens of men no one's thought to bring up—boys she went to high school with, her teachers, the men who worked at the grocery store where she shopped, her next-door neighbors when she was growing up. Then there are the men we do know about. There's Allen, but we know he can't be the father. And Tom," she said quickly, one eye on Charlie, "but of course it can't be him." She saved her best idea for last. "But what about Howard? Howard lived right next door to Elizabeth. He can't even talk about her without breaking down. But what if he's crying, not because she's dead, but because he's sorry he did it?"

"Howard?" Charlie slowly shook her head. But she seemed stronger than she had earlier in the afternoon, and Claire hoped that all the talk of a long-ago crime had taken her mind off the present-day one. "It just does not feel right. I think it must have been someone else. Maybe the reason this man did not talk of marrying her was that he was already married. Who might know is her brother. Let us go ask Frank who he thinks it might have been. Back in those days, all he did was watch us. Perhaps now that will turn out to have some value."

When they rang the bell at Frank's house, he came to the door looking old-man sharp in a golf shirt, yellow pants, and white loafers. Claire gave a little start when she saw her mother was with him, standing as close to him as his shadow. Jean had her hand hooked in the belt on the back of his pants, as if Frank were some kind of life-size puppet. She maneuvered him back to the couch, and they both sat down in a space more suited to one person.

"Hi, Mom," Claire said weakly. "I didn't realize you were over here, too."

"Oh, we're practically living in each other's pockets," Jean said. She and Frank smiled at each other, a smile so sweet, it made Claire's teeth ache just to see it.

"So," Frank said, "what brings you ladies by?"

"We have learned something new," Charlie said. "Something about your sister's baby. It was not Allen's."

"What?" Frank looked startled. "That can't be right. Who told you that?"

Claire sketched out what Nova had said, then leaned forward. "But what I'm wondering is, do you think it could have been Howard?"

Frank seemed taken aback. "Are you thinking that he might be the father of her baby or that he might have killed her?"

"If he was the first, he might have had reason to do the second."

"Not to be a wet blanket here, but aren't you missing something?"

"What do you mean?" Charlie asked.

Frank hesitated. "Um, because Howard's gay?" There was no doubt he was using the word in its modern sense.

"Howard loves women," Charlie protested, but Claire could tell she was turning the idea over in her mind. "He was always the biggest flirt."

"Every time I've talked to him, he's given me the once-over," Claire said.

"Haven't you noticed he's a little bit much?" Frank said, shaking his head. "He's like the preacher on TV proclaiming that adultery is a sin when he's secretly sleeping with his secretary and all the women who come to him for counseling."

"It is true he never was with one woman for more than a date or two," Charlie said.

Even Jean was looking interested in this turn of events. "Didn't you say he was a teacher? And coached the school's baseball team?"

Charlie and Frank both nodded.

"Maybe that's your answer. Fifty years ago, any teacher who came out of the closet would have been fired the next day. Especially one who spent time in the locker room with kids. Heck, twenty years ago. Maybe even now. People get nervous when it comes to their kids, even though it's usually the married scoutmaster or the priest who seems to be the worst offender."

Claire thought of her own high school PE teachers, women

who were invariably addressed with a "Miss" and who shared apartments with other female PE teachers to "save on rent." "I don't know, though. I mean, just because Howard never got married doesn't make him gay. Maybe he's just inept."

Frank sighed. "There's more to it than that. Howard is definitely gay."

"And you know because...?" Jean prompted.

Frank looked down at his lap. "Once Howard and I got really drunk when we were down by the river. Nova had this flask she had brought along, and Howard and I made off with it and drank it all ourselves. We ended up talking together, sitting on the edge of the riverbank, while the rest of them were off doing something else. It was one of those conversations that appears quite meaningful at the moment, due to a complete lack of sobriety. Anyway, after it got dark and we were getting ready to go, he leaned forward and tried to kiss me."

"What did you do?" Jean asked.

"I just turned my head away. And neither of us ever said anything about it." Frank sighed, then looked down at his small white hands. "The world is cruel to short men. I was never an athlete. They used to call me girly in high school. For a long time, I worried that Howard knew something about me that I didn't know myself."

Jean patted him on the thigh, rather high up, Claire thought, but it brought a smile to Frank's face. His shoulders relaxed.

Claire wasn't quite ready to drop the idea. "Just because Howard is gay, it doesn't mean he couldn't have fathered her child."

Frank shrugged. "I guess anything is theoretically possible, but I think Liz would have needed a lot of coaxing before she had sex. She was very modest and shy when we were growing up. And she never got Nova's off-color jokes. Why would a gay man go to all the bother of seducing a female virgin?"

"Well, if it wasn't Howard, then who could it have been?" Claire asked. "Did your sister ever date anyone else besides Allen?"

"Allen was Liz's first boyfriend. They had only gone on a few dates when suddenly she was flashing this big ring around. Anybody who grew up in my house was eager to vacate it as soon as they could. Maybe after he shipped out, Liz found another boyfriend that none of us knew about. It would have to have been someone she saw frequently, though, someone who might be able to get her to the point she let down her guard." Frank snapped his fingers. "Wait a minute. I just thought of something. Remember that Tom guy? The one who was building the wall? What about him? I mean, think about it, Charlie. As far as you know, they were the only two at the house before you came over that day you found my sister. And day after day he was out there working on the wall. She used to watch him work, find excuses to bring him glasses of lemonade. And I still remember the way he used to look at her."

Charlie didn't say anything for a minute, but Claire knew she was forcing herself to imagine the scene. Tom was certainly strong enough and resourceful enough to have staged a suicide if he had accidentally killed Elizabeth. Had they argued about the baby just beforehand, and then there had been a fall, a shove, a sudden panic? And then had Tom hurriedly strung her up, one eye on his watch?

"He liked her," Charlie said slowly. "But I saw his face when we found her, and he was just as shocked as I was. It is true that Tom watched her, but so did everyone. Elizabeth was beautiful. You cannot turn your eye away from such beauty. It was the beauty of a young girl. I used to envy her that beauty, because I could not be innocent like that. She was like a princess in a fairy tale for children. The kind of girl who had learned her life from books, not living."

"Oops!" Frank said. "I forgot that you and Tom used to be an item. Well, I'm sure you're correct." His tone implied that he wasn't sure at all.

Claire thought of another possibility, but waited until she and Charlie were in the car to voice it. "I didn't want to say this in front of Frank—but what did Nova say again about Elizabeth?

That she was worried she had sinned and the baby would be a monster? Maybe that's the reason no one can figure out who the father of her baby was. You said Elizabeth's dad was drunk and violent. Could the child have possibly been his?"

Charlie seemed to be turning this idea over. "It is possible, but I do not honestly think he was clever enough to cover his tracks. I keep returning to the idea that no matter who fathered Elizabeth's baby, it must have been Allen who killed her when she told him."

FORTY

BACK AT THE HOUSE, Claire and Charlie found Dante and Tom busy in the kitchen. The house was filled with the good smells of sweet onions, tomatoes, and basil.

"You missed yourself on TV," Dante told Charlie. "Not just the local news. They even put a little clip of you on the *NBC Nightly News*. You sounded very articulate."

Charlie colored. "Who would want to be known for this?"

Tom looked up from the cutting board. "It's six thirty-five. Aren't you girls going to go to the rally?"

Everyone looked at Charlie. There was a long pause while she considered it. Finally she nodded.

"If Tom thinks he can hold down the fort," Dante said, "I'll come with you."

Tom waved a wooden spoon at them. "You go on. I'll keep an eye on the house."

They walked the seven blocks in silence. Dante and Claire carried umbrellas, but kept them furled, as the clouds had been emptied of rain. Twilight was settling in. The closer they got to the park, the more cars were parked along the road. In the low grassy bowl that usually held soccer or baseball games, there were several dozen people, perhaps as many as a hundred, standing in a rough semicircle. They faced, not the road, but the canopy of maples and firs that edged the rising slope at the back of the park. A few people carried signs: NO HATE. WE ARE GOD'S CHILDREN. HATE IS NOT THE ANSWER. NO SKINHEADS IN OUR TOWN! Almost everyone held either a cupped candle or a flashlight. A few held disposable lighters. The flickering light reminded Claire of an ancient church. Even the TV crews were keeping a respectful distance.

Charlie, Dante, and Claire walked to the outer edge of the crowd, their shoes sinking slightly into the wet grass. Heads turned, and there was a murmur as people recognized the sight of the slight figure of Charlie and elbowed their neighbors.

The rain had stopped, but people were still dressed in slickers and hooded raincoats. There were many children, wide-eyed and silent.

From somewhere in the middle of the gathering, a woman began to sing in a rich contralto voice. "Let There Be Peace on Earth." A few voices joined in, then others took courage, until finally the whole crowd was singing. When they came to the end of the first verse, they simply repeated it. Even without accompaniment, their voices were in perfect harmony, with not a single off note.

FORTY-ONE

"THE MORE I TRY to figure things out, the more confused I become," Dante told Claire, Charlie, and Tom over breakfast. He rubbed his eyes and stretched. All of them had spent a restless night, alert for the sounds that would tell them the spraypainters had returned to cause more and worse damage. "And the other curators I've been talking to have nothing but rumors to pass along. They all agree there are a lot of drawings on the market right now, but some of them think it's just rising prices that have caused them to be put on offer. Only a couple of people are telling me that they've had their doubts about a particular piece. And no one will own up to acquiring one."

The phone rang, and Claire went to answer it. It was only after she picked it up that she noticed the caller ID read Riverwalk.

"May I speak to Charlie, please?" a woman said.

"Could I tell her what this is regarding?" Claire asked, ready to run interference. Damn! She thought they had been careful not to leave any trace of themselves behind when they toured the Riverwalk campus, but clearly Riverwalk had still somehow scavenged their number. Maybe Jean had given it to them. Now the only question was how rude Claire would have to be to get Charlie's name back off the list.

"Her?" the woman echoed, clearly surprised.

"Are you calling for Charlie Heidenbruch? Her given name is Charlotte, but she goes by Charlie."

"I guess so. I just have this name and a number. This is M. E. Froehlich, the head nurse at Riverwalk's skilled nursing facility. I'm calling about Nova Sweeney. We found the words

'Must call Charlie!' and this phone number written on a pad next to her phone."

"Is she dead?" Claire asked. Charlie, Dante, and Tom stopped eating and turned to stare at her.

"Sorry, I should have said that to begin with. Nova's not dead, but she did have a stroke last night. A pretty bad one."

Claire thought of Nova's continual cigarette. Was any pleasure worth such a terrible price?

"What's Nova's current condition, then?" Claire chose words that answered some of the questions she could see in the others' eyes. Slowly, Tom let his breath out and then put his arm around Charlie's shoulders.

"Fair. Luckily, she managed to pull the emergency cord over the bed, or it could have been much worse. As it is, she's facing a long stretch of rehab."

"Can we come see her? We're old friends of hers. That's why Charlie's number was by the phone."

"You could come to visit, but she's pretty worn out, so you can't stay very long. But I'm sure she would be comforted by your presence. Visiting hours end at two."

DANTE HAD NEVER met Nova, and they figured a hospital ward wasn't the best place for introductions. He planned to spend the time they were gone continuing to make circumspect inquiries about faked drawings on the phone and Internet.

Riverwalk's skilled nursing facility hadn't been one of the buildings they toured. Claire could see why. While its airy foyer, marble floors, and fresh flowers made it look more like a luxury hotel than a nursing home, it still smelled like the latter, an amalgam of cleaning products, overcooked food, and the subtle tang of urine.

"We're here to see Nova Sweeney," Claire said to the young woman sitting behind the highly polished mahogany counter. She wore a white fitted dress and white hose, and even had a white nurse's cap bobby-pinned onto her hair. Claire wondered if the woman was really even a nurse. Maybe Riverwalk just asked her to dress in order to fit a ninety-year-old's idea of a nurse, formed back in the days when women didn't want to be doctors, they wanted to marry them, or be a nurse all dressed in white.

The young woman's smile could have been used to sell toothpaste, and she had the swooping intonations of a commercial announcer. Claire figured she probably whiled away her days behind the desk dreaming of being a spokesmodel. "Ms. Sweeney's in Room 102, which is the first door on the right behind me." Her gesture would have been perfect for emphasizing the lines of a convertible on a TV game show.

They walked around the lobby divider. A row of about a dozen doors, all closed, faced an empty nurses' station. The three of them were standing in front of the door marked 102, uncertain of whether to knock, when a doctor came walking briskly down the corridor that formed a T with the one where they stood.

"Can I help you folks?"

"We are here to see Nova Sweeney," Charlie said. "Can you tell me how she is doing, Doctor?"

Even to Claire's eyes, the doctor, with his short brown hair dyed to yellow spikes at the tips, seemed very young. Claire had the disconcerting thought that she was probably two or three years older than he was. Without his crisp white coat and the stethoscope around his neck, she would have taken him for some resident's grandson.

"Are you her family?"

Was he aware that Nova's only child had died years ago? Yet he might not tell them anything if they weren't relatives. Claire claimed the middle ground. "Great-niece," she said.

"And I'm Nova's sister-in-law," Charlie added. She squeezed Tom's arm. "And this is her stepbrother."

The doctor didn't seem to question their kinship. "Her condition is fair. She's had a fairly severe stroke. In many ways, it was to be expected. She was sixty-seven"—Claire noted with amusement that Nova hadn't been above lying to her own doc-

tor—"and she's been smoking two packs a day since she was
fourteen, most of those in the years when they didn't even
make cigarettes with filters. Like everyone else I see, she was
in denial. I was afraid it would come to what did happen, which
is an occlusion. In layman's terms, a blockage. She had some
warning symptoms. What we call TIAs, transient ischemic attacks. The last time I saw her she admitted to occasionally having double vision, tingling in her legs, and once she was unable
to speak for a few minutes. So I ordered a brain angiogram.
Even though it showed some damage, she refused to moderate
her habits. I put her on some medications to dilate her blood
vessels, but I suspect she never filled the prescription."

"Will Nova recover?" Charlie asked.

"To put it frankly, your sister-in-law's stroke has caused
some brain damage to the left side which has left her with aphasia for speech." He finally noticed their blank looks. "Right now,
the part of her brain that controls communication is damaged."

"She can't talk?" Tom asked.

"Not at the present time."

Claire saw Charlie's hand tighten on Tom's arm. She was
probably thinking, as Claire was, that Nova loved talking more
than anything, more than men, even more than cigarettes. Was
a Nova who couldn't talk really the same person?

"She can't communicate at all?" Claire felt her stomach
turn over.

"Well, she makes sounds. It almost sounds like she's saying
a word, but we haven't been able to figure it out yet. I'm fairly
certain she knows what she would like to say. It's just that
she's lost contact with the part of her brain that would allow
her to say it. So don't be surprised if she seems upset when you
go in there. For a patient, it's very frustrating not to be able to
communicate. Of course, she can still nod or shake her head,
but anything more complicated than that, well…" His voice
trailed off and he looked down at his scuffed shoes.

"Is she brain-damaged?" Tom asked.

"Perhaps not in the way you mean. Ms. Sweeney doesn't

seem to have any trouble thinking. If we ask her to roll over, she can do it, or at least try to do it, since the right side of her body was also affected. We think she's 'all there.'" He made quote marks with his fingers. "What's damaged is her ability to communicate. While she understands everything you say to her, she can't answer you just yet. She's also very weak, so you'll need to keep your time with her to under fifteen minutes to avoid tiring her out. In fact, she's probably asleep right now."

He knocked on the door, then called out, "Ms. Sweeney?" and opened it, although Claire hadn't heard anyone answer. "Go on in," he said, holding the door for them. "I'm sure she'll wake up once she realizes you're here. She's hardly slept at all, jumps at the slightest sound. I think..." He lowered his voice to a whisper that still carried. "I think she's afraid of dying."

Who wouldn't be? Claire thought. This wasn't the kind of place they took you for miraculous recoveries.

Charlie went into the room first, followed by Tom and then Claire. The room was furnished in dark cherry pieces, but nothing could hide the fact that at the center was a hospital bed with stainless steel railings. Nova lay flat and unmoving on the bed, her eyes closed. Her body barely made a bump under the blanket. Her arms lay on top of the covers, and Claire had the uncomfortable feeling they had been placed there. Her left hand was open and relaxed, but her right looked as if someone had tightened invisible strings inside of it, drawing up her fingers until they curled almost to her wrist, like a shrimp. Against the white of the sheet, her skin was gray, and her hair looked as dead and artificial as a Barbie doll's. Two clear plastic tubes snaked into her nose. Her mouth was drawn down on the right, the stroke still gripping her tightly even in her sleep. A thin line of drool snaked down from her lips to the flat pillow. Nova looked more dead than asleep, as if she were halfway into the next world already.

As she turned to softly close the door behind them, Claire noticed the plush white terry-cloth robe that hung on the back. The pocket was embroidered with the words "Nora Sweeney."

Claire guessed the robe was supposed to make even the hospital wing of Riverwalk feel upscale, but the misspelling just made it feel all the more impersonal.

"Hello," Charlie said softly.

Nova jerked. Her eyes opened wide. The one side of her face that was mobile pulled backward as if she were opening her mouth to scream.

Charlie quickly patted her hand while leaning over so that Nova could see her face. "It is just Claire and Tom and I, Nova-le. You remember Tom, from the old days? Were you having a bad dream?" She soothed the wisps of dyed blond hair back from Nova's brow. "Would you like us to fix your hair up for you, perhaps put some makeup on? You always told me a woman feels best fully armored."

Nova's left hand shot out and grabbed at Charlie's arm with curled fingers. Her mouth opened, but the only sound that came out sounded like a groan.

"Maybe we're upsetting her, Charlie," Claire said. "Maybe we should go."

Charlie, who was presumably more comfortable with the way life could warp you on the way to death, said, "We will just stay and keep her company for a little while. Maybe Nova cannot talk to us right now, but she hears and understands, right, Nova-le?" She sat down in a chair next to the bed.

Nova nodded vigorously. She stared first at Tom, then Charlie, then Claire. When she opened her mouth, all that came out was a loud string of vowels, the sound insistent even if it was meaningless.

"Gosh, Nova, it's been a long time, hasn't it?" Tom perched on the arm of Charlie's chair. "Still, it's almost like I can hear you, Nova, at least in my mind. Your eyes are so expressive."

Nova shook her head and uttered another long-drawn-out groaning series of sounds. Frustration twisted her features. A steady stream of drool ran from the corner of her sagging lip and down her chin. Charlie took a tissue from the bedside box and wiped it up.

God, Claire didn't want to get old. Not if it meant being like this. And Nova hadn't wanted to be healthy, not if it meant giving up all the things she enjoyed. Looking at her, Claire resolved to give up Doritos entirely. And Snickers. And Payday bars. No more Cheez n Breadstix packs, no matter how good the little breadsticks tasted after a dip in the bright orange "cheez," sweet and fatty and salty all at once. She would eat a dozen servings of vegetables a day. Two dozen. Maybe it was already too late. Was some fatty deposit just hanging on to the wall of an artery by a thread, ready to break free and clog up something important?

While Claire was worrying, Charlie was nattering on, about how nice the weather was outside, about how Jean was still dating Frank, about how she and Tom had found each other again. Tom told Nova about his two children, the loss of his first wife (Claire heard the word "first" and wondered if he meant anything by it), and about his produce stand at the Hillsboro farmer's market. In the middle of one of Tom's sentences, Nova began to moan again.

"Is she okay?" Claire shifted from foot to foot. She hoped they left soon.

Tom said, "I think she's trying to tell us something."

Nova nodded. Her lips strained, her tongue flicked in and out, and she uttered what seemed to be the same series of sounds she had made before. Linked vowels.

"Is it to do with Elizabeth?" Charlie asked. "Do you know who killed her? Did you remember something?"

Nova nodded vigorously, her features straining, her mouth writhing as she tried to force sound from lips that were half-dead.

Was it a word? Was Nova croaking the name of Elizabeth's murderer, or the father of her child? Claire leaned forward. The sounds made a pattern, and she thought the pattern might make a word. *Ih-uh-ah-uh.* Claire ran through the list of suspects in her head. Allen, Howard, Tom, even Mary—none of them had names with four syllables.

Nova repeated the sounds again, more insistently. The consonants were merely suggested, the vowels slurred. "Nih-cuh-wah-gwah."

"Yes, Nova, yes. There's no hurry," Charlie said gently. "We have all the time in the world."

Nova rolled her eyes at that, as if she didn't have the time. She tried again, the same series of sounds. "Nih-cuh-wah-gwah."

Suddenly Claire understood. "I've got it! She's saying 'Nicaragua.' Right, Nova, is that what you are saying?" But if that *was* what she was saying, what did it mean? Nova had said she suggested Elizabeth take a quick trip to Mexico for an abortion, but as far as Claire knew, Elizabeth had never been out of the country in her short life.

What looked like anger twisted the features on the right side of Nova's face. She made the sounds again, but they were the same sounds, and Claire heard the same meaningless meaning to the pattern. *Nih-cuh-wah-gwah.*

"That's what I hear, too," Tom said. "Nicaragua. But I don't understand what it means."

"Did Elizabeth go to Nicaragua?" Claire asked.

Nova shook her head.

"Was the man who got her pregnant from Nicaragua?" Tom asked. He added, more to himself, "Although I never met anyone from Nicaragua until about five years ago."

The old woman shook her head again. Her lips still formed the word, softer now, her tone sounding hopeless. Tears leaked from her eyes. Was she confused, disoriented? Was she stuck back in a time when Reagan was president and Nicaragua was the enemy? In her confused brain, could "Nicaragua" be a code word for all that was wrong, for the warring factions of her body?

"I think she is…stuck. Is that right, Nova? Is your brain stuck?" Charlie looked at Nova for confirmation.

Nova nodded, and half her face curved into a smile, making it look oddly like a tragedy/comedy theatrical mask.

Charlie took the pen and paper from beside the telephone that sat on an otherwise empty desk. "Nova-le, could you write for us? Could you write what you are trying to say?"

For an answer, Nova held up her right hand, twisted like a claw.

"Could you attempt with your left hand?" Charlie asked. "I will hold the paper for you."

Tom helped Nova sit up, careful of the lines that ran into her nose, then supported her with his arm around her shoulders. Charlie held up the pad of paper and put the pen in Nova's left hand. Nova's hand shook so hard that Charlie tried to curve her own hand around it. "Go on, now, Nova-le," Charlie urged gently. "What are you trying to tell us about Elizabeth?" They all leaned in closer to see.

Nova drew one shaky line down the paper, about three inches in length. Charlie helped Nova lift her quivering hand off the page again. A second line, starting out an inch or two to the right of the first, then leaning in to the first line as it went up until they touched near the top of the page of paper. Charlie helped her lift the pen again. Nova's hand wobbled violently over the page as she strove to put the pen back down again where she wanted it.

A voice from the doorway made them all jump. "What exactly is going on here? I will not have my patients disturbed." It was a tall, gaunt woman with steel-gray hair pulled back into a tight bun underneath her cap. She was also dressed in a dated-looking nurse's uniform, but she inhabited it completely as the young woman had not. On her, it didn't look like a costume, but rather armor.

Nova's voice took on a tone of protest, but she used the same sounds as before. Now that Claire was sure what it was, it was easy enough to hear the syllables build one by one into the meaningless word. "Nicaragua!"

"Well, I was just visiting my great-aunt, and she—" Claire began, only to be immediately interrupted.

"I've read her chart. Nova has no living relatives." Claire watched as a new thought occurred to the nurse, pulling her mouth down into a frown so deep the lines on either side made her look like a nutcracker. "Wait a minute! Are you trying to get this poor woman to sign an altered will?" She snatched the paper and pen away.

Everyone but the nurse looked shocked. "No!" Claire said. "She was trying to tell us something! Listen to her. She kept trying to tell us something, but she can only say the word 'Nicaragua.'"

Obligingly, Nova croaked out the syllables again.

"See," Tom said. "We're old friends of Nova's. We know she doesn't have any family, but we were afraid the doctor wouldn't talk to us unless we said we were related to her. And she's been trying to tell us something. Something that seems to be very important to her." Claire noticed Tom left out the part about it being very important to them, and to a girl who had been murdered fifty years before. "But it's like she is stuck. All she can say is one word. And we finally figured out it was Nicaragua. So we were hoping she could write down whatever she was trying to say."

From the bed, Nova spoke again. Now that Claire had heard her say "Nicaragua" a dozen times, she noticed that Nova was able to shade it with meaning. This time, there seemed to be hope in her voice.

"Hm," the nurse said, her tone not completely convinced. "I've heard of this. It's a variant on Broca's aphasia. Word perseveration. In time, Nova may regain her language. But as for today, I'm afraid you'll have to leave. You're upsetting her. For all you know, she's asking you to leave. And even if she's not, you'll just have to wait to try to communicate with her. She's very fragile just now."

Nova repeated her one word, imbuing it this time with a tone of protest.

The nurse leaned over the bed. "Your friends can come back in a couple of days, Nova." The tone was like one you would use with a toddler. "When you've had some time to rest and recover your strength."

"We will be back, Nova-le," Charlie said. She squeezed Nova's hand.

Tom and Claire also said good-bye. Claire leaned down to smooth the hair off Nova's forehead, but she kept her eyes on the notepad the nurse held loosely in her hand. The new line Nova had added ran perpendicular to the other two. She had drawn a very shaky letter *A*. As in Allen.

FORTY-TWO

TRAFFIC WAS SLOW on Barbur Boulevard, and it took a couple
of stoplights before Claire could see why. The TV crews were
out again, only this time they weren't filming Charlie and
Claire's house. Instead, they were all clustered around a cheap
apartment complex, the kind with peeling paint and aluminum-
framed windows. The walls on one corner of the building had
been defaced with the now-familiar black spray paint. Only the
words were different. "Nigger!" "White Power!" "Go back to
Afrika!"

Standing in front of two TV cameras was a small figure Claire
recognized. "That's Jason from Capitol Hill Elementary!"

Charlie made a noise that was either the word "no" or a
moan. When Claire looked over at her, she looked pale and ill.
Tom patted her knee.

Feeling sick herself, Claire pulled over. Jason had nothing,
but now he would have even less. The criminologist was right.
These people were cowards. They attacked the old, the young,
the homeless, those who couldn't fight back. She looked again
at the words. Something about them bothered her, but maybe
it was the horrific sameness of what had happened to her own
house: the black runny paint, the misspellings, the hate the
words conveyed.

People milled about in the parking lot—reporters, photog-
raphers, apartment residents, neighbors, and the curious who
had just been driving by. Claire got out of the car, but Charlie
hung back, as if she couldn't stand to be so close to evil again.
Tom turned in his seat, put his hand on her knee, and began to
murmur in her ear.

Claire saw Jason's brother, Matt, wearing a Seattle Mariners baseball cap and talking to an earnest-looking woman with a tan reporter's notebook. "I'm joining the Marines next year, when I turn eighteen. Some of my buddies just got back from serving in the Gulf." Maybe the military would work out better for him than the other things he'd tried.

Jason hadn't noticed her yet. He was still being interviewed, his voice so soft that she couldn't hear his answers, only the reporter's ridiculous questions about how he felt. How did the reporter suppose he felt? Frightened, vulnerable, all alone. Claire's heart felt like it was turning over in her chest when she realized that he was wearing the T-shirt silk-screened with a dragon that she had given him—and no coat, despite the fact that it was probably about fifty degrees outside.

Someone had set up a card table near the spray-painted words. While she waited for Jason to finish talking to the reporters, Claire went over to it. On it was a petition demanding tolerance, peace, and justice, signed by two dozen people, and addressed to nobody in particular. Next to it sat a bucket, with a sign taped to it that read "Donations." There were a lot of bills in it, most of them ones, but a few tens and twenties, too. Claire put in a twenty-dollar bill.

The reporters had turned their cameras on the crowd, so Claire went up to Jason and gave him a hug. He hugged her back, hard, his shoulders and arms feeling as tight as a stretched wire. "Jace—I am so sorry!" She opened her mouth to offer him a place to stay, but then closed it. Really, was her house any safer than his apartment?

He looked past her to focus on her car and Charlie. "I know that lady with you! She's the lady on TV. My brother and I watched her. The same thing happened to her, and everybody helped her, like they're gonna help us."

Claire blinked. Matt must have tried to put a positive spin on things, to keep his brother from focusing on the frightening reality.

Even though Jason might not be safe at her home, she could

still put him up in one of the hotels on Barbur. Although the Bridge City Motel would presumably be a bad idea. "Do you need a place to stay, honey? 'Cause you could tell your dad I could put you up someplace."

"We're gonna stay right here. Matt says we'll be safe."

Claire shot a glance at Matt, who was ducking his head while an older woman gave him a hug. Seventeen years old and trying to put on a brave front for his little brother. "Honey, I don't know if that's such a good idea," Claire began.

Jason set his jaw. "Matt promised that we would be safe. He said he could guarantee that nothing would happen."

Claire gave up arguing. She didn't want to tarnish his obvious hero worship. Jason clearly needed heroes right now. An adult would be more likely to listen to reason. "Why don't I talk to your dad?" She looked around, although she didn't know what kind of man to look for. "Where is he, anyway?"

"He hasn't exactly been around for a while."

"What do you mean?" Although the pieces were beginning to fall into place. The ever-present dirty red flannel shirt, the two boys alone at Fred Meyer, the evident lack of supervision Jason was receiving in the hair-combing and teeth-brushing departments.

Clearly uncomfortable, Jason looked around for his brother. Matt hurried over and put his hand on his brother's shoulder. "Hey, you're the teacher lady, right?"

"I do volunteer work at the school."

Jason said in a monotone, "She was asking about Dad."

Matt's green eyes met Claire's, then he looked away. "He's out of town on a business trip."

What kind of mechanic went out of town on a business trip? "I'm thinking it might be better for you two if you stayed someplace else for a few days. Until the police have had a chance to investigate this more."

Matt started shaking his head, then stopped when he saw Claire get out her wallet. "Well, if you want to help, that would be great."

She gave him forty-seven dollars, all she had left in her wallet, then excused herself for a minute and went to the car to talk to Charlie and Tom, who contributed an additional eighty-one dollars. She pressed the small bundle of bills into Matt's hand.

He was looking past her, at Charlie, with an odd look on his face. "I don't feel right taking it from her. She got picked on, too, same as us. Is she okay?"

Claire hesitated. "It's taken it out of her, that's for sure."

He pressed the money back in her hands. "It wouldn't be right. Tell her…" He hesitated, as if trying to find the right words. "Tell her I'm really sorry for everything. And that I'm sure nothing else will happen to her."

But Charlie didn't want her money back. So Claire waited until Matt was busy talking to another reporter before she went and put the money in the bucket.

FORTY-THREE

AFTER CLAIRE DROVE HOME, Charlie and Tom decided to go out to lunch in Tom's car. They didn't say anything, but by their body language, Claire knew they didn't want or need company. She found Dante sitting in the living room, making a list of what he had learned so far about the drawings. In the kitchen to make sandwiches, she hadn't gotten any further than slicing some of Charlie's bread when a sound cut through the air.

The noise was high-pitched, not quite a wail or a scream, but a pure ululation. A shiver tugged Claire's shoulders up to her ears. The sound was of fear and horror past words.

They ran outside. In the driveway stood McKenzie, the girl Claire had met earlier. Now she stood staring openmouthed at her dog. Looking agitated, brown eyes rolling, it was walking stiff-legged down Claire's driveway. Clearly something was terribly wrong with it.

"What happened, honey?"

McKenzie opened her mouth to speak, but then she looked at her dog again. No sound came out beyond a new wail. To Claire's horror, the muscles in the dog's legs began to twitch so hard that she could see them jumping from ten feet away. The dog fell over in the driveway. Dante bent over it, touched it lightly on the forehead, and its legs began to paddle the air.

Claire took the girl's hot, wet face and turned it toward her, holding her hands like blinders so the girl couldn't see the dog. She leaned down until their faces were only a few inches apart. With an effort she kept her face calm, her voice steady. "McKenzie, tell me what happened."

"Bailey and I were by Gabriel Park. I had him off the leash, but then I couldn't find him for a minute. When he came up, he had found this squirrel. It was dead. I think it was already dead when he found it. It was really gross. Bailey had bit into it and I could see its insides. I yelled at him and yelled at him, and finally I pulled it out of his mouth. He growled at me, and he never growls." Tears leaked steadily down her face, but at least now she was talking. Claire had tugged on McKenzie's arm until she turned, so that her back was to the dog. "Then on the way home he started acting funny, jerking at every sound, and walking all weird, stiff-legged, so I tried to hurry. And then he started doing…that."

Dante stood up. The dog was finally still. Claire thought it must be dead.

"Sounds like some kind of poison," Dante said. He looked at Claire. "Is there a veterinary hospital you can call?"

"There's Dove Lewis in Northwest."

"Take her into the house and give them a call." He patted McKenzie's back. "Go on inside with Claire, honey." Then his mouth opened as he had thought of something else.

"You said you touched that squirrel?"

McKenzie's mouth started to quiver again. "Yes—but I threw it in some bushes."

"You'd better wash your hands with soap and hot water. For a long time. And be careful not to touch your eyes or mouth."

"But what about Bailey?"

At the sound of the girl's raised voice, the dog began to jerk again. Claire was relieved that it was alive, even though part of her wished it would die.

Dante kept his voice soft. "I'll stay here with Bailey, honey. You go on in with Claire." Over her head, he gave Claire a significant look that she translated as, *Keep her away from the window.*

It seemed to take Claire an eternity to find the number for Dove Lewis and dial it. When they answered, she explained what had happened. "And now the dog keeps having seizures every time there's a loud noise."

The woman's voice on the other end of the line was professionally calm. "It sounds like some kind of poisoning. You'd better get that dog in here as fast as you can. As gently as you can, cover the dog with a blanket, pick it up, and put it in the car. I'll alert the vet you're bringing your dog in."

Dante folded down the seats of the hatchback and then rode crouched in back with the dog, although he was careful not to touch it. They had covered Bailey with a dark gray wool blanket Claire kept in the back for the freak snowstorm that would never happen in Portland. Trying to ignore how her hands trembled on the wheel, Claire drove as quickly and as cautiously as possible.

At a stoplight, she looked in the rearview mirror. The blanket trembled as underneath it tremors raced across the dog's flanks.

At the veterinary hospital, Claire didn't even have time to come to a complete stop before McKenzie was racing in the door. The first few seconds were a blur of action, as two vets whisked the dog away to the back.

While they waited, Claire used Dante's cell phone to call McKenzie's aunt and uncle and explain what had happened. At first they were angry, an anger fed by fear, but they gradually calmed down as Claire explained what had happened. In the middle of the conversation, a vet with a dark ponytail and a name tag that read LOUISE came out. Claire handed over the phone so that Louise could talk to McKenzie's aunt and uncle.

"Bailey's not out of the woods yet, but he's doing better than I would have initially expected. We've given him some Valium and he's stopped seizing. We're still running some tests, but with the clinical signs he was exhibiting, those seizures, and the sawhorse stance, our best guess is strychnine poisoning. It's possible that the squirrel may have been poisoned by strychnine, and then Bailey scavenged it and got a secondary poisoning."

McKenzie tapped the vet's elbow to get her attention. Claire watched the girl struggle to be brave. "Will my dog live?"

Louise put a hand on her shoulder. "I can't promise anything honey, but I hope so. Now I need to get permission to do some more tests and pump his stomach." Then she finished her business on the phone and handed it back to Claire.

Thirty minutes later, Louise reported that the dog's vital signs had stabilized. "I'm cautiously optimistic Bailey will pull through. You should go on home now and get some rest. We're going to keep giving drugs to make him stay asleep until tomorrow. That will keep him from having any more of those seizures. We'll call you tomorrow first thing, or if anything changes. And of course you can call anytime to see how he's doing."

Once they got back to McKenzie's aunt and uncle's house, the two snatched the girl and held her close. McKenzie, who had been quiet in the way that only complete exhaustion can bring, began to cry again. Claire gave them her phone number and asked them to call her with an update on the dog's condition.

When they got back to the house, Charlie and Tom were there. Dante and Claire explained what had happened. "What kind of sick person would poison a squirrel?" Dante asked.

"Maybe it wasn't the squirrel they were after," Tom said. "I think strychnine is usually used to poison gophers or rats. Maybe the squirrel just got hold of some accidentally."

"Maybe," Claire said. "But I've been thinking about how many dead animals I've been seeing lately when I go running. Squirrels, rats, crows—and I never used to see dead things." A memory flashed through her mind—somebody complaining about rats—but it slipped away again before she could place it.

CLAIRE HAD BEEN HOME for a half-hour before she noticed the answering machine's green light was blinking.

Nova Sweeney had had a second stroke, a fatal one.

The memorial service was scheduled for Riverwalk's chapel in two days' time.

FORTY-FOUR

CLAIRE WAS ASLEEP that night, her head on Dante's shoulder, when a sound like a car backfiring pierced her dreams. Near and very loud, it was accompanied by the crash and tinkle of broken glass. She started up, groggily wondering if she was still dreaming. But Dante was also awake, raised up on one elbow beside her, his eyes wide.

Then Charlie began to scream.

Down the stairs, in the dark, Claire's feet unerring from years of living in the same house. Dante one pace behind. Claire heard him trip over the last step, the grunt as he sprawled full length in the hall, but she didn't stop, pulled on inexorably by the sound of Charlie's screams. Was Charlie injured? Dying?

Yanking open Charlie's bedroom door, Claire flipped on the light, then froze. Tom lay with his blood-drenched upper body sprawled across the bed, his heels drumming the floor. Charlie cradled him in her arms. There was so much blood Claire couldn't tell whether Charlie was hurt or not. On Charlie's face was an expression Claire had never seen there before. Fear.

"Are you all right, Charlie?" Claire shouted as Dante ran in behind her. She could hear the gasp of his indrawn breath.

Charlie shook her head. "Help Thomas!" The word said the German way, with no "h," *Toe-mahs*. "He has been shot in the chest."

Dante knelt down in front of Tom.

Claire snatched up the phone to call 911. No dial tone.

Dante's hands fumbled with Tom's buttons.

Claire clicked the talk button off and on, off and on, but still heard only silence. She looked at it again. The power light glowed green.

Dante gave up and tore. A button bounced off Claire's cheek.

Pressing the phone to her ear again, Claire still heard nothing. "The phone's not working!"

"I'll go find my cell," Dante's voice was measured, even though his face was pale and his fingers dripped blood onto the wood floor. "Try to find where he's bleeding and get it to stop. Press on it hard with your hands. He's losing too much blood. We've got to get an ambulance here fast." He ran from the room.

Charlie seemed in shock, her face white. All she was doing was stroking Tom's hair while his blood soaked into the bed and wicked up the sleeves of her pink cotton pajamas. Claire leaned over Tom. His lips were an eerie lavender, his skin gray underneath his tan. His breath came in shallow gasps. The veins in his neck bulged purple.

Tom's eyes pleaded with her. "Can't breathe! Can't!" Claire grabbed a pillow and used it to wipe the blood away so she could find its source. There was a neat round hole two inches below his left nipple. Tom gasped for breath, the cords on his neck standing out. To her horror Claire saw bright red blood foam from the wound as he tried to exhale. Then came a terrible wet sucking sound as he breathed in. On the right side, his chest rose normally, but on the left it stayed flat. Claire pressed her hand over the hole and felt air bubbling out. Like some obscene mouth, the wound suckled on her palm when Tom struggled again to inhale. The blood was so red it was nearly mesmerizing. Putting one knee on the mattress to gain leverage, Claire pressed down harder, trying to seal the wound.

Tom's lips were still moving, but there was no sound. His eyes pleaded with her.

"Don't talk." Somehow, Claire managed to make her voice calm, hoping her expression was reassuring. "Save your breath." The phrase took on a new meaning.

Dante ran back into the room, his feet crunching on the splinters of broken glass. "What is the address here? I can't remember!" Charlie told him while Claire kept trying—and failing—to stop the bleeding. He relayed the information, thanked the person on the other end, and then put down the phone. "Since it was a cell phone, they couldn't use the automatic locator. She said they should be here in a couple of minutes."

Claire realized where Dante was standing—right next to the shattered window, its ivory curtains billowing in the breeze. "Get away from the window!" she yelled. Dante backed away quickly. "Whoever did this could still be out there!"

Underneath her, Tom gasped for breath again. Despite how hard she was pressing, Claire felt the flesh again draw down under her hand. The wet sound filled the room.

"That's a sucking chest wound," Dante said. He came to her side. "We've got to get it sealed up. Here. My hand's bigger. Let me try." Dante slid his hand under hers, then pressed so hard the skin of Tom's chest whitened around his hand, but at least the terrible slurping sound stopped. "Quick, do you have any Saran Wrap, you know, plastic wrap? And some kind of tape that will stick to his skin—medical tape or even duct tape?" He leaned in to speak to Tom, although Claire didn't know if he was past hearing. "Tom! Try to breathe as little and as shallowly as possible. Your lung has collapsed."

Claire ran into the kitchen, but felt like she was moving in slow motion as she fumbled open the kitchen drawer for the plastic wrap and then had to open two more drawers before she found the silver roll of duct tape. Her feet threatened to slide out from under her as she made a quick detour to throw open the front door for the paramedics. As she scrambled back to the bedroom, her mind was filled with a wordless prayer that the ambulance would show up right now. Only when she saw Tom again, awash in blood, did Claire realize that whoever had shot him could easily have been standing on the other side of the front door. Between her shoulder blades, she felt an itching like crosshairs.

"How long a piece of plastic do you need?" she asked Dante.

"At least two feet. And four strips of duct tape about ten or twelve inches long. Hurry."

When she tried to tear off a piece of plastic wrap, it twisted and clung to itself. The more she tried to straighten it out, the worse it got. Finally, Claire ripped off the first balled-up piece and started again, forcing her hands to move slowly. Then she tore off the four strips of duct tape and tacked them onto the headboard.

"That's good. Now fold the plastic wrap in half. Okay, I'm going to lift my hand up. Charlie, I want you to wipe up the blood with a blanket or something as fast as you can. And Claire, you slap that plastic into place as soon as Tom exhales and you see his chest fall to its lowest point. Make sure it completely covers the wound. Move as fast as you can, but we want a good seal." Dante looked at both of them to make sure they were ready. "And now!"

Everything went as smoothly as if they had done it all many times before. The blood was wiped up, the plastic slapped down. Dante quickly fastened it into place with the duct tape, but he left one corner loose. "Now he'll be able to exhale without sucking air through the wound when he inhales."

Claire took a second to look at him in amazement. "How do you know all this?"

"Ex-Boy Scout who remembers the goriest lessons the best." Something that under normal circumstances might have been a grin flashed across Dante's face. "See if you can get his pulse."

Claire picked up Tom's bony wrist and set her fingers on it, probing for the groove just underneath the wrist bone. Under her fingertips there didn't seem to be even a flutter. She quickly looked up at Tom. His face didn't look as gray, and the veins on his neck were no longer as prominent. And as she watched, he drew a breath, this time a quiet one. So why couldn't she find his pulse? She pressed harder, and there it was, weak and irregular and way too fast, so fast, she had trouble counting it. Shutting out all distractions, she focused on her wristwatch for thirty seconds, then announced, "One hundred thirty." Claire knew her own resting pulse was around sixty, but then again, she had never taken it after having just been shot.

Charlie leaned over him. "But his color looks already better."

Tom stirred and spoke, his words slurred. "What happened?" He blinked and looked around, tried to straighten up.

Dante put a hand on his shoulder. "Shh, stay still. You've been shot. The ambulance is on its way. Hang on, now, don't talk, and try to breathe slowly and shallowly. You've got a collapsed lung." Dante straightened up. "Okay, okay, let me see if I can remember. I think if we prop Tom up we can make it easier for him to breathe. You guys stick those pillows behind him. I'll go grab the cushions from the couch. We want to get him in a sitting position."

Charlie put one arm around Tom's shoulder while Claire picked up the three blood-spattered pillows and shoved them behind his back. Her hand came away slick with hot blood.

Oh, shit, she thought, they had forgotten all about the possibility of an exit wound.

"Dante?" she called, and heard her voice rising. Tom was curled forward now, his head resting on his bent knees. She lifted his pajama top. His back looked like hamburger. It was going to take more than duct tape and plastic wrap to fix this. "Dante, can you come in here?"

At that moment, sirens converged on the house and she heard Dante yelling from the porch. For a second, Claire again worried about him being shot, but then she realized that whoever had done this, fired a shot through a darkened window into a man dazed with sleep, wouldn't be brave enough to wait around for the cops.

Footsteps pounded down the hall and two paramedics and a cop ran into the bedroom, with Dante on their heels. The room was suddenly too crowded. The cop was yelling, "Where's the shooter?"

"We never saw anyone. They were outside and shot him through that window." Dante pointed at the shattered glass. The cop turned and ran from the room, his gun drawn.

The tension in the room was escalating even as the man at the center of it seemed to be collapsing like a leaky balloon.

The paramedics converged on Tom, shouting commands and facts at each other, ripping open medical supplies they yanked from their bags, barking into the two-way radios they wore on their shoulders. They pushed Claire and Dante out into the hall, where they hovered in the doorway, watching anxiously. When Claire got a glimpse of Tom's face, it was twisted into a grimace. Charlie was still on the bed. She had refused to leave. They had made her scoot back to give them room to work. She sat now in a corner, her shoulders braced by the walls, her knees drawn up to her chest.

And then the next time one of the paramedics stood back and Claire saw Tom's face, it was clear that he was…gone. His eyes were still open, but it was like a light behind them had been put out.

The paramedics' rush slowed, and then stopped. They stepped away from Tom, their hands dropping to their sides.

"Can't you do something?" Claire pleaded from the doorway, even though she knew it was hopeless. "Can't you shock him with those paddles or something?"

The older one turned his head in her direction, but she noticed he didn't quite meet her eye. "The bullet severed one of the main arteries. Even if he had been rushed into surgery the second after it happened, I don't think they could have saved him. There was just too much damage, ma'am. I'm sorry."

Charlie moved then. Across the bloody mattress, she crawled forward on her hands and knees and kissed Tom's blue lips.

FORTY-FIVE

FOR YEARS, Charlie fought not to feel resentment toward the living. Why should they be alive when everyone else was dead?

As time passed, she got to the point where she could bear to hear people say, "I'm starving," as they sat down at the restaurant, their eyes scanning the menu. Or "I was so frightened," when they spoke about a movie.

They used words so lightly, as if they were weightless. *I'm hungry, I'm scared, I'm cold, I'm sick, I thought I would die.*

For a long time, everything felt beside the point. Was this freedom, this unbearable solitariness? Why should she live?

In time, Charlie knew she had to choose: to die or to forget. To continue to breathe was to forget.

Even to remember was to forget.

FORTY-SIX

THE POLICE SEEMED to think it was likely that the person or persons who had shot Tom had been the same ones who spray-painted the house. They talked about an escalation of violence. Worried for Jason, Claire was relieved when they talked about moving the other hate-crime victims to safe houses. But most of her fears were for Charlie. Claire sat next to her friend, one arm around her shoulder, one hand on Charlie's knee, as they answered the same questions again and again. The older woman seemed weightless, as if grief had left her an empty husk. Claire had the feeling that, if it hadn't been for her, Charlie would have simply floated away.

"We were asleep," Charlie explained again for the third time. "Then I heard a rap on the window. I was not sure if I heard it or I was dreaming it. Tom got up and went to see what the noise was. The next thing I know, there was shooting, and the glass, it was everywhere flying. And then Tom fell and I was holding him, I was trying to hold him."

Since Charlie hadn't seen anything, nor had any of the neighbors, the police had little to go on. Someone had disconnected the line at the junction box. There were no fingerprints on Charlie's bedroom window, only smudges thought to be from gloves. Before they left, the police said they would be in touch later for more questioning, and gave Dante the name of a cleaning company that specialized in crime scenes.

"There is one thing," Claire said on the porch. "Could you check the photos of the other crime scenes? The photos of the writing?"

"Why?"

"The writing on our house was both in upper- and lowercase. But the writing at Jason's and Matt's apartment is in all capital letters. It's probably nothing, but—"

The detective straightened up. "You know those kids?"

"Mostly the younger one. I tutor Jason at school two days a week."

"Did you tell us that?"

"Ours happened first, so no, I didn't."

"Do you know any of the other victims?"

Claire shook her head. "I don't think so. I might have seen that one homeless guy around, but I'm not sure."

EVEN THOUGH NONE of them had slept for two days, Charlie insisted on attending Nova's funeral. Gingerly, Claire had ventured into Charlie's bedroom to find a black dress. Dante was paying a small fortune for the cleaning company to come in while Claire and Charlie were at the funeral. Even if they repainted it and replaced all the furniture, Claire wasn't certain if Charlie would ever want to sleep there again.

Claire was getting to be an old hand at finding her way around the Riverwalk campus. The parking lot was crowded. Once they were out of the car, Claire had to temper her stride to match Charlie's. The older woman moved slowly and seemed unsteady on her feet, but shrugged off all offers of assistance.

Inside, the small chapel was carefully nondenominational. The stained-glass windows showed curving abstract shapes, not images of saints. In front was a lectern but no cross. There were six rows of pews on both sides of a wide aisle, carpeted in sky blue.

Given how Nova had complained about the lack of men in her life, there were an amazing number of them in the pews—silver-haired, bald, even a couple with hair the color of shoe polish. They outnumbered the women three to two. Claire was glad to see that they had had to break out the folding chairs.

They had to squeeze past people to reach the only open seats, in the middle of one of the rows of folding chairs. As they inched their way in, Charlie stumbled. Claire reached out and caught her shoulder, steadying her. Underneath her fingers, Charlie's arm seemed impossibly fragile, the bones no bigger than a child's. Even McKenzie must have had twenty pounds on Charlie.

Charlie's eyes were shadowed, and she had not spoken a single unnecessary word since the police interview. Dante was just as concerned about her as Claire was. In an odd way, Tom's murder and their concern about Charlie had pulled them back together, made them a team again. If Charlie could barely make it through this funeral, then how would she be able to bear Tom's later in the week?

The service was brief and nondescript. It was clear that the speaker had never heard of Nova until after she was dead. In well-practiced cadences, he combined a few not-very-revealing tales of Nova—obviously fed to him by others—with quotations from Kahlil Gibran, e. e. cummings, and a child's bedtime story.

Afterward, they gathered for punch and cookies out in the lobby. It was here that the real Nova was revealed. Claire heard stories about the men Nova had dated, the hearts she had broken, the trysts she had consummated in unlikely places, the clever ways she had snatched a man right out from under his girlfriend's unsuspecting nose. Everyone brightened at these tales. Color appeared in wrinkled cheeks, laughs were low and knowing, winks and nods were used as often as words, and someone produced a flask to "freshen up" people's cups of punch. Just talking about Nova seemed to make the twenty or so men and women who remained feel more alive themselves.

One of the ladies leaned toward Claire. She was dressed to the nines, in a black Chanel-style suit and a black hat with a large brim and a small dotted veil that covered her eyes. In a Brooklyn accent, she said, "I'm Jean Rivin. I live across the way from Nova. I saw you and your friend visiting her the other day, didn't I?"

"Yes, I'm Claire. I'm so sorry that she died. I'm so glad I never took up smoking. It's such a hard habit to break."

Jean's laugh was surprisingly low. "Cigarettes! Nova? I don't think so. I've seen all those guys coming and going. It was too much s-e-x." She spelled out the word.

Claire said, "The doctor said she had a stroke."

The older woman shook her head. "But what brought it on, hmm? The night she had her first stroke, I heard her cry out. I looked through my peephole and I saw a man leaving in a big hurry. When he saw that she was getting sick, he must have pulled the emergency bell and then turned tail and run." She dropped her voice lower. "And when I went to visit her in the nursing unit, outside her door I heard her making these little moans, and a man's voice, too low for me to catch the words. I couldn't believe that she was still fooling around in her condition. I just turned and went on back to my condo. An hour later, I heard she was dead."

Charlie's voice startled Claire. "You saw a man running from her home the night she had a stroke?" Her voice was a rasp, rusty from disuse.

"Yes," Nova's neighbor said. Her tone was nervous now, as if she had been caught telling tales out of school. "I'd never seen him before. He must have been a new one. Of course, she has—had—a new one every month."

"What did he look like?" Charlie's words were speeding up. "How old was he?"

"I only saw him for a second," Nova's neighbor protested. Charlie's eyes drilled into her. "Well, he was about our age. Tall. Thin. White hair." There was a long pause. "Oh—and I think he was carrying a cane."

FORTY-SEVEN

"ALLEN KILLED THEM. He killed them all," Charlie said as they hurried out to Claire's car. "Elizabeth, Nova, Tom." It wasn't sorrow that strengthened her voice, but anger. "First he killed Elizabeth. Then he killed Nova to stop her from figuring out the truth. It's the same reason he tried to kill me and ended up killing Tom."

"And that's the reason the spray-painting looked different at our house. Allen must have read about the skinheads, and decided to play copycat. It was a cover for what he planned to do later." Even as she said the words, a doubt teased Claire, but it slipped away when she tried to pin it down. "But I don't know how we can prove it."

"We will ask for Howard's help. He did love Elizabeth, even if it wasn't how a man loves a woman. All these years, he has lived next to the Lisacs. He has watched them. If we put our heads together, perhaps he will remember something that will give us a clue we can take to the police."

Claire felt a flash of doubt again as she thought about Howard, his desperate loneliness. There was something else about Howard, but what was it? "I don't know, Charlie," she said slowly, "aren't they old friends? Why would he betray him?"

Charlie said grimly, "I will make him afraid not to. Everyone else who knew the truth is dead. Howard has got to see that he is next."

They parked on the street, then hurried up Howard's driveway, which paralleled the Lisacs'. Claire had a hard time keeping up with Charlie, who was practically running. Howard was polishing his car, his back to them. Mary looked up from her garden next door. She was on her knees, a basket of cut flowers beside her.

"Howard," Charlie called, her voice low and urgent. He turned. "We're here to talk to you, Howard. To talk to you about the truth."

In the next second, everything changed.

Howard dropped the yellow sponge he was holding. In five long strides, he was at Mary's side, leaning over her. Hooking his left arm around her neck, he pulled Mary to her feet. At the same time, his right hand grabbed something from her basket. There was a single sharp scream, abruptly cut off. Then Claire saw why Mary had frozen, her scream dying in her throat. Something that flashed silver in the sunlight. The tip of a pair of garden shears was pressed against the loose skin of Mary's throat.

"Back off or I kill her!"

Mary let out a tiny strangled gasp. Claire didn't know if Howard had been proving his seriousness or Mary had shifted, but now a thin line of blood began to snake slowly down her neck.

Allen appeared on the front step, his empty hands spread wide as he patted the air, the way you might calm an overexcited dog.

"Howard, what are you doing?"

Howard tightened his arm around Mary's neck, raising her chin to the sky.

"Howard, can't we—"

"Shut up and let me think!"

A few of the pieces fell into place. Nova inquiring eagerly into Howard's marital status, then saying, *Better the devil you know,* as she prepared to go on a date the night she was to have a "stroke." And there had been a thunderstorm the night Nova died, Claire thought. She remembered the old-fashioned umbrella in Howard's living room, the one that, furled, might have looked like a cane to an old woman peering out a peephole. Howard's big hand suddenly slapping the window, scaring away the squirrel. Howard asking if there had been anything else in the wall, as if he had already known the answer. And how Nova had tried to tell them in a note. A note that had started with H, not A, Claire realized now.

Charlie must have been thinking some of the same thoughts. Now she said, "It was you." It wasn't a question.

Howard said, "What Warren didn't know was that his lies were true. He told everyone that Elizabeth had slipped, fallen, and hit her head. But that's what really happened. I didn't mean to kill her." His grip on Mary loosened a fraction. Her eyes rolled as she tried to see where the garden shears were, but otherwise she was as still as a statue.

Charlie shook her head. "But why? Why kill Elizabeth?"

"School had just started up again, and the class was very unruly. I got this terrible headache that got worse as the morning went on. At lunchtime, I asked the principal to sub for me, then walked home. As I came up the hill, I saw Tom and Charlie walking away. He was carrying a picnic basket and had his arm around her. I called to you," Howard said to Charlie, "but you didn't hear me.

"But Liz did. She came out on the front porch. She was wearing only a nightgown, so I hurried inside before the neighbors saw her. I knew she and Allen had had a big fight the night before. I had heard them yelling at each other. She looked terrible. Her eyes were swollen from crying. And she told me that she was pregnant. And that it wasn't Allen's baby."

"Whose baby was it, Howard?"

Howard sighed noisily. "Liz had been too much the innocent to ever notice how old Warren looked at her when she started dating Allen. At first she wouldn't tell me who it was, but when I asked her if it was Warren's, she started to cry. And then Liz told me she had gone to Warren, and he had refused to help her get rid of it. It was like he was proud of himself, not ashamed at all. He told her she should just pass it off as Allen's baby. It would even look like him—because it would be his brother or sister." Howard looked directly at Allen. "The only thing your father hadn't counted on was you, Allen. That you would say no. That you would tell Elizabeth that you wouldn't marry her, that the wedding was off. She was...lost.

"And then I came walking into the picture. And Liz begged me to marry her. She poured me a glass of wine, and she rubbed herself all over me like she was a cat and I was catnip. But I just pushed her away. Her touch made me feel dirty. And then I could see her changing, making herself get harder. Liz started telling me that she had guessed the truth about me. She said it didn't matter to her what I was or who I was with. That all she needed was for someone to give her baby a name, someone to marry her and make her a respectable woman. That we could even sleep in separate rooms."

Claire was listening to Howard's story, but part of her was also watching Howard. The shears no longer dimpled Mary's neck, as the pressure he applied began to ease.

"And I argued with her. I told her I didn't know what she was talking about, that I wasn't that way at all. But I guess old Warren, he had taken a bit of that innocent shine off of Liz. She just looked at me, and I saw that her eyes were old. And that there wasn't anything anymore that she couldn't or wouldn't do, if she thought it was necessary.

"I still told her no. And then Liz was like an animal, cornered and desperate. She said if I didn't marry her, she would march down to the school right that very moment and tell them the truth about me. She knew it would get me fired, even though I had never even looked crossways at those kids. They were children! Just because I'm not meant to be with a woman doesn't mean I'm a monster, preying on babies. But she knew no one would understand that. Back then, nobody made those distinctions. Even now they don't."

Howard was lost in his story now, the point of the shears drooping toward the ground. Still, even if Claire rushed him, it would only take a second for those shears to sink into Mary's neck.

"Liz was right up in my face, screaming at me, pounding at me with her fists, saying she wouldn't let her life be ruined, and that if it was, she would ruin mine as well. And I shoved her away. I had to get her away from me." Tears began to slip silently down Howard's face. "You have to believe me, Allen. I didn't mean for it to happen. When I pushed her away, she fell backward over the ottoman and hit her head on the wooden arm of the couch. And then she lay there and she didn't move. She didn't move at all. And I looked at her mouth and I thought about how when she woke up she would use that mouth to ruin my life. So I took my hand and put it over her mouth and nose. She barely struggled. And in a minute or two, when I took my hand away, she was quiet and still, and I knew she would never talk again.

"And then I panicked. I ran out of the house. I knew my life was over. Still, I made myself go back to the school. I told the principal I was feeling okay now, that he didn't need to sub for me. I taught all afternoon, not even hearing what I was saying. I knew I was going to be found out, but I kept hoping if I kept to my old routines, then maybe no one would know. I hid my head in the sand."

Claire could see Mary was gathering herself. Slowly, her hands began to rise, an agonizing inch at a time. But Howard had eyes only for Allen.

"But then, when I came home, someone had taken care of everything for me. They had hung up her dead body so it would look like she killed herself. And I realized who it was. It was you, Allen. You did it for me. And afterward, you pulled away from me. I understood why. That you had done this one thing for me, but that was all."

Allen's eyes had gotten wider and wider as Howard talked. His lips parted, but no sound came out. His eyes were like stones. When he finally spoke, it was almost a stutter.

"It was you that killed her? You killed her? You sick bastard—you killed her?"

Mary's hands froze, still at least a foot from where Howard's hand held the haft of the shears. She let out a little moan, like a sigh, like a warning, but Allen was blazing with fury now, too far gone to hold back.

"Didn't you? Because of…of…" Howard's voice trailed off.

"What? You think I did it for you? You think I would have covered up for you?" Howard flinched at the sarcastic emphasis Allen gave each "you," but Allen didn't notice "All these years, I thought it was my father who killed her. I thought I had cleaned up after him. You think I covered up for you because of that one night before I shipped out? You think that meant anything? I was just horny, and drunk, and stupid. That's all. It didn't mean anything. It didn't mean anything about me. It certainly didn't mean anything about us. Any cat in the dark, isn't that what they say? But not in the light, Howard, not in the light."

"It wasn't for me?" Howard said slowly.

"Why would I have done it for you?" Allen didn't seem to notice Howard flinching at his blunt words. "And the way my father acted afterward, I was sure it had been him. He must have been thinking the same thing about me. Making sure to keep the cops out. Making sure to get everything cleaned up and as smoothed over as possible. Making sure nobody talked. He thought he was saving me. And I thought I was saving him. When we were really saving you—the sack of shit who killed Elizabeth in the first place!"

"Allen, don't!" Mary croaked, but her husband was past heeding her.

"He picked Liz out for me, you know. Or did he really pick her out for himself? I never knew. I still remember the last time I saw her alive. My parents were at the opera. I was in the living room when she walked in wearing only a silk gown." Allen's eyes seemed focused someplace far away, as if he saw Elizabeth walking toward him, slowly putting one foot in front of another as if balanced on a tightrope. "She came and took my hand and placed it on her breast and she trembled under my touch. In my ear, she whispered words that even the whores in Seoul had never said. But Elizabeth's eyes were old and sad, just like the eyes of those whores had been."

Claire didn't know if it was intentional, but with every sentence, Allen took a half-step closer to Howard and Mary.

"I pushed her away, but she wouldn't leave me alone. I knew I had to tell her. Tell her that we couldn't get married, that I wasn't really a man anymore. But then she blurted out she was pregnant. Whose baby was it? I asked her, but she refused to say, just stood there with her shoulders curled over and tears running down her cheeks. I couldn't believe that after all those letters she wrote, all those promises she made, she had taken up with someone else. And then she begged me to marry her, said she would be the best wife a woman had ever been. I told her I wouldn't marry her, that I couldn't, not after this. She got hysterical, pounded my chest with her fists. I just turned away from her, went to my room, closed the door, and lay there staring at the ceiling. Everything had shut down inside of me."

He took another half-step forward. Charlie let out a small sound, no louder than a sigh, and Claire followed the direction of her gaze.

"All night I laid awake thinking about it. And in the morning I got up and drank three cups of coffee and went to work before my parents realized something was wrong. And at the job site I thought about it and thought about it, turning it over in my mind. I was going crazy. Whose baby could it be? Which one of my friends had betrayed me? Or was it someone I didn't even know—a clerk at a shoe store, a bus driver, the priest where Liz still went to Mass? I thought of everything, but nothing really seemed possible."

Claire saw what Charlie had seen. Tucked into the small of Allen's back, where Howard couldn't see it, was a handgun.

"Whoever had done it must have talked her into it. Before I left, Liz was shy, scared of her own desires. I knew it had to be someone who had contact with her every day, who could whittle away her defenses a little at a time. Someone who could wear her down like water trickling over a stone."

The next words tumbled out of Allen's mouth. "And then I knew. I knew whose baby it was. My father's! He had always been a hound, sleeping with his secretary, a barmaid, even the woman who played the church organ. He would come home with alcohol on his breath, his tie off, and suck marks on his neck. Before I went to Korea, he had even been sneaking around with Nova. He hadn't even cared that I knew."

Did Claire hear a siren? She strained to hear, as if she could squint her ears.

"That day at lunch, I went home to make Liz tell me if I was right. Instead"—Allen's words slowed—"I found her lying on her back next to the couch. Her body was still warm, but she wasn't breathing. I knew who had done it. My father. She must have told him that I wouldn't marry her, and he had been afraid that everything would all come tumbling out, that he wouldn't be able to live his double life any longer. He had done this thing, and run away. After all the years I had grown up listening to him tell me that a man always cleaned up after his own messes, that a man doesn't run away from a problem, that a man doesn't cry, that a man's not afraid of a little blood. But he had been afraid and he had run away and he had left behind a mess."

Beside Claire, Charlie lifted her head. It was clear there were sirens now, more than one.

"That's when I knew that I was better than my father. I was more man than he would ever be. So I did what had to be done. Her body was so slack and heavy. But I cut the curtain cord to make a noose, hauled her body up, tipped over a chair underneath her, wiped the blood off the wooden arm of the couch. As I worked, I thought. It was no secret that Elizabeth had been upset and nervous. I decided to say she had broken up with me because of my leg. And afterward, I didn't owe my father anything anymore. Elizabeth's death set me free, in an odd way. Not just from her, but from owing my father."

The sirens were close now, Claire thought. Maybe only a block away. But Allen and Howard seemed too caught up in their own personal drama to notice.

"You didn't do it for me?" Howard asked.

Allen shook his head, disgust pulling his features into a mask. "Can't you get it straight? It's never been about you, Howard."

Two cop cars skidded to a stop at the bottom of the driveway. Doors opened, radios crackled, commands were issued in low voices. Claire tensed, fearing that everything was about to change, and not for the better.

"All those years, I held on to that one thought, that you had cared enough for me to risk yourself for me," Howard said slowly. "And I understood how what I had forced you to do had made you turn away from me."

Allen shook his head, his expression one of disbelief. "All because of one time that lasted fifteen minutes and that didn't mean anything? Are you crazy?"

"It was more than once," Howard said, his lower lip jutting forward. "You can lie to anyone else, Allen, but don't lie to yourself. And you liked it!"

"Was that enough to ruin my life? My father used to call me a fag. Why do you think I went to Korea? To get away from you. Everything you touched, you ruined! Me, Elizabeth, your own pathetic, messed-up life!"

Tears still slid down Howard's face, but his gaze hardened. He began to drag Mary backward, her head tucked right underneath his chin. His lips seemed to be moving, but Claire couldn't hear what he was saying. Then his voice got louder, although it still shook. "I'm going to kill her," he called out, loud enough that the cops on the street could hear. "I'm going to kill her right in front of you. She stood between you and me, Allen, and now she's going to pay!"

"Down, down!" came the cries from the street. "Get down!"

Claire fell to her knees, then had to tug on Charlie's pants leg to get her to move. They flopped forward onto their stomachs, but both of them kept their heads raised a little bit. Rather than obeying the shouts of the cops, Allen rushed forward.

"I'm going to kill her! Now!" Howard shouted.

Everything happened in a blur. Allen pulling out his gun. The shears jerking upward. Mary collapsing to the ground, suddenly boneless. The bullet that caught Howard square in the throat, before Allen threw himself over his wife's body. And the volley of shots that spun Howard around, blood flowering on his shirt, and then flung him to the dirt, his body a few feet away from Mary's. He twitched once and then was still.

And then Mary moaned. Allen rolled off her and she pushed herself to her knees. Her neck had only one scratch on it, and a single pearl of blood.

And on his knees beside her, Allen embraced Mary and began to sob.

FORTY-EIGHT

FROM THE OREGONIAN

They had meetings at Shari's Restaurant, two National Guard buddies fresh from peacekeeping duties in the Middle East, and one a high school student who had looked up to them ever since they were all in grade school and living in the same apartment building. The soldiers, accused of torching their own barracks in Egypt, had returned in disgrace. Together again, they shared a late-night meal to plot the latest in a string of attacks police are calling a stateside "mission" of hate.

Police and family members spent Friday trying to piece together why the three—Jeff Reynolds, 19, Pat Caruthers, 19, and a 17-year-old juvenile—would take part in such attacks. The three appeared Friday afternoon before Multnomah County Circuit Judge Jesse Gonzalez wearing forest-green jail uniforms and sandals, their hair cropped short in military style. Some victims of the hate crimes said their attackers looked like skinheads.

To family members, the two soldiers and the teen had seemed like gung-ho military types, not bigots. The two soldiers had dreamed aloud of combat in Iraq. Instead they had been sent home early from the Oregon National Guard. The soldiers were among the troops sent to the Sinai Peninsula in July for peacekeeping duty on the border between Egypt and Israel. There, just after midnight August 13, Reynolds, accompanied by Caruthers, took part in an arson. Reynolds pleaded the military equiva-

APRIL HENRY   261

lent of no contest to accusations that he squirted lighter
fluid on the side of his $100,000 barracks and set it
ablaze. Other soldiers were inside, asleep. The two were
caught in the act, and the fire was quickly extinguished.
They were confined to barracks, sent home early and de-
moted in rank to private. Once stateside, the two buddies
violated a direct order not to associate with each other.

A few weeks after returning from Egypt, Reynolds
and Caruthers confronted an African-American man and
two African-American teenagers in a car. The soldiers
brandished a handgun and shouted racist slurs from their
car, according to police. The victims fled to a shopping
center.

A week later, the two, joined by the teen, jumped a
Hispanic man as he waited at a bus stop. They beat him
with a baseball bat, breaking his nose and cheekbone
and leaving him covered in blood, police said. One of the
men yelled, "You're leaving tonight in a casket!" Later
they attacked a white homeless man for being a "race traitor," and an Indian motel owner whom they mistakenly
thought was Muslim. (A fourth crime, which defaced the
home of a Jewish woman, is now thought to be the work
of a copycat.)

The most disturbing part about those crimes, according to Lt. Mike Calkum, a Portland police detective who
interviewed Reynolds, is that the two soldiers referred to
their actions as "missions." Their crime spree began to
unravel when the teen, whose brother had an African-
American mother, decided to spray-paint his own apartment in hopes of reaping a windfall of donations. All
three are now behind bars.

FORTY-NINE

WHEN HOWARD HAD begun to drag Mary backward, he had put his lips against her ear and told her to drop when he yelled out the word, "Now!" The short, sharp movement of the shears they had all witnessed and been horrified by had been a ruse—he wrapped his own fingers around the closed blades before the point even touched Mary's throat. As instructed, though, she had crumpled to the ground. Believing Mary dead or dying, the cops—and Allen— had fired. The grand jury had been convened to hear the evidence, but it was a foregone conclusion that the shooting was justified. Suicide by others' hands—a quick way out rather than face the shame of a trial.

Things were not nearly as clear-cut at the Oregon Art Museum. In disarray, the board of directors had postponed the planning for the new Allen Lisac Wing and the hiring of the curator to oversee it. Part of their discomfort had to do with the donor's shooting his next-door neighbor to death over what, rumor had it, had been a longstanding homosexual affair. Dante said the board's discomfort was proof that he wasn't in New York anymore, where publicity of any kind was always welcome.

But the Oregon Art Museum's board had another reason for rethinking their plans. As Claire and Charlie had been confronting Howard, Dante had been hitting the send button on an e-mail to the board. In it, he detailed his discomfort with the three drawings in Allen Lisac's collection, and suggested that all the drawings and paintings needed to undergo a more thorough review.

In his e-mail, Dante had proposed a novel solution to the problem he believed the museum faced. He advocated that they hold the investigation out in the open, in a show similar to one the Met had held in the late nineties called "Rembrandt, Not Rembrandt." The popular exhibition had invited viewers to decide for themselves which paintings were Rembrandts and which weren't by presenting them with scientific evidence and expert opinion, some of it conflicting.

In a similar vein, Dante proposed that visitors to the Allen Lisac Wing of the Oregon Art Museum could not only be shown the paintings and drawings themselves, but also the corresponding X-rays, autoradiographs, and other technical ways of seeing under a work of art. The museum could bring in teams of experts to evaluate the drawings and the paintings as well as letting kids peer into microscopes. At the core of the concept was the idea that the Oregon Art Museum borrow similar paintings or drawings from other museums and then display them side by side with the ones from Allen Lisac's collection—both suspect and not suspect.

The board was still considering the proposal. Even though they admitted it would draw the worldwide attention they craved, they still stumbled over the fact that some of the attention might not be of the type they had hoped for. While hinting that Dante was their top candidate, they had promised to reach a decision as soon as possible. Unable to wait, Dante was returning to New York. Claire ached every time she thought about it. She had finally decided to commit to him, but how could she, if he were to stay in New York? There was no way, especially now, that she could leave Charlie alone.

"DO YOU WANT a bag for that?" the cashier asked.

Claire looked down at the book in her hand. *How to Heal Grief and Loss.* She didn't want Charlie to see it. The fact that she would buy an advice book at all seemed to somehow trivialize Tom's death.

"Yes, please."

"Claire!"

She turned at the touch on her shoulder. Mary. The two

women embraced, Claire's tentativeness engulfed by Mary's greater enthusiasm.

"How are you doing?" they said simultaneously, and they both laughed. Then Mary invited Claire to split a cinnamon roll with her at Fat City. Claire was ashamed by how eagerly she took her up on the offer, by how unwilling she was to go home.

"Can I ask you something, Mary?" Claire said after the waitress had taken their order. "I still don't understand why the ring was in the wall. Who put it there?"

"Howard did." Mary lined up her fork, knife, and spoon until they were perfectly parallel. "He hid the ring and the purse in the wall, hoping that everyone would think a thief had attacked Elizabeth. I'm sure the reason there wasn't any money in it was because he took it. He's always been sneaky and devious, although it took me a long time to see it."

"What will you do with it now?"

Mary stretched out her right hand, her fingers tucked under her thumb. On her ring finger was a silver band set with a single diamond nearly as big as a dime.

She answered Claire's unspoken question. "We had the stones reset into two rings. We each wear one. What the jeweler did when he melted down the ring is kind of like what happened to us. We went through fire and came out different on the other side."

"Didn't it bother you to find out Allen's role in your sister's death?"

Mary leaned forward, her voice pitched low to match Claire's. "But he didn't have a role. Elizabeth was dead before he walked in that door. And before we were married, he told me about what had happened. The truth as he knew it, that it had been his father who had killed her. This was after Warren died. He was sick with cancer even when he was carrying on with my sister. It might explain things." Mary shrugged. "Then again, it might not. When he told me what had happened, Allen said he would understand if I didn't marry him. Because of…what happened with Elizabeth, and other…things." The two women met each other's gaze. "Because of how his father raised him, Allen never realized his own value. But I looked at him and knew he was what I wanted."

"I guess you weren't the only one," Claire said, thinking of Howard. For so long, Howard had gotten away with murder. Howard had known the how, if not the real reason why. Every look he and Allen exchanged had been heavy with meaning as far as Howard was concerned, weighted down by the extraordinary thing Allen had done for him out of love. And if Allen had chosen never to acknowledge this out loud, well, Howard must have comforted himself with the idea that actions spoke louder than words. And if Allen had entered into a sham of a marriage, well, Howard knew from Elizabeth just how hollow that marriage must be.

"The police showed them to us, you know. His notebooks." Mary turned her hands over, and Claire noticed that her nails were bitten to the quick. "They were scary. They were supposed to be birding notebooks, but really there were just hundreds of sketches of Allen, with only a couple of drawings of a flicker or a warbler. But mostly just Allen. Every mood, every smile, every expression. Interspersed with notes about every conversation the two of them had, which weren't many. Even so, Howard read something into everything Allen told him. Not that they spent that much time together. We never did that much together socially, unless Howard managed to engineer it."

Claire nodded, thinking of how Howard hadn't been able to bear to live in a world where Allen had never loved him. And when he had realized that his falsehoods were unraveling, he had made the split-second decision that it would be better to die—and engineered it so that the man he had always loved was also his killer.

"You know the other thing he recorded in those notebooks? How many"—Mary leaned forward and made quote marks with her fingers—"'vermin' he killed. He hated rats, squirrels, what he called 'trash birds,' like crows and jays. And every year the total was higher."

Claire shuddered. "It sounds like he was so closed off, living tighter and tighter in a world of his own imagination."

"I think he liked controlling things, or thinking he did. It gave him an odd sense of power," Mary said. Claire nodded.

"Just like after he realized Matt was one of the boys carrying out those attacks, he liked the power of not turning him in. Instead, he paid him to spray-paint Charlie's house. But he couldn't talk him into killing her, so Howard had to do it." Claire took a sip of her coffee. "Matt's not actually that bad a kid. I've been to visit him in jail a couple of times. And I'm trying to see what steps I would need to go through to maybe take his seven-year-old brother into foster care. It seems the dad took off last month sometime, right around when this all started. I can't bear to think of Jason being all alone in the world."

"So you're starting a family," Mary said without irony. "Congratulations."

Claire hadn't thought about it like that, and she wasn't sure she was ready for anything that permanent. Still, any reluctance she felt vanished when she thought about Jason's hugs. "Maybe I am."

"And how's Charlie doing?"

"Not well," Claire said. "Not well at all." Which was an understatement. Charlie was disappearing before Claire's eyes. She doubted that her friend even weighed eighty pounds. The last two nights Claire had come downstairs to find her sitting in a chair in the living room in the dark.

"Tell her I'm thinking of her," Mary said, as she laid down a ten-dollar bill next to the check. When Claire started to reach for her wallet, she said, "No, let me get this."

When Claire opened the front door of her house, the air smelled like smoke. She hurried toward the kitchen. She found Charlie wiping the counter with a sponge, while Dante swept the floor. There was spilled flour everywhere, and the air was thick with both the smell of burned butter and another smell. Claire sniffed. Something sweet was cooking in the oven.

"What happened here?" Claire asked, pretending dismay

with her hands on her hips. Charlie wasn't smiling, exactly, but it was clear she was back from wherever she had gone.

"I tried to make some banana bread, but I guess I got a few things messed up," Dante said. "I was trying to melt the butter, but the next thing I knew, the pan was on fire."

Charlie interrupted, feigning indignation. "The next thing you knew? There was a fire in my house, and I had to come out of my room to tell him the smoke alarm was making a noise." She shook her head at Dante. "If you are going to cook, watch what it is you are cooking. You could make a catastrophe with one stick of butter. I do not need such excitement."

"Yes'm," Dante said primly.

Claire swiped at her eyes, hoping to hide the evidence before Charlie noticed the tears sliding down her cheeks.

Charlie hugged Claire fiercely. "To be alive is to be alive even to pain," she whispered in Claire's ear. "I choose to live."

The oven timer binged. In a normal tone of voice, Charlie asked, "Who wants banana bread?"

Both of them said yes.

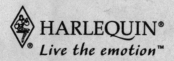

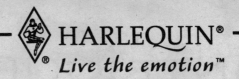

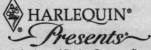